THE FALLIBLE ENCHANTMENT

Two of the northern soldiers hung back, and Valder quickly realized why. The third was a superb swordsman, probably the divisional champion. His blade flashed like heat lightning. But this did not bother the magic sword Wirikidor in the slightest. It countered each blow with supernatural speed, then swept past the guard and plunged into the soldier's throat.

Valder wrenched the blade away, and the northerner collapsed in a lifeless heap. Then Valder stood waiting for Wirikidor to take on the next swordsman.

Wirikidor did nothing. As the second northerner swung at him, it was all Valder could do to bring the suddenly sluggish Wirikidor up in time to parry. The sword was utterly inanimate.

There was no trace of the spell that should have protected him!

The Misenchanted Sword

Lawrence Watt-Evans

A Del Rey Book
BALLANTINE BOOKS • NEW YORK

*Dedicated to
Richard Evan Reis
and the old gang at P.I.C.*

PART ONE

Wirikidor

CHAPTER 1

The marsh stank, with a sharp, briny stench that seemed to fill Valder's head. He stared out across the maze of tall grass and shallow water for a long moment and then reluctantly marched onward, into it. The ground gave beneath him; his boot sank past the ankle in gray-brown muck. He muttered an obscenity, then smiled weakly at his own annoyance and slogged forward.

The enemy, he knew, was no more than an hour behind him. The marsh was nothing but a minor inconvenience by comparison.

To his left lay the open sea, and to his right was endless empty forest that was probably full of northern patrols and sentinels, human or otherwise. Behind him somewhere were the three northerners who had been pursuing him for the past four days. Ahead of him, wet and green and stinking, lay the coastal marshes.

He could, he supposed, have turned to the right and avoided the marshes, tried to lose his pursuers in the forest, but he had been running through forests for four days without being able to shake them off his trail. At least the marshes would be different.

After half a dozen long, slow steps through the mud, he struck a patch of solid ground and hauled himself up onto it; dirty seawater poured from his boots, which had not been watertight in more than a sixnight. The marsh grass rustled loudly as he pushed his way across the little hummock; he froze, peered back over his shoulder, and, seeing nothing but the unbroken line of pine trees, sank to the ground for a moment's rest.

The marsh was probably a mistake, he told himself as the foul smell saturated his nostrils. He could not move through it without making noise, it seemed—the rustling grass was far more audible than the crunch of pine needles, and the suck of mud wasn't much better—and the enemy sorcerer almost certainly had some sort of spell or talisman that augmented his hearing. Even the other two northerners might have hearing more than normally acute; from what he had seen of their movements, Valder was quite certain that at least one of them was *shatra*—half man, half demon, though human in appearance. That eerily smooth, flowing motion was unmistakable.

All three might be *shatra*; the demon warriors could disguise their movements if they chose. One of his pursuers was a sorcerer, but he had heard it said around the barracks that some sorcerers were *shatra*. It seemed grossly unfair for a single enemy soldier to have both advantages, but life, he knew, was sometimes very unfair.

Nobody knew exactly what *shatra* were capable of, but it was generally believed that they possessed magically acute senses—though not, probably, up to the level a good sorcerer could achieve. Valder had to assume that the northerners chasing him could see and hear and smell far better than he could.

He had managed to stay ahead of the enemy patrol for four days now, but it had been due to luck as much as to anything else. He had exhausted his last few prepared spells in diverting the pursuit, but none of the diversions had lasted very long, and his company's wizard had not provided him with anything useful for actual combat. Valder was supposed to be a scout, after all; his job, if he encountered the enemy, had been to run back to base camp to warn his superiors, not to fight. He was not interested in a glorious death in combat. He was just another of Ethshar's three million conscript soldiers trying to survive, and, for an ordinary human against *shatra*, that meant flight.

He had been able to travel at night as he fled because the greater moon had been almost full when the chase began, but the wizard-sight he had been given when he first went out on his routine solo patrol had worn off six nights ago.

Thick morning fogs had helped him, as much as the moon had; he was running blind to begin with, with no intended destination, and therefore was not concerned about losing his way in the mist, so long as he didn't walk off a cliff. His pursuers, however, had had to grope carefully along his trail, using their sorcerous tracking a few steps at a time. They did not seem to have any unnatural means of penetrating the fog, either sorcerous or demonic.

And, of course, the enemy had stopped for meals every so often, or for water, while he had had no need of food or drink. That was the only bit of wizardry he still had going for him, the only spell remaining; if that were to wear off, he knew he would be doomed. His outfit's wizard had known his job, though, and Valder had so far felt not the slightest twinge of hunger or thirst. He felt the charmed bloodstone in his belt pouch, making certain it was still secure.

Now, though, he had come to this stinking salt marsh and he wondered if his luck had run out. He settled himself on the grassy hummock and pulled his boots off, letting the foul water run out.

His luck had really run out two months ago, he decided, when the enemy had launched a surprise offensive out of nowhere and cut through to the sea, driving the Ethsharitic forces back down the coast, away from the forests and into the open plain. It had been phenomenally bad luck for Valder to have been out on solo patrol, checking the woods for signs of the enemy, when the assault came.

He had been looking for saboteurs and guerrillas, not the whole northern army.

Valder still did not understand how the enemy had cut through so quickly; all he knew was that, when he headed back toward camp, he had found northerners marching back and forth across the smoldering ruins of his home base, between himself and the Ethsharitic lines. He had encountered no scouts, no advance units, had had no warning. The fact that he had been sent out alone, in itself, indicated that his superiors hadn't thought the enemy had any significant forces within a dozen leagues, at the very least.

With the enemy to the south, the sea to the west, and nothing to the east but forest wilderness clear to the borders of the Northern Empire itself, he had headed north. He had hoped to get well away from the enemy, then find or build himself a boat and work his way south along the coast until he reached the Ethsharitic lines—surely the enemy could not have driven very far to the south, certainly not as far as General Gor's fortress. He knew nothing about boats, but he was reasonably sure that the enemy knew no more than he did. The Northern Empire was an inland nation; he doubted that there was any northern navy to worry about.

Unfortunately, the enemy had followed him northward along the shoreline, not because they knew he was there, but, as best he could guess, because they were afraid of Ethsharitic landings. He had kept moving north, staying ahead of the enemy scouts; four times he had settled in one spot long enough to start work on a raft, but each time a northern patrol had come along and driven him away long before he had a seaworthy craft.

Finally, four days ago, he had been careless, and a northerner who moved with the inhumanly smooth grace and speed of a *shatra* had spotted him. He had been running ever since, snatching naps when he could and using every ruse he could think of and every spell in his pouch.

He pulled off his right sock and wrung it out, then draped it on the grass to dry; he knew that it would just get wet again when he moved on, as he would have to do quickly, but while he rested he wanted it dry. He was tugging at his left sock when he heard the rustle of grass. He froze.

The sound came again, from somewhere behind him,

to the north—he had seated himself facing back the way he had come so as to have a better chance of spotting his pursuers.

It didn't seem likely that even *shatra* could have circled around behind him already. Perhaps, he told himself, it was just a bird or an animal of some sort. Carefully, with his right foot bare and his left sock hanging halfway off, he rose, trying not to rustle, and peered through the waving stalks.

Something tall was moving about, something dark gray and pointed at the top. Not *shatra*, or at least not the sort he was familiar with; they customarily wore round, close-fitting helmets that covered almost the entire head. Enemy sorcerers usually wore similar black helmets festooned with talismans, and the common soldiers made do with whatever they could scrounge up—most often ancient, rusty relics passed down through generations of warfare. This gray object did not look like any of those. It didn't look like a helmet at all; it looked like a cloth hat.

He wondered whether it might be some unfamiliar variety of beast, perhaps a magically created one or some odd kind of small dragon. He had seen pointed hats; they had once, he understood, been the standard issue for wizards until someone pointed out that they made excellent targets, but he could not imagine what one would be doing here, far to the north and west of anything resembling civilization. Who would be wearing such a thing in a marsh on the edge of nowhere?

He sank back to the ground and pulled his left sock back up, ignoring the fact that it was still soaking wet, and then pulled on his other sock and both boots.

The rustling noise continued; whatever the tall thing with the gray point was, it didn't seem to have noticed him. He stood up again, then crouched and began inching his way toward whatever it was, parting the grass carefully with his hands.

As careful as he was, however, his movement was not silent. He stopped again and listened.

The other had also stopped. For a tense moment, Valder waited. Then the rustling began again, and the other moved away. Valder followed, trying to move only when the other moved, but the rustling of his own passage drowned out the other's noise and made it very difficult to judge when the other had stopped.

A few feet from the spot where he had sat and dumped out his boots Valder found himself at the northern edge of the dry hummock, facing a wide, shallow channel. He eased his foot into it until the sole of his boot was resting on solid bottom, sunk an inch or two into muck. His other foot followed, until he was standing in six inches of foul-smelling water and three inches of goo. Both feet were once again thoroughly soaked.

He waded across the channel, moving slowly so as not to splash. No grass grew in the center of the channel, and the reeds were not thick, so that he was able to proceed without making very much noise. He heard new sounds ahead, not rustlings, but clatterings, as if things were being casually moved about.

He reached the far side of the channel and slogged up the bank, pushing aside reeds and grass; he paused at the top to peer ahead.

The gray point was not in sight, but something else was, something yellow-brown, warm and inviting in the setting sun. It looked very much like a thatched roof. From his previous viewpoint it had blended with the surrounding foliage.

He was so intrigued by this evidence of a human habitation where he had expected none that he forgot his pursuers for the moment and made his way toward the roof without first checking behind. He knew that the inhabitant was just as likely to be a northerner as an Ethsharite, but if the gray thing had indeed been a hat, then whoever wore it was probably not a soldier. Valder was armed and reasonably capable. He had the sword on his hip and a dagger on his belt; a sling was tucked away. He wore a breastplate of good steel. His helmet had been lost two days earlier, and he had abandoned his bow when he had run out of reusable arrows, but he still felt confident that he could handle any civilian, whether northerner, Ethsharite, or unknown.

One reason for his intense interest in the roof was that

its mysterious owner might well have a boat, since he or she lived here in a coastal marsh—and that might save Valder the trouble of building a raft, as well as being safer and more comfortable.

He crept forward through the tall grass, across another dry patch, then through a reed-clogged expanse of water and mud and over another hummock, and found himself looking at a tidy little hut. The walls were plastered over with yellowish baked mud or clay; wooden shutters covered the two small windows on the near side. The roof, as he had thought, was thatch. A doorway faced the ocean, with a heavy drape hooked back to leave it mostly open. Seated in the doorway opening was the hut's inhabitant, an old man in a gray robe, his tall, pointed hat perched on one knee. He was leaning back against the frame, staring out over the sea at the setting sun. The hut was built on the highest bit of land in the marsh, but faced down a short, steep, bare slope, giving a fine view of rolling waves and crying gulls.

Valder saw no weapons, but that didn't mean the old man had none; he had no way of knowing what might be inside the hut. The hat and robe did seem to resemble an archaic wizard's costume, and wizards of any sort could be dangerous.

He saw nothing to indicate the man's nationality, unless he counted the fact that the Northern Empire had very few wizards, archaic or otherwise—but then, the garb could easily be that of some obscure variety of sorcerer or other northern magician. He debated with himself what action he should take. He was not about to turn and leave, with the patrol still somewhere behind him. He could approach by stealth, try to take the old man by surprise, but that would appear definitely hostile and might cost him an ally, and, with the rustling grass, stealth might not be possible. Far better, he decided, to make his presence known and then see how the hut-dweller reacted.

With that resolve, he stood up straight, waved a hand in the air, and called, "Hello, there!"

The old man started violently, grabbed at his rope belt, and looked about wildly.

"Hello! Over here!" Valder called.

Spotting him at last, the man got to his feet and stared at Valder in open astonishment. "Who in Hell are *you*?" he demanded.

He spoke in Ethsharitic; Valder relaxed somewhat and looked the old man over.

He was short and scrawny, with unkempt white hair hacked off raggedly at shoulder length and a messy beard. The gray robe he wore was clean but badly worn, with faded patches at each elbow and faint stains here and there. The pointed gray hat had fallen unnoticed to the ground when its owner arose. A rope belt encircled his waist and carried a large leather pouch on one side, a sheathed dagger on the other, where it had been hidden from Valder before; the old man's right hand rested on the hilt of the knife. His feet were bare, his eyes wide, and his mouth open with surprise.

He did not look dangerous, despite the dagger; for one thing, the weapon was still sheathed, where an experienced fighter would have drawn it automatically. Valder guessed the man to be a hermit, someone who hadn't seen another human being in years. His amazement at Valder's presence was very evident.

"I'm lost and alone," Valder replied.

The old man stared at him for a moment, then called, "Didn't ask that." He sounded peevish; his surprise was fading into irritation at Valder's intrusion.

"I'm a soldier; I got separated from my unit. You don't expect me to give my name, do you? For all I know you're an enemy magician; if I tell you my name, you might have power over me."

The old man squinted, nodded an acknowledgment of the truth of Valder's words, and then motioned with his left hand for Valder to approach. His right hand remained on the hilt of his knife. "Come here, soldier," he said.

With his own right hand on the hilt of his sword, Valder made his way through a few feet of grass and several yards of mud and reeds and eventually splashed up out of the marsh onto the little island of dry ground surrounding the hut. He stood waiting while the old man looked him over carefully. As he waited, he remembered the three northerners somewhere behind him and suppressed an urge to tell the old man to hurry up; there was no need to frighten him yet.

"Ethsharitic, hah?" the old man said at last.

"Yes. Scout First Class, with the Western Command under General Gor."

"What are you doing out here, then? Nothing to scout around here." Before Valder could reply, he added with sudden harshness, "Isn't any fighting around here, is there?"

"I got cut off from my unit, far south of here, and got chased north. The fighting is still a long way off. I thought maybe you could help me—loan me a boat or something."

"Maybe I can. No boat, but come in and tell me about it and we'll see." He gestured and led the way into the hut.

Valder smiled. The old man's face was as easy to read as a baby's. He had obviously forgotten how to control or conceal his emotions after being alone for so long; Valder had plainly seen his initial surprise and confusion turn first to annoyance at this unexpected disruption of his routine and then to eager curiosity. Valder could not be sure, but he guessed the old man was also eager for a little human companionship. Even a hermit might get lonely eventually.

He followed the old man into the hut, ducking his head to clear the low doorframe.

CHAPTER 2

*A*s they stepped inside, the old man asked, "You want something to eat?"

"No," Valder answered tersely.

The hermit paused and turned to look at him. "The old bloodstone charm? Spell of Sustenance, that one?"

Reluctantly, Valder nodded. He hadn't expected the old man to guess the reason for his abstinence so readily. If any food or drink were to pass his lips, or even if he salivated too much, the spell would be broken and he would need to forage or carry supplies like any ordinary wanderer; accepting anything from the hermit was therefore out of the question. Unfortunately, the old man now knew that Valder carried a bloodstone, which, although not exactly a fortune in gems, was a fairly rare and precious item, particularly in this northern wilderness so far from the mines of Akalla.

The old man obviously had some acquaintance with magic, as Valder had suspected, to realize so quickly why a weary traveler might refuse an offer of food.

Then the hermit stepped aside and opened the shutters, allowing his guest a good look at the hut's interior, and

Valder knew that his host had far more than a passing acquaintance with magic.

The basic furnishings were simple and practical. A bed consisting of a mattress, pillow, and furs lay against the base of one wall; a table against another wall held a basin, pitcher, and assorted pots, pans, and kitchen implements. A cozy wicker armchair stood beside the table and a large wooden chest that could serve as either another chair or a low table was nearby. Those were the only ordinary furniture, but the remaining space was by no means empty. Shelves and cabinets lined every wall, and free-standing sets of shelves occupied much of the floor. Every shelf and cabinet was crammed to overflowing with bottles, jars, boxes, vials, and bizarre paraphernalia. It was obvious why the hermit had been able to identify the Spell of Sustenance so easily.

"You're a wizard, aren't you?" Valder said. Only a wizard had any use for such things as mummified bats and bottled organs, so far as Valder was aware. Sorcery, witchcraft, demonology, and theurgy all had their own ceremonial trappings, but those were not among them.

The old man glanced at the cluttered shelves as he sank into the wicker chair. "Yes, I am," he said. "Are you?"

"No," Valder answered, "I'm just a soldier."

"You've got that spell."

"They issue that to any scout who's going out on patrol for more than a day and a night." He looked around again, impressed by the arcane bric-a-brac.

"Sit down," the hermit said, pointing at the wooden chest. "Sit down, and tell me what's happening in the world."

Valder's feet were tired and sore—in fact, his entire body was tired and sore. He settled gratefully onto the wooden trunk, allowing himself to forget momentarily that he had no time to rest while the northerners were after him. His boots made a wet squeaking as his weight was removed.

"Get those off," the wizard said. "I'll light a fire and you can dry them out. And *I'm* hungry, even if *you* can't eat; I don't use that charm if I can help it. It wears you down if you keep it going too long, you know; it can ruin your health. If you don't think the smell will break the enchantment, I'm going to make my dinner."

"A fire would be wonderful," Valder said, reaching down to remove his boots. "Please don't let me interfere; you go right ahead and eat."

As he pulled off his second boot, however, he suddenly remembered his pursuers. They might, he realized, arrive at any moment, if he had not lost them by entering the marsh. "Ah . . . Wizard?" he asked, "Do you speak the northern tongue?"

The sun had set and the light was beginning to fade; the old man was lighting a fish-oil lamp with a flame that sprang from the tip of his finger. When the wick was alight, he curled his finger into his palm, snuffing the flame, and turned to look at his guest. "No," he said. "Haven't needed it. Why?"

"Because there's a northern patrol after me. I should have told you sooner. They spotted me four days ago and have been following ever since. There are three of them; one's a sorcerer, and at least one is *shatra*."

"You led them *here*?" The old man's voice became a screech.

"Well, I'm not sure of that. I may have lost them. I'm hoping they wouldn't expect me to try and cross the marsh and that their trackers, if they have any, can't follow me across water. If you could speak their language, I was hoping you could convince them that I'm not here; after all, this far north, one of their people would be just as likely as one of ours, even out here on the coast. If you hadn't spoken Ethsharitic when I hailed you, I wouldn't have known which side you were on and I might have gone around you. Maybe you can convince them that I *did* go around."

"I wish I *hadn't* spoken Ethsharitic! I don't know any of their speech; I can't fool them for a minute. I came out here to get away from the war, damn it, not to get tangled up with *shatra*!"

"I wondered why you were here. Well, if you deserted,

here's a chance to get yourself a pardon; just help me get away from these three."

"I didn't..."

A voice called from outside, and the wizard stopped abruptly in mid-sentence. The call was in the harsh northern tongue.

"Oh, damn it!" the hermit said. He reached for a thick leather-bound book on one of the nearby shelves.

"Look, I'll see if I can slip out and lead them away," Valder said, suddenly contrite. "I never meant to get anyone else into trouble." As he spoke he got to his feet, leaving his boots behind and stumbling toward the doorway. The wizard ignored him, fully occupied as he was in pawing desperately through the fat, leather-bound volume and muttering to himself.

Valder leaned out the door, then jumped back in as a streak of red flame flashed past, tearing through the twilight inches from his face.

Seconds later, three sharp smacks sounded, followed by an instant of uncanny whistling screams as sorcerous projectiles tore across the interior of the hut at roughly the level of a man's chest, narrowly missing Valder's arm as he fell back. The sound ended in a second three-part snap as they exited through the north wall.

Not quite sure how he got there, Valder found himself sprawled on the hard-packed dirt of the hut floor. He looked up and realized that the wizard was still standing, book in hand, staring nonplussed at the holes in his wall.

"Get down, wizard!" Valder called.

The wizard still stood motionless.

Concerned, Valder shouted, "Are you all right?"

"What?" The magician stirred uncertainly.

"Wizard, I think you had better get down, quickly; they're certain to try again."

"Oh." Slowly, the wizard sank to his hands and knees, keeping the book nearby. "What *was* that?" he asked, staring at the holes.

"*I* don't know," Valder answered. "Some damned northern sorcery."

The wizard peered at the soldier in the dim light of the

flickering fish-oil lamp and the last gray twilight; his scraggly beard almost reached the floor, and his robe was bunched up around him, revealing bony ankles. "Sorcery? I don't know any sorcery."

"Neither do I," Valder replied. "But they do." He jerked a thumb at the south wall.

The wizard looked at the three entry holes. A wisp of smoke trailed up from a book that had been pierced by one; the other two had gone through jars, strewing shards of glass. "Protections," he said. "We need protections, ones that will work against sorcery." He began desperately turning pages in his book.

Valder watched him warily. No new assault had immediately followed the projectiles, and that seemed like a good sign. The northerners might be waiting for someone to move and provide them with a target, he thought. If so, they would have a good long wait; he was not that foolish.

The wizard stopped, slammed a hand down on the open book, and looked at Valder, anger and fear on his face. "What were those things?" he asked. "I have to know what I'm defending against."

"I don't know what those things that came through the wall were, but I know what sent them. I told you, a northern patrol is after me. *Shatra*—you know what *shatra* are, don't you?"

"I'm not a fool, soldier; *shatra* are demon warriors."

"More or less; they look like men, but fight like demons."

"Damn you, soldier, I came here to get away from the war!" the wizard burst out.

"You told me that. Tell *them* that; maybe they won't bother you. I doubt they have anything against Ethsharitic deserters."

"You have no call to insult me; I am *not* a deserter. I was never enlisted. I served my apprenticeship under a civilian advisor, not a combat wizard, and worked thirty years as an advisor myself before I retired and came out here to do my own research."

"Research?" Valder ducked his head instinctively as another projectile whistled through the hut; this one entered through an open window and departed through a box of gray-brown powder, leaving a slowly settling cloud of dust hanging in the air above them. "You mean *magical* research?"

"Yes, magical research." He waved a hand in the direction of the nearest jam-packed shelves.

"Oh." Valder stared at the old man. "And I thought you were a coward, hiding out here! I apologize, wizard, for wronging you. You've got far more courage than I do if you've been experimenting in wizardry."

"Oh, it's not that bad," the wizard replied modestly, brushing at the dust that had settled on his sleeve and open book.

"I've heard that the life expectancy of a research wizard is just twenty-three working days," Valder argued.

"Oh, but that's for *military* research! I don't do anything like that—no flame spells or death-runes or juggernauts. I've been working with animations and I've been very careful. Besides, I use a lot of protective spells. That's what most of this book is. They were my old master's specialty."

"Protective spells?"

"Yes, of course."

"Have you got spells there that will stop those three?"

"I don't know. Look, soldier, you must know what wizardry is like; it's tricky, unreliable stuff, and there's no telling what a new spell will do—if it does anything at all. I haven't gotten any of the results I wanted in my research so far. I've come up with some interesting things, but I don't know what will work against *shatra*. Demons aren't like men or beasts, and *shatra* are half demon, aren't they? I've got a spell here that *may* help us; it's not much, but it's the best I could find in a hurry that won't take more time than we've got or ingredients I don't have. It's an aversion charm." He rose to his knees and snatched a jar and a small wooden box from a low shelf.

Valder paused and listened before replying, then said, "I hope you can do it fast, wizard; I hear something moving out there."

The hermit paused, a pinch of malodorous green powder in one hand. "I don't hear..." he began.

The rest of his words were lost in a whooshing roar as the roof of the hut vanished in a ball of flame. Blinking and shielding his eyes against the sudden glare, Valder grabbed one of the old man's bony arms and dragged him unceremoniously across the dirt floor, keeping his head low and dodging scraps of flaming debris that spattered down on all sides.

The wizard flung the powder across both of them, gestured with his free hand, and said something incomprehensible. Something flashed pale blue where the powder fell, cool against the orange blaze of burning thatch; the old man grabbed at the knife on his belt and yelled, "The door is the other way!"

"I know," Valder shouted back over the roar of the flames. "That's why we're going this way! They're probably waiting out front!" With his left hand still locked around the old man's wrist, Valder drew his sword with his right and jabbed at the back wall above the wizard's bedding.

As he had thought, the smooth coating was a thin layer of baked mud, and the wall itself just bundled reeds; the mud broke away easily, allowing him to hack an opening through the dried reeds with his blade. A moment later the two men were outside, tumbling down into the brackish water of the marsh; the wizard spluttered angrily while Valder scanned the surrounding area for the enemy.

Someone was visible off to the left; Valder whispered in the old man's ear, "Lie still."

The hermit started to protest; Valder jabbed him with the hilt of his sword.

"No, listen," the wizard insisted, "I have a spell that can help here."

Valder glanced at the shadowy figure of the enemy soldier, standing well back and apparently unaware of their presence, and then at the blazing fury of the thatch roof. "Go ahead," he said. "But hurry, and keep it quiet."

The wizard nodded, splashing, then drew his dagger and stabbed the back of Valder's hand.

"What the hell . . ." The soldier snatched his hand away; the wound was only a scratch, but it hurt.

"I need a little of your blood," the wizard explained.

He smeared a streak of blood along Valder's forearm, dabbed a few drops on the soldier's face and neck, then pricked his own arm and distributed a little of his own blood similarly on himself.

Behind them, the fire was eating its way down the walls of the wizard's hut, lighting the surrounding circle of marsh a vivid orange, its reflections in the murky water a labyrinth of flame. Valder knew that somewhere in the blackness beyond the illuminated area the northerners were watching; he could not see them anymore, as the fire's glow kept his eyes from adapting sufficiently to the dark, and nothing at all remained of his night-sight spell. He wished that he had one of the sorcerers' masks that the enemy used for night vision; they were awkward to wear and carry, but they seemed never to wear out the way wizard-sight did.

The old man was muttering an incantation, working his wizardry, whatever it was. Valder wondered, as he had before, why Ethshar used wizardry so much more than the Empire did and sorcery so much less. This difference in magical preferences was hardly a new question; he and his comrades had mulled it over dozens of times back in camp. Everybody knew that the Empire used demonology and Ethshar used theurgy, but that just made sense, since the gods were on Ethshar's side, and the demons on the Empire's. Wizardry and sorcery seemed to have no such inherent bias, yet a northern wizard was rare indeed, and southern sorcerers almost as scarce. Neither side, it seemed, got much use from witchcraft, and that was another mystery.

He peered out at the surrounding gloom and again spotted the northerner he had seen before, at the very edge of the circle of light. That, Valder thought, was probably the one who had ignited the hut. He was slowly circling closer to the burning structure, obviously looking for any sign that his intended victims had escaped. Valder could make out one of the intricate metal wands used by combat sorcerers cradled in the northerner's arms; he gave up any thought of fighting the man on even terms and perhaps killing him before his companions could arrive. One of those wands could rip a man to pieces almost instantaneously, from a dozen paces away.

Something exploded with a bang and a tinkling of glass somewhere inside the flaming hut, and Valder remembered the shelves and cabinets crowded with jars and boxes. He guessed that several more would probably explode when the flames reached them.

The northerner turned at the sound, wand held ready, and Valder looked desperately for some way to take advantage of the instant of surprise. He found none.

If the man came closer, Valder estimated, ambush was a possibility; at close enough range, sorcery would be no better than a sword, and a knife might be better than either. Thinking of the wizard's dagger, he realized that the sound of the old man's incantation had stopped. That reminded him of the drawn blood, and he glanced at his injured hand.

His mouth fell open in horror; instead of a simple scratch, he saw the flesh laid open to the bone, blood spilling out thickly, as if half-congealed. When his jaw fell, more blood poured out, running down his beard and into the mud—yet he felt no pain save for a slight twinge in his hand.

Confused and frightened, he looked at the wizard and shrank back involuntarily; the old man was obviously horribly dead. His skin was corpse-white, splotched with cyanotic blue-gray, and blood dribbled from his nose and mouth. His arm was a mangled ruin, and his throat cut open clear to his spine.

"Gods!" Valder gasped. The spell must have gone wrong, he thought; he had heard of spells backfiring. Backfires were what made magical research so deadly.

The old man smiled, his expression unspeakably hideous through the half-dried blood. "The Sanguinary Deception," he whispered. "Looks awful, doesn't it?"

"You're alive?" Valder had difficulty accepting it, despite the old man's movement and speech.

"Of course I'm alive. So are you, and you probably look worse than I do. It's a simple trick, but effective; doesn't the army use it any more?"

"I don't know," Valder said, staring in fascination at the hermit.

"Well, it's a good trick, and if they aren't using it, they're fools. Now, shut up and lie still, and they'll think we're dead."

Valder stared at the old man for another second, then slumped back and did his best to look dead.

Something else shattered amid the flames, and a loud clatter followed; Valder guessed that a shelf had given way, spilling its entire contents. He stole a glance at the hermit and saw that the old man was no longer smiling at his ruse; instead his face was contorted with anger and pain at the destruction of his home and his work.

From the corner of one eye Valder noticed the northerner doing something with his wand, perhaps making a mystical gesture or perhaps only adjusting something; then he lifted it to chest height and pointed it at the fiery remains of the hut. Red streaks of light scarred the air, etching themselves into Valder's vision, and the burning ruin fell inward all at once with a roar, collapsing into a smoldering heap less than two feet high.

A seething hiss sounded.

The northerner did something else to his wand and pointed it again; something seemed to leap from the wand to the wreckage. With a white flash and a sound like tearing metal, the smoldering heap vanished in a shower of burning fragments, leaving only a crater.

For several seconds lumps of hot mud and burning reeds splashed into the marsh around the two fugitives, sprinkling them liberally with salt water and mud, but not actually striking either of them. It seemed to Valder that some pieces actually dodged aside in mid-air in order to miss them. "That aversion spell," the wizard whispered beside him.

After what seemed like hours, quiet and darkness descended again. Valder lay absolutely still. For a long moment the only sound was the hissing of burning debris as it was extinguished by the marsh; then a voice called out. Valder could not understand the words. He whispered, "Do you know what he's saying?"

"No," the old man answered. "I told you, I don't know their language."

Another voice called back to the first, and both laughed.

Then came the sound of feet slogging through the marsh with no attempt at stealth.

"They must think we're dead," Valder whispered.

"That's the idea," the wizard replied.

They lay still as footsteps splashed about; when the sound stopped for a moment Valder risked a glance and saw two of the northerners poking about the smoking crater, carrying torches. One stopped, knelt, then stood, holding out something for his companion to see. Valder squinted. He couldn't be sure, but the object looked like a scorched bone.

The northerners exchanged a few words in their own language, and one gave a short, unpleasant laugh, then glanced around at the surrounding marshland. Valder froze. The northerner's eyes came to rest looking directly at the spot where the two Ethsharites lay. The man called something to his companion, then marched toward them, moving out of Valder's line of sight. Valder did not dare to shift his eyes.

A moment later a boot splashed into the marsh beside him and a hand gripped his hair and pulled him up. The pull hurt, but Valder kept himself limp, refusing to react, playing dead. Blood dripped from his beard.

He toyed briefly with the idea of pulling his knife and taking the northerner by surprise, but the sorcerer was waiting, watching from the rim of the crater, and Valder did not think much of the idea of suicide, even when taking an enemy with him. He had too much to live for. He hung limp in the northerner's grasp.

Then the man dropped him, and he fell heavily to the mud; the side of his face stung with the impact, but he kept still.

Done with Valder, the northerner rolled the wizard over with his foot; the old man's arm fell splashing into the water.

Satisfied, the northerner called something, then turned and slogged off across the marsh. A moment later Valder made out two other sets of footsteps moving away. The torchlight, too, receded, leaving the Ethsharites in darkness.

When the footsteps were safely out of earshot, Valder

waited for another long moment to be certain, his face in the mud and his nose full of the stench of decaying aquatic life. Finally, he cautiously raised his head and peered about. He saw no sign of anyone anywhere, save himself and the wizard. A few sparks still smoldered here and there among the grasses, insects chirped, and both moons were in the sky, but in general the night was dark and silent.

Slowly and carefully he rose to his knees and then to his feet, water streaming from the folds of his drenched tunic and kilt and pouring out from inside his breastplate. When no one shouted and no lights or sorcerous weapon-flashes appeared, he reached down and helped the bedraggled and gory little wizard up.

The old man stood, a trifle unsteady at first, and brushed at the mud that caked the front of his robe, shaking mud and water from his hands between strokes. He ignored the torrents of drying blood. When he decided that he had removed what he could, he stood, dripping, and gazed through the smoky gloom at the crater where his home had been.

When the sight had had time to sink in, he turned on Valder, fists clenched and shaking, and screamed, "You stupid fool! You led them right to me! Now look what they've done!"

"Don't shout," Valder whispered desperately. "We don't know how far they've gone, or how well *shatra* can hear."

The wizard ceased shouting and glanced at the distant line of trees, faintly visible in the moonlight. When no menacing figures appeared, he pointed an accusing finger at the crater. "Look at that!" he cried.

"I'm sorry," Valder said with genuine contrition, uncomfortable speaking to what looked like a mangled corpse. "I didn't know they would do anything like that."

"You didn't know," the wizard mocked. "Well, soldier, you know now. And what do I do, now that they've blown my house to powder looking for you? Do you know that? I haven't even had my dinner!"

"I'm sorry," Valder repeated helplessly. "What can I do?"

"Haven't you done enough? Why don't you just go

away and leave me alone? The moons are up; you'll be able to see."

"Oh, I can't just leave; what would *you* do, here alone?"

"What would *I* do? I'll tell you what I'll do; I'll rebuild my house, just as I built it before, restock my supplies somehow, though I don't know how, and go on with my research just as if you had never come along, you blundering idiot!"

"Your supplies? All those bottles and jars?"

"That's right, all those jars. I had everything from dragon's blood to virgin's tears, twenty years of careful scrimping and saving and pilfering, and the gods alone can know how I'll ever replace it all!"

"I'll stay and do what I can to help..."

"I don't want your help! Just go away!"

"Where am I supposed to go? The patrol thinks I'm dead, but I'm still cut off, a hundred miles behind enemy lines. I might as well stay here and help you rebuild; I can't go home."

I don't want your help." The wizard's tone had changed from righteous fury to petulance.

"You're stuck with it, unless you can figure out how to get me back to friendly territory."

The wizard stared at him resentfully. "Just walk back. No one will bother a walking corpse."

"The spell is permanent?" Valder was horrified. The idea of spending the rest of his life gushing illusory blood was unappetizing, to say the least.

"No," the wizard admitted. "It wears off in a day or so."

"It took me two months to come this far north!"

"Well, I can't fly you out with my supplies all gone! Even the simplest levitation I know needs ingredients I haven't got any more." He paused; before Valder could speak, he continued, "I have an idea, though. Give me your sword. You've been waving it about; we might as well use it."

"What?" Valder realized he was still holding his drawn sword; he had never sheathed it after cutting through the wall of the hut and had picked it up without thinking when he got to his feet. "What do you want it for?"

"I want to get rid of you, idiot."

"How? By killing me?"

"No, of course not. You may be a fool, but that's not enough reason to kill you. I don't kill anybody. Besides, you are an Ethsharite, even if you are an idiot, and I'm still a loyal Ethsharite myself, even out here."

"Then what do you want my sword for?"

"I'm going to enchant it. I'm going to put every spell I can find on it, every enchantment I can come up with that might help you fight your way back and out of my life forever."

"Can you do that without your supplies?"

"I can do *something*; I know a few spells that don't take anything fancy, and a couple of them are good ones. It may not be the greatest magic sword in the world when I'm done, but it will get you home, I promise you. I've got one spell I invented myself that I'm sure will do it, and it doesn't need any ingredients I can't find here in the marsh. If you stay around here very long, I *may* kill you, Ethsharite or not—and neither of us wants that to happen."

Valder was still reluctant to give up his weapon, though the offer was tempting. He had not really wanted to build a boat and sail down the coast; he was no sailor, and storm season was approaching. He couldn't even swim. "How do I know I can trust you?" he asked.

The wizard snorted. "You don't need to trust me. You're twice my size and a third my age; I'm a feeble little old man and you're a trained, healthy young soldier. Even if I had the sword, you could handle me, couldn't you? You've got the knife on your belt; I'm not leaving you defenseless."

Valder remained wary. "You're a wizard, though, not just an old man."

"Well, then, if I'm a powerful enough wizard to handle you, how much difference can that stupid sword make? I've already got my own dagger, if I need a blade for some spell. You can't have it both ways; either I'm too old and feeble to worry about, or I already have the advantage. Look, soldier, I'm in no hurry. I can't do any magic to speak of until morning, because I'll need to see what I'm doing. You can either get yourself out of here before dawn, or you can stay and let me enchant your sword—or you can stay and annoy me enough that I'll turn you into . . . into something unpleasant. That would be better than killing you, at least. You suit yourself. Right now I'm going to try and get some sleep and see if I can forget that I haven't had my dinner and that my house is a pile of ash. You do as you please." He turned and stamped his way up out of the marsh onto the mounded rim of the crater.

Valder stood for a moment, sword in hand and his bare feet in briny muck, thinking it over.

After due consideration he shrugged and followed the old man.

CHAPTER 3

The rain began around midnight, Valder judged, though
after the clouds covered the moons it was hard to be sure
of the time. It trailed off into morning mist an hour or
two before dawn. He was soaked through and had slept
very little when the sun's rays managed to slip through
the trees to the southeast and spill across the marsh, slowly
burning away the mist. Worst of all, he was dreadfully
thirsty and ravenously hungry; he was unsure whether a
splash of marsh water was responsible, or the blood of
the Sanguinary Deception, but something had disrupted
his Spell of Sustenance. The bloodstone was still secure
in its pouch, but his fast had been broken.

The wizard had stayed dry throughout the rain, Valder
noticed when the morning light illuminated the old man's
white hair; it was still a tangle of knots and fluff smeared
with phantasmal blood but not plastered to his head as
Valder's was. The soldier assumed that the hermit had
achieved this enviable state of desiccation by somehow
keeping the aversion spell going.

The old man did not appear very comfortable, though;

at first light he was up and pawing through the debris that lined the crater where his house had stood, spattering unreal gore in all directions.

He did not appear to be performing a spell, but Valder never felt very confident when dealing with unfamiliar magicians of any sort and knew better than to risk interrupting a wizard at work. Besides, by daylight the lingering effects of the Deception made the little hermit unspeakably repulsive.

Valder had spent the night curled up between two grassy mounds, above the waterline but still fairly sheltered. Now he climbed up atop one of the hillocks and settled down to watch the old man.

The hermit heard the rustling and looked up. "Oh, there you are, soldier," he said. "Have you seen anything to eat?"

"No," Valder said. "Have you?"

"No, and I'm hungry. My stomach has been growling for hours. I missed my dinner, you know."

"I know. I'm hungry, too, and thirsty."

"Oh. Spell broke, did it? Can't say I'm really sorry, after all the trouble you've brought me. There's a clean stream back in the woods, over that way," he said, pointing vaguely northeast. "If you can find something that will hold water, go fetch some. You can drink your fill while you're there; I don't care. I'm going to see about catching some breakfast, since I can't find anything left of my pantry. You might bring back some firewood, too, so I can cook whatever I find; everything here is either soaked or already burned."

Valder nodded. The old man's tone was not very friendly, but at least he was willing to talk. "I'll do my best," he answered.

"Do that," the hermit replied. "Oh, and give me your sword; I want to look it over."

"You still intend to enchant it somehow?"

"Oh, yes; how else can I get rid of you quickly? I've found a few things here; I'll manage. Now, give me that thing and see if you can find something that doesn't leak."

Valder shrugged; he made his way across the blasted

remains of the hut to where the wizard prowled and handed over his sword and sheath. After all, he told himself, he wouldn't need it while fetching water, and he *would* need both hands. The northerners were gone, and he could handle most other dangers, either by running or with his dagger.

The old man accepted the weapon and looked it over casually, noting the ugly but serviceable workmanship— bow grip, straight blade, without any frills or ornamentation. He nodded. "It should do very well. Go get some water."

Valder said nothing, but began looking for a container.

A quick circuit of the crater showed nothing suitable for the job, but a second glance at one of the outer slopes turned up the top half of a very large glass jar, the lid still screwed tightly in place; Valder hoped that would serve. Careful of the jagged edge, he cradled it in one arm and headed off in the direction the old man had indicated.

Unlike the old man, however, he had not spent years living in the marsh and learning its every twist and turn; he found himself slogging across muddy ditches, climbing over crumbling sandpiles, wading through branches of the sea, and pushing through reeds and rough grasses. His unshod feet acquired a variety of cuts, scrapes, and bites; his socks were soaked through and rapidly falling to tatters.

Eventually he gave up following the direct route through the marsh and instead turned his path toward the nearest dry land. Once firmly ashore on solid ground, under the familiar pines, he turned north and made his way along the edge of the marsh until he came to a stream he assumed to be the one the old man had pointed out.

The water was clear, but salty and brackish; he turned and walked upstream, cursing the wizard.

Roughly a hundred yards from where he had first tasted the water, the stream poured down across a rocky outcropping, spilling exuberantly from one pool into another along a narrow stony path down the face of a rise in the ground. The water in the upper pool was fresh, sweet, and cold; Valder lay on his belly and drank eagerly.

When he lifted his face, he was momentarily shocked to see blood swirling downstream; then he remembered the Deception and laughed.

He rinsed out his broken jar, then filled it, and was relieved to see that it could still hold a decent quantity of water. He left the jar on the bank of the stream while he looked for firewood.

Fresh pine, he knew, smoked and spat. Any wood was less than ideal when green, but pine was especially unsatisfactory. He looked about in hopes of finding something better.

The best he could do was a fallen limb, perhaps once the top of a tree but now a crooked, dried-out chunk of wood as long as he was tall and as thick as his forearm. Broken up, with kindling beneath, he judged it would serve well enough.

He gathered a pouchful of twigs and dry needles to start the fire with, then tucked the full jar in the bend of one arm, hefted the limb in his other hand, and headed back toward the marsh.

The journey back was even more difficult than the trip out. Although he knew better where he was going and what terrain he faced, he had the added problems of keeping the water in the inverted half of a jar and keeping the wood, already wet from the night's rain, from becoming even wetter. This last proved virtually impossible in crossing the marsh, but he managed to reach the crater with only one end of the branch newly soaked and with several inches of water still in his makeshift container.

The old man did not immediately acknowledge his return; the wizard was bent over the sword, inscribing blue-glowing runes in the air an inch above the blade with the tip of his finger. His false wounds appeared to be healing, Valder noticed, and some color had returned to his face. Valder dropped the tree-limb on a convenient mound of earth, placed the water container nearby, and glanced around.

Some semblance of organization had been created, turning the crater from simple desolation to a camp among the ruins. A small pile of crabs lay to one side of the wizard; that, Valder guessed, would be breakfast, though he could not imagine how anyone could have found so many crabs so quickly in such northern waters as these. Arranged about the wizard were various elements of his arcane paraphernalia—a fragmentary skull, small glittering stones, shards of this and that, and five broken candlestubs. Valder marveled that any candles could have survived the preceding night's inferno.

After a long moment, as he was beginning to wonder whether there was anything he should be doing, the wizard looked up at Valder and said, "Cook the crabs, why don't you? Boil them, if you think that thing will hold water well enough."

Valder looked at the crabs, then looked at the broken jar, and then looked back at the wizard. "I thought you were thirsty," he said.

"No, I'm hungry; *you* were thirsty. Cook the crabs."

Annoyed, Valder scooped four of the crabs into the broken jar and set about building a fire. He had no trouble in breaking the wood into suitable lengths and arranging it over the tinder, but found that the twigs and needles were still damp from the rain, though he had chosen the driest he could find, and would not light readily. He knelt, smothering curses lest he accidentally say something that might let demons interfere with the wizard's spell-making, and struck spark after spark without success.

After several minutes he sat back on his haunches and found the old man standing beside him. Without a word, the wizard extended a forefinger that flamed at the tip like a candle, his nail serving as the wick, as he had the night before when lighting the lamp. He thrust it into the little heap of tinder, which flared up immediately.

That done, he snuffed his finger by curling it into his palm, then used his other hand to flick a yellowish powder on the young flames. He said one unfamiliar word. With a sudden roar, the fire leaped up and engulfed wood and jar alike; a second later the wood was burning steadily and naturally, the water beginning to steam slightly.

"Call me when they're ready," the old man said as he turned back toward Valder's sword.

Valder watched him leave, trying to tell himself that the wizard was not accustomed to dealing with people and could not know how annoying his behavior was. When the old man had settled cross-legged beside the sword and begun making a new series of mystical gestures, Valder turned back to the improvised cooking pot and poked at the crabs with his dagger far more viciously than culinary concerns required.

He tried to force himself to relax. He had escaped the northern patrol—in fact, the old fool had saved his life with his spells. The wizard had told him where to find water, had provided food, and had lighted the fire when Valder could not. There was no cause for annoyance save for the old man's utter disregard for the little diplomacies of everyday life. Valder had always had a healthy respect for such niceties and had used them to forestall a few barracks brawls; he wondered whether two months alone in the woods and four days of desperate flight might have impaired his own behavior sufficiently to justify the hermit's rudeness.

By the time he judged the crabs to be fit to eat, he was calm again. The heat of the fire had dried most of the rain, mist, and marsh out of his hair and clothing, and the improvement in his comfort had contributed to his improvement in mood.

He called, "Wizard! Breakfast is ready!"

For several seconds the only reply Valder received was the bubbling of the water in the broken jar, and the crackle of the flames. Finally, the wizard paused in his mysterious gesturing and called, "Keep it warm, will you? I can't stop here."

Valder shrugged. "Please yourself," he answered. He fished out a crab with his knife and sat down to eat.

When he had eaten three of the four—as might be expected so far north, none were very large—he threw three more in the pot and settled back against a hillock, feeling reasonably content. Settled comfortably, he watched the old man.

The candle-stubs were burning, and the smoke was weaving about unnaturally, forming something resembling blue tatted lace hanging in mid-air; his sword stood upright, unsupported, in the center of the tangle. Valder had no doubt that the wizard was doing *something* to the weapon, though he had no idea what.

The old man barked a single word that Valder didn't quite catch, in a voice surprisingly powerful for so short and thin a body; the sword and smoke froze, hanging immobile in the air. The wizard rose to his feet, arms spread wide, walked sideways around the column of petrified smoke, then turned away from it and strolled over to the cookfire.

"Let me use your knife, soldier; all mine are either lost or in use." He gestured, and Valder noticed for the first time that the wizard's own dagger was balanced on its tip below the sword, spinning about and gleaming more brightly silver than the light of the sun could explain. He shrugged and handed the old man his knife.

The wizard ate all four of the cooked crabs in silence, wolfing down the flesh eagerly. When he had finished and tossed the shells in the marsh, he remarked, "Magic is hungry work, and that smoke is making my throat dry. Go for some more water, soldier, if you aren't doing anything else."

"Give me back my knife first," Valder replied. He saw no point in wasting argument or courtesy on the old man.

The wizard handed back the dagger, and Valder reluctantly set out for the stream.

He spent the rest of the day alternately sitting doing nothing, and fetching wood or water—or, once, three black pine cones, an item the wizard needed for his spells. Valder discovered that black pine cones were a scarce item; most were brown or gray. Eventually he located an odd bluish tree that yielded the desired objects.

The sun crawled across the cloud-strewn heavens and sank toward the sea, and still the wizard continued with his spell-casting. Glowing runes and weaving smoke were just two of the myriad odd effects Valder observed, and he wondered more and more just what the old man was doing to the sword.

Well after the sun went down, Valder finally dozed off,

not far from the fire, while the wizard was etching fiery red lines in the dirt with a golden something-or-other that was oddly unpleasant to look at.

He was awakened suddenly by a loud whooshing sound and a shout. He started up, reaching automatically for a sword that wasn't there. He glanced about wildly.

The fire had almost died, and there was no longer any magical glow anywhere—no runes in the air nor lines on the earth nor glittering blades. It took him a few moments to interpret the dim shapes he could make out.

The wizard was walking toward him, the sword sheathed and cradled in his arms.

"Here, soldier," he said, thrusting the weapon forward. "Take your damned sword and get out of here!"

"What?" Valder was not at his best when suddenly awakened. He looked blankly at the completely ordinary-looking scabbard and hilt in the wizard's arms.

"I'm finished with your sword, I said. It's carrying all the enchantments I could put on it under the circumstances. If it won't get you home safely, then nothing I know will. Take it and go. And don't draw it until you're over the horizon."

Still befuddled, Valder accepted the sword and looked at it stupidly for a moment before hanging it in its accustomed place on his belt. It looked no different, as far as he could see by the fire's faint glow, from what it had been when he arrived. When it was securely in place, he reached for the hilt to check the draw; a soldier needed to be able to get his blade out quickly.

"No, I said!" the wizard barked at him; a bony hand clamped around his wrist. Irrelevantly, as he looked at the hand, Valder noticed that the last traces of the Sanguinary Deception had vanished. "You mustn't draw it here! It's dangerous! Don't draw it until you need it, and you won't need it until you're well away from here."

"Whatever you say," Valder said, taking his hand off the sword.

The wizard calmed. "That's better. Ah...I gave it a name."

"What?" Valder was still too sleepy to keep up with this apparent change of subject.

"I gave the sword a name; it's to be called Wirikidor."

"Wirikidor? What kind of a name is Wirikidor?"

"An old one, soldier. It's from a language so old that the name of the tongue is forgotten and no trace remains of the people who spoke it. It means 'slayer of warriors,' and it was part of the spell I put on the thing, so now that's its name."

Valder glanced down and resisted the temptation to grip the hilt again. "I was never much for naming swords; some of the men do, but it never seemed to do them any good."

"I didn't say it will do you any good, but that sword's name is Wirikidor now, and I thought you ought to know, since it will be yours. Ah . . . that is, it should be. It's got an untriggered spell on it, a variant of the Spell of True Ownership; whoever draws it next will be its owner for as long as he lives. Make sure that's you, soldier, and the blade will protect you."

"Protect me how?"

"Ah . . . I'm not quite sure, actually."

"It will protect me once I draw it, but I mustn't draw it until I'm leagues from here?"

"That's right."

"What's to protect me until then?"

The wizard glared at him. "Your native wits, of course—except that leaves you unarmed, doesn't it? We'll just have to hope you won't need protection, I guess."

Valder was becoming more awake and alert, awake enough to decide that arguing with the wizard might not be wise. Still, he asked, "That's all you can tell me about it, that it will protect me?"

"That's all I'm *going* to tell you, you blasted fool! Now take your sword and get out of here!"

Valder looked around at the darkness surrounding them; the fire's glow faded within a yard or two, and the clouds were thick enough to hide the moons and stars. He saw no trace of the sun's light to either east or west.

"What time is it?" he asked.

"How should I know? I finished the spell at midnight exactly, or at least I intended to, but you've kept me here arguing long enough that I have no idea what time it might be. It's after midnight, and it's not yet dawn."

Valder said, "I don't know what time it is either, old man, but I do know that I'm not going anywhere until dawn. An enchanted sword isn't going to do me much good if I trip and drown in this stinking marsh."

The wizard glared at him for a long moment, then growled. "Please yourself," he said as he turned and stalked off.

Valder watched his back fade into the gloom, thinking how absurd so small a man looked when angry, then sat down and looked at the familiar scabbard on his belt. He saw nothing different about it, yet the wizard had undeniably worked over it for a day and half a night, with indisputably real magic. The urge to draw it and see if the blade was visibly altered was strong, but Valder had a healthy respect for magic of all sorts; if the old man said it was dangerous, it probably *was* dangerous. Perhaps enough magic lingered in the air from the spell-making to react with the sword's enchantment.

Or perhaps, the thought crept in, the wizard had decided to retaliate for the destruction of his home, and the sword would work some terrible vengeance when drawn, a vengeance the old man did not wish to see.

Valder drove that idea back down; he had little choice but to trust the hermit. He settled back against the hump of ground and was quickly asleep.

CHAPTER 4

*H*is *legs were stiff and cramped when he awoke; he* unfolded them slowly, then flexed them again, working out the stiffness as best he could. When he felt up to it, he pushed himself up onto his battered feet and looked around.

The sun, he was appalled to discover, was halfway up the eastern sky; he had not intended to sleep so long as that. He saw no sign of the old hermit.

He told himself that the wizard had probably gone off to fetch water or food. He decided to wait for the old man's return so that he might say his farewells before heading southward. With that resolved, his next concern was breakfast. He glanced about casually.

The handful of crabs that had not been eaten the day before were gone; Valder supposed they had served as the old man's breakfast. The broken jar was also gone, which supported his theory that the hermit had gone after water. As he continued to look, however, it gradually sank in that *everything* that might be of use was gone. Nothing remained on the site of the destroyed hut but ash and

37

broken glass. The piles of salvaged magical paraphernalia had vanished with their owner.

An automatic check told him that his sword was still securely in its sheath on his belt; he was relieved by that.

He could not imagine how the old man could have cleared everything away so completely, or where he might have gone with it all. Puzzled, he clambered up the rim of the crater, wincing at the scratching of shards of glass against his bare feet.

Runes were gouged into the ash in the center of the crater, showing black against white. They were nothing magical, but merely a message in common Ethsharitic runes.

"Found new place," they said. "Not returning. Good luck."

No signature was included, but one was hardly necessary under the circumstances. Valder stared at the words for a moment, then shrugged. It might be that the wizard was actually somewhere nearby and would return as soon as Valder was gone, he thought, but if so it was none of his concern. The hermit obviously wanted him to leave without further contact, and he saw no reason to argue about it. He took a final look about, then marched southward into the marsh.

He reached dry land without incident. By noon he could no longer see or smell the salt marsh, though a faint whiff of the sea could still be detected on the breeze from the west. Although he was eager to return to his comrades in the south and get out of the wilderness, he stopped when the sun was at its zenith and sat down abruptly on a moss-covered log.

His feet were blistered and would carry him no further without a rest; the day's walk of a mere two or three hours was not so much responsible as was the prior day's abuse and the lack of footwear. He had not taken the time to rig any sort of substitute for the boots that had been burned to ash in the wizard's hut, and his weight was distributed differently without them, putting pressure on parts of his feet that were not accustomed to it.

He was not sure what sort of a substitute he *could*

improvise; he had never before lost a pair of boots while out in the country. It was not a subject that he remembered hearing discussed, either in his training or in barracks chatter; when a pair of boots gave out, they were replaced with another pair of boots. That was one item that had never been subject to shortage, so far as he knew.

His socks, which he had left on for lack of replacements, had worn down to absolute uselessness, their soles consisting of a few stray threads; he peeled them off and hurled them away.

As if aching feet were not sufficient annoyance, he was ravenously hungry. Enough streams had crossed his path to make thirst no problem, but he could not eat pine cones, and the only wildlife he had seen had been a chipmunk he had not thought to pursue.

He stared around at the empty forest, the sun dappling the thick bed of pine needles that covered the ground. He had no food—he had been out on a two-day reconnaissance, and with the sustenance spell, at that—who would have thought he might need food? He had survived for two months without any, thanks to the bloodstone's magic, but that enchantment was broken and gone now.

He did not have any ready means of acquiring food, either. He had his belt, his sling, his knife, and his magicked sword, but that was almost the full extent of his supplies. He had a silver bit tucked away, not so much as a lucky piece as because one never knew what might happen, and even a single coin might bribe a peasant— not that any peasants lived in the northern forests. He had managed to hang onto his flint and steel and he still wore kilt, tunic, and breastplate, though his helmet was long gone. The bloodstone was still safe in its pouch, but useless until he found another wizard to renew the spell.

He wondered if the hermit might be able to cast a Spell of Sustenance and upbraided himself for not asking when he had the chance. If he went back, he would probably be unable to find the old man.

Of course, it was unlikely that he would have been able to help in any case. Valder knew that casting the spell required a mysterious powder or two, and the little hermit's supply of whatever it was had probably burned and would not be readily replaced.

He ran through a quick mental inventory of what he had and decided that the sling was his best bet for obtaining food. He would need to find some pebbles, or at least wood chips, for ammunition, and he would need to find some sort of game to use it on.

A sword was too big to be of much use against a chipmunk, but he looked down thoughtfully at the hilt on his belt. Something larger than a chipmunk might happen along eventually, after all.

The hilt looked just as it always had—simple, functional, and rather ugly, gray metal bare of any ornamentation or finesse, the sweat-softened leather of the grip bound in place with dulled brass wires. There was no gleam, no glamor about it, and he suddenly wondered whether the wizard had actually done anything to it. Spells existed, he knew, that did nothing at all save to look impressively magical, and the old man had had no supplies to speak of. Perhaps, in his fully understandable annoyance at the loss of his home, he had deceived his unwelcome visitor with play-pretties and phantasms. That would explain why he hadn't wanted the blade drawn until he had had time to disappear; use would surely show that there was no real enchantment.

That, Valder said to himself, would be just his luck. Overcome with suspicion, he drew the sword.

It slid smoothly from the scabbard, the blade bright in the sun—but no brighter than might be expected. Valder saw no unnatural glow, no sparkling silver, just the shine of well-kept steel. He held it out, made a few passes, even got to his feet for a quick, if slightly clumsy, parry-riposte against an imaginary foe; there was no sign of any magic. The blade looked and felt just as it always had.

He lowered the sword and looked down at it in mild disappointment. He was not really angry; after all, the old man had probably not trusted him and had merely wanted to be rid of a serious nuisance. Quite possibly the old hermit was not as great a wizard as he might pretend to be—although he had certainly done well enough with minor spells like the Sanguinary Deception or the Finger of Flame.

A magical weapon would have been very nice to have, though, very reassuring. It would not save him from starvation, but he would have liked it all the same.

He briefly considered turning north again and trying to find the wizard, but dismissed the thought. The hermit was gone and probably not worth tracking down. And if Valder *did* manage to find him, what would he do with him? The old man had his own problems, just as Valder did; there was no point in combining the two sets.

The thought of turning north again did remind Valder that he was not yet very far from the salt marsh, and that meant that he was not far from the sea. Pine forests might not provide food, but the ocean would. Even if he found no crabs, no clams, no oysters, even if he could catch no fish and hit no gulls, he could always eat seaweed. Rather than north, he would head west and stick to the coast henceforth. His route south would wiggle back and forth, detouring around every bay and inlet, but he would not need to fear starvation or becoming lost.

That decided, he tried to sheathe the sword.

The blade turned away from the mouth of the scabbard.

Thinking he had slipped, due to weariness, he tried again. Again, the tip of the sword refused to enter the sheath, sliding to one side instead.

Still not actually thinking about it and with a trace of irritation, Valder formed his left hand into a ring around the top of the scabbard to guide the blade in and keep it from moving to either side. That worked, in that the blade did not move away, but he still could not sheathe the sword; instead of dodging, it now simply refused to slide home.

He pressed harder, building up until he had all the strength he could muster, shoving sword and sheath together, but whatever was holding it refused to yield.

His initial irritation gave way quickly to puzzlement; he took off his belt and held the scabbard up so that he could study it closely, inside and out. He saw nothing amiss, nothing in any way out of the ordinary, and felt a small tingle of excitement in his gut. The wizard had *not* lied!

He sat down again and very slowly, very carefully brought the sword and the sheath together. They behaved ordinarily, like any inanimate objects, until the tip of the blade reached the mouth of the scabbard, and then *something* stopped any further motion. It did not matter whether the point was in the center of the opening, at either end, or to one side or the other; it would not enter the scabbard.

Fascinated, Valder put the sword down and then discovered that he could not remove his hand from its hilt. He picked it up again and stared at it.

No difference was visible. It was the same standard military-issue sword he had had since becoming a scout. He could open his hand and wiggle his fingers, but could not, he found, pull his hand away from the grip entirely. Something held it, magically. He lifted his hand, fingers outstretched and palm down, and the sword clung to the middle of his palm as if glued there.

It was not glued there, however; he wrapped his hand around it again, then unwrapped, and this time had it hanging from his fingertips.

There was no discomfort involved; the sword simply refused to leave his hand. Experimentally, as it hung from two fingers, he reached up with his left hand and pulled at it.

It came away readily in his grip—but now adhered to his left hand just as it had to his right.

He passed it back and forth a few times, then decided to try something else. With the sword clinging to the tips of his fingers, he braced both feet against it, leaning back against a tree, and pushed.

His hand came free; both hands were now unencumbered. The sword was now attached to the bottom of his right foot.

He stared at it, unsure whether to laugh or scream. Laughter won; he smiled broadly and chuckled. The sword looked incredibly foolish stuck to the sole of his foot.

He played with it and found that, although the sword insisted on always being in contact with some part of his body, it did not seem to care very much *which* part. He could hang it from his nose, if he so desired—although it would swing toward his right hand, as if preferring that and trying to get back to it. Nor did it matter visibly which part of the sword touched him, hilt, blade, or guard.

Tiring of the game at last, he stuck the sword to the bottom of his foot again while he studied the scabbard. A quick experiment showed that his dagger would slip into it with no trouble; pine needles could be stuffed into it and then scraped out again. Obviously, the sword was the culprit, not the sheath.

He satisfied himself that this was indeed the case by trying to force the dagger's sheath onto the tip of the sword's blade; it would not go, any more than the sword's own scabbard would.

An attempt to wrap the sword in his kilt showed him that the weapon refused to be covered; the cloth slid away from making contact with the metal of the blade; although Valder could force a few square inches into contact with the steel for a couple of seconds, something would not let them stay. The sword refused to be put away, and that was all there was to it.

This peculiar behavior was so intriguing that Valder spent well over an hour playing with the sword, experimenting in various ways and ignoring the growling of his stomach. Valder could no longer doubt that the old hermit had put an enchantment on the sword, but he was still puzzled regarding the exact nature of the magic. He tried everything he could think of short of risking breaking the blade by chopping at trees or rocks, but nothing caused the sword to manifest any useful abilities. The only signs of magic were its refusal to be covered or sheathed and its insistence upon remaining in contact with its owner at all times. The latter trait, Valder realized, could be useful—he would never need to worry about being disarmed in battle. On the other hand, he might have a hard time surrendering, should he need to do so. All in all, he doubted that the sword's odd pair of magical characteristics would be enough to protect him if he ran afoul of another enemy patrol. He suspected that the magic must be far more extensive, but he could not determine anything more of its nature.

He risked a more daring experiment, nicking the little finger of his left hand on the blade; this demonstrated that the sword did not protect him from all harm, that the sword was exceptionally sharp but not unstoppable, since he did not lose the finger, and that the sword did not change its behavior upon tasting blood. It behaved exactly as any ordinary sword would, as far as the edge was concerned, save that most swords were not as sharp.

Of course, as he was its owner, his blood and his finger might not produce the same reactions as someone else's would.

After that, he could think of nothing more to try. He got to his feet and began walking again, this time heading west by southwest toward the ocean, with the sword dangling in his hand.

By the time he reached the rocky shore, the sun was sinking toward the waves, drawing a broad stripe of golden light from the land to the horizon, and Valder's belly was knotted with hunger. Forgetting himself for a moment, he tried again, unsuccessfully, to sheathe the sword, so that he might wade out among the rocks in pursuit of something to eat. When the blade's refusal to slide home reminded him of the enchantment, he looked the weapon over thoughtfully, wondering whether it might be of help in obtaining food.

He could think of no way to use its known peculiarities and decided on a little random experimentation. He swirled the blade through a tidal pool without result, but was interested to discover, when he drew it out again, that it was dry. The metal had shed the water completely, in a way ordinary steel did not. Valder supposed that this meant he need never worry about rust.

Further experimentation demonstrated that a sword was not an ideal tool for digging clams, but it worked, and sand did not mar the blade, nor did prying up rocks bend it or dull the edge. Valder no longer doubted that the sword had special virtues; he was not as yet convinced, however, that they were anything that would be of much use in getting him safely home.

He ate his dinner of clams fried on fire-heated rocks slowly and thoughtfully, considering the sword. He knew so very little about it, he thought.

"Wirikidor," he said aloud. Nothing happened. The hilt still clung to his hand, as it had since he first drew it.

"Ho, Wirikidor!" he cried, more loudly, holding the sword aloft.

Nothing happened.

"Wirikidor, take me home!" he shouted.

Nothing happened; the sword gleamed dully in the fading daylight. The sun had dropped below the horizon while he ate.

"Wirikidor, bring me food!" The clams had not completely filled the yawning void in his gut.

Nothing happened.

"Damn you, Wirikidor, do something!"

The sword did nothing; the sky dimmed further as he waited.

Thinking that perhaps the sword's abilities, such as they were, might be linked to the sun, Valder tried to drop the sword; it remained adhered to his palm.

It occurred to him that he might be doomed to hold the thing for the rest of his life, which was hardly an appealing prospect. Of course, there were plenty of wizards around; he would certainly be able to find one eventually who could reverse the spell and free him of the sword's grip.

Still, he was apparently stuck with it until he could return to civilization.

Disgusted, Valder stopped playing with the sword and turned his attention to making camp amid the black rocks above the high tide mark.

CHAPTER 5

In the eleven days that followed his drawing of the sword, Valder made his way down the coast, living mostly on clams, crabs, and an occasional fish. He tried every experiment he could devise on the sword, with no discernable result. The blade remained sharp and clean, the hilt refused to leave his hand, and he was unable to force it into the scabbard. His feet toughened considerably, calluses replacing his blisters. He got very tired of carrying an unsheathed sword, and his hands, too, grew calloused.

In all that time and in all the leagues he traveled, he saw no sign of any other human beings—or semihumans, for that matter. He had expected to make frequent detours around northern coast-watchers but did not; apparently those he had encountered on his way north had been withdrawn. He saw only the endless sea to his right and the forests to his left, while the shoreline he traveled varied from sandy beach to bare rock to sheer cliff and back again.

As he made his way southward, the nights grew warmer and the stars more familiar; the pine forest began to give way slowly to other trees, and birds in ever-increasing numbers sang in their branches or swooped overhead. Beasts, too, increased in number—mostly small ones such as squirrels and rabbits, but he did glimpse a deer once and, on another occasion, thought he saw a boar. His bow and arrow were long gone, and he did not feel like tackling deer or boar with his sling, but twice, by persistence and luck more than skill, he added rabbit to his diet.

He was in pursuit of a third such delicacy a hundred yards inland, in mid-afternoon of his twelfth day of travel, when he heard a rustling in the underbrush ahead of him, a rustling far too loud to be caused by his quarry. He froze, the sling hanging from his right hand, the sword bare in his left, a handful of sea-rounded pebbles clutched against the hilt.

The rustling stopped, to be followed by other small sounds. Valder judged the source to be somewhere to his right, hidden by a tangle of flowering bushes. He peered intently at the foliage and, as the rustling began again, he made out the outline of something moving through the bushes, something roughly human in size and shape.

For the first time in days, Valder remembered that he was in enemy territory. He adjusted his grip on the sling and slipped a stone into the pocket, ready to swing and let fly at the first threatening move.

Whoever or whatever was hidden in the bushes did not seem to have spotted him, but was moving away with no attempt at stealth, back out toward the sea.

As it emerged from behind the leafy barrier, Valder got a good look. The mysterious figure was, as he had expected, a northerner, but rather than a *shatra* or combat sorcerer or some other deadly menace, it appeared to be a very ordinary young man, with no helmet and no adornments or personalizations on his standard-issue uniform and weapons.

He did not look threatening. His back was almost directly toward Valder, and he was totally off guard, oblivious to any lurking danger. Still, he was an enemy. Valder hesitated.

The northerner was a hundred feet away and widening

the gap. Valder was not good enough with a sling to be sure of hitting him, let alone downing him; if he missed, the sound of the stone would almost certainly alert the man—who, like most northern soldiers, carried a crossbow slung on his back.

Valder did not care to become a crossbow target. He decided to wait where he was and hope the young man went away without seeing him.

Wirikidor seemed to tremble slightly in his hand, and the grip felt warmer than usual; the Ethsharite remembered for the first time since spotting the northerner that he held a magic sword, a sword whose enchantment was supposed to see him safely home. He glanced at it and, without thinking, shifted his grip for a better hold.

One of his sling-stones fell to the ground and by mischance bounced from a half-buried rock with a loud click.

The northerner paused and started to turn. His movements were casual and unhurried; he was obviously thinking more in terms of small game than possible enemies, but Valder knew the man could hardly fail to see him. He brought his sling up and set it whirling.

The northerner's mouth fell open in astonishment at the sight of the Ethsharite. He ducked hurriedly as he recognized the sling for what it was, falling first to his knees and then flat to the ground. He struggled awkwardly to bring the crossbow around to where he could use it.

Valder let fly, knowing as he did that his stone would miss. It whizzed away, two feet above the northerner's head and a foot to the side.

As the pellet left the sling, Valder dove for cover behind a nearby oak. Once there, he stuffed the sling into his belt and passed Wirikidor from his left hand to his right, to have it ready for use.

The enemy soldier had not given an alarm, had not yelled for help; to Valder, that meant that there were no more northerners within earshot. He depended on that. If he could close with this man and kill him, he would be safe, at least for the moment. If he could disarm the northerner somehow and convince him to surrender, better still—assuming the man knew at least a little Ethsharitic, since Valder spoke not a single word of the northern tongue.

He was not even sure that all northerners spoke the same language.

The man looked younger than himself, probably still in his teens, and not particularly formidable. Had they been matched in weaponry, Valder would have been fairly confident of victory; as it was, however, the northerner had a crossbow, and Valder had his enchanted sword. Crossbows were very effective weapons—but very slow to load. The enchanted sword was an unknown quantity.

"Well, Wirikidor," Valder muttered. "What do we do now?"

The sword did nothing in reply, but it seemed somehow unsteady in his hand, as if it were struggling within itself.

Cautiously, he peered around the tree. The northern soldier was still flat on the ground, but now held the crossbow aimed and ready. As he saw Valder, he pulled the trigger.

The Ethsharite ducked back, and the quarrel whirred harmlessly past, vanishing into the woods beyond.

Seizing the opportunity provided by the northerner's nervous impatience, Valder emerged from concealment running, charging straight through the bushes toward his frightened foe.

The northerner was in the undignified process of discovering that it was impossible to load a crossbow properly while lying flat on one's belly with nothing to brace it against when he looked up and saw Valder plunging toward him. Terrified, he flung the crossbow aside—exactly the reaction Valder had hoped for—and snatched at his sword while rolling over onto his back.

The distance between them had been greater than Valder had realized; the enemy soldier was on his feet, sword drawn, before the Ethsharite could reach him. Valder slowed his headlong charge and came to a wary halt a few steps away.

The two faced each other for a long moment, while Wirikidor twitched and strained in Valder's hand.

Valder was in no hurry. He wanted to take his time, see what his opponent was capable of, before getting down to serious combat. Youth did not always mean inexperience, and the northerner's reflexes were surely at least as fast as his own. Valder was bigger, with a longer reach, and was fairly sure he was trickier and more determined, but preferred not just to hack away; he was not a great swordsman and he knew it. The northerner might be faster or more skillful. Or both.

The northerner moved a step to the side. Valder turned slightly to keep facing him, but did not follow.

The northerner crouched lower. Valder did not move.

The northerner took a swipe at him. Although Valder was not aware of trying to respond, Wirikidor came up, meeting the enemy's blade, turning it aside, and sliding past it, in a twisting lightning-fast stroke that thrust the sword's point through the northerner's throat.

Valder had definitely not intended that. Both men stared in astonishment at the gleaming steel that joined them. The northerner's mouth opened and a sick croak emerged, followed by a gush of blood.

Valder tried to pull his blade free; he saw no need to do more to the northerner, whose wound was probably fatal. The fellow was little more than a boy, and, if there were any chance he might live, Valder wanted him to have it. The man was obviously not going to fight anymore; already his sword had lowered, and, as the blood spilled from his mouth, his fingers opened, dropping the weapon to the petal-strewn ground.

Wirikidor's blade would not come free. Instead, the sword twisted in Valder's hand, ripping through the northerner's neck.

Valder stared at the blade in horror. His hand had not moved. The sword had moved, certainly, but his hand had not. Wirikidor had killed the northerner of its own volition.

The northerner fell free of Wirikidor's blade and crumpled to the ground, obviously dead. With a shudder, Valder dropped the unnatural weapon. Wirikidor fell from his hand and lay on the ground inches from the dead man's face.

Valder stared at it, his earlier horror giving way to astonishment. The sword had left his hand! Was the enchantment broken?

Cautiously he picked it up, then put it down again.

There was no resistance or adhesion; the sword behaved like any other inanimate piece of steel.

Puzzled, Valder picked it up again and looked it over carefully. It appeared unchanged, except that the victim's blood, unlike water, clung to it. He wiped the blade on his dead opponent's sleeve and then cautiously slid it into the scabbard on his belt.

The blade fell smoothly into place without resistance of any sort.

He stared at the hilt. Had the enchantment been good only for a single use? Had using the sword broken the spell? The wizard had said that "Wirikidor" meant "slayer of warriors"; well, it had indeed slain someone, although Valder was not convinced that the northerner had been much of a warrior.

He considered for a moment and then drew the sword again and looked at it closely. He saw nothing enlightening, merely the simple steel blade he had always had. With a shrug, he attempted to return it to its sheath.

The blade turned away from the opening.

He stared at it for a long moment. "Damn it," he said, "and may demons carry off that idiot wizard!" He knew there was no point in disputing anything with Wirikidor. If it chose not to be sheathed, he would not be able to sheathe it.

He stripped the northerner's body of provisions and other useful items, such as the discarded crossbow. Although he had little hope, given their relative sizes, he tried unsuccessfully to pull on the man's battered boots; as he had expected, none of the clothing was big enough to be of any use to him.

As he worked he told himself that at least he had learned something about his magical defense. The sword was bloodthirsty, for one thing. For another, blood apparently canceled some of the spell but only until the sword was sheathed and then drawn again.

He paused. No, he told himself, it wasn't that simple. He had cut himself to test the blade, and that had had no effect. It was not just blood that was responsible but something else.

He had heard legends of foul weapons, demonic or

sorcerous in origin, that sucked the souls from their victims; could it be that he now carried such a weapon? He had never heard of such a weapon being created by wizardry—but then, the old hermit had been using spells of his own invention.

One part of the usual version of the story said that the victims invariably died with their faces frozen in expressions of unspeakable terror. He glanced at the dead northerner's face; while scarcely calm, the expression of shock and pain did not live up to the descriptions of those whose souls had been stolen.

No, he didn't think it was the northerner's soul that had appeased Wirikidor and allowed it to be sheathed—albeit briefly. Perhaps the blood of the sword's owner would not work, but any other would. The hermit had told him that the sword had some sort of an ownership spell on it.

He remembered the sickening sensation as the sword had twisted in his hand, determined to cut the northerner's throat out; no, the sword was not satisfied with just a little blood. It had wanted the man's life. Not his soul, perhaps, but his life.

That was not a pleasant thought. Wirikidor might indeed protect Valder, but he did not think he would enjoy owning it. For one thing, it was a nuisance carrying it about unsheathed. He promised himself that the next time he got it into the scabbard he would leave it there until he needed it again.

Putting aside for the moment his consideration of the sword's nature, the next important question was what this northern soldier had been doing here. From the man's nonchalant attitude, it was obvious that he had not been expecting any Ethsharitic activity—at any rate, not on land close at hand. Valder could guess well enough what he had been doing skulking in the bushes, from the sound if nothing else—even northerners needed to relieve themselves—but where had he come from? As nearly as Valder could estimate, he was still several leagues behind the northern lines—unless the Ethsharitic forces had successfully counterattacked.

That was an encouraging thought, but Valder was not

at all sure it was justified. He glanced about, hoping to pick up the northerner's trail.

He found it with surprising ease. The man had made no attempt to conceal it and had, in fact, obviously used the same path several times, judging by the amount of wear. Mosses and creepers had been thoroughly trampled. With Wirikidor in hand, Valder followed the trail southwestward through the forest and in only minutes emerged onto the top of a rocky bluff and found the northerner's little encampment, overlooking the sea. The dead man's duty was clear; he had been stationed to watch for Ethsharitic landings along this stretch of coastline. The elevated position gave him a clear view of several miles of beach.

He had not expected an attack on land, of course. Valder's presence must have been a shock.

This realization left Valder with only guesswork to tell him how far behind the northern lines he might still be. He had no way of knowing how much of the coastline the enemy would consider worth guarding. His own army might be a league away, or a hundred. All he could be certain of was that the war was still being fought, as it had always been, or else there would have been no need to post a coastal watch at all.

Any number of questions were now vital. When was the soldier's relief due? How far apart were the shore-watchers posted? Would it be worthwhile to travel inland to avoid them?

He glanced at Wirikidor. He was protected, he told himself; he could go where he pleased. That was not really a major concern, after all.

No, he corrected himself, there were still crossbows, not to mention the arcane weaponry of sorcerers and *shatra*. He did not want to encounter any more of the enemy than he had to, and where possible it would be best to meet at close quarters, where Wirikidor would, it seemed, do his fighting for him.

Besides, he had no particular desire to kill northerners—though he felt a twinge of guilt at making that unpatriotic admission to himself. Creating a disturbance back here behind the Empire's lines might draw troops away from his countrymen and comrades; he knew that and told himself that he probably *should* try to cause trouble, but he was still not eager to kill anyone. Better by far, in his opinion, to avoid trouble.

The sentry's relief might be along any minute, he thought—or perhaps not for days, but he saw no reason to take unnecessary chances. He turned and walked back into the forest, away from the sea.

CHAPTER 6

Two days later Valder was beginning to wish an enemy would find him, just so that he could sheathe his sword after killing someone. He had been carrying the weapon bare in his hand for thirteen days, against his will, and was sincerely tired of it. He had tried putting it under his belt, or along one shin, but these had proved much too uncomfortable to use for any length of time.

He was well away from the shoreline now and had no intention of veering back in hopes of picking off another coast-watcher, but the thought of coming across a lone northern scout had a certain appeal. The sweaty palms and tired wrists were overcoming his distaste for bloodshed.

With that in mind, he was taking pains to move quietly, lest thoughts of an enemy might tempt the gods to bring him one; he did not want to be caught off-guard. The forest had thickened, and a profusion of rhododendrons limited the easily available paths, so that he found himself picking his way carefully, watching his feet, his head bent low to avoid overhanging branches. That let his hair, woefully unkempt after two and a half months without a mirror, hang down across his eyes, and, with his hands as tired as they were, he did not bother to brush it aside very often. It was sheer luck that he saw the northern patrol before they saw him; he happened to glance up at exactly the right moment. None of the three enemy soldiers was as fortunate.

Valder froze for a moment and watched them. All three moved with the normal clumsiness of ordinary men; none had the smooth, gliding grace that marked *shatra*. That was a relief.

Valder wondered what they were doing out here; what made a patrol behind the lines necessary? Were there Ethsharitic scouts—other than himself—operating in the area? Even as he wondered, he reached up slowly for the captured crossbow slung on back.

The sword in his hand made him awkward; the blade struck an overhanging branch as he struggled to bring the bow around where he could use it. The sound was not loud, but one of the northerners, sixty yards away, apparently heard it. He paused in his stride, turned, and saw the Ethsharite.

He shouted something in the northern tongue, then began running toward Valder, his hand reaching for the sword on his belt. Valder guessed that he did not care to use a bow; not all soldiers, on either side, were marksmen.

The other two northerners followed. The first, Valder saw, was grinning with excitement. Like the sentry on the shore, these three were young, very young—and, Valder thought, not likely to grow old if they were always so careless. They obviously hoped to capture him alive, forcing a surrender by virtue of their superior numbers, but were completely oblivious to the possibility of an ambush or magical defense. They saw a man in the gray breastplate and green kilt of an Ethsharitic soldier and forgot everything but that they faced an enemy and an opportunity for glory.

He got the crossbow free, but the bowstring fouled on the same overhanging branch the sword had hit. With a curse, Valder dropped it, leaving it hanging, and stepped forward. He had the magic sword Wirikidor, the slayer of warriors, he told himself; what had he to fear?

The first northerner stopped a dozen feet away, apparently puzzled that the quarry had not run off to be chased down like a fleeing deer. His comrades came up behind him. All three stared at Valder and the naked steel in his hand.

The leader called something; Valder guessed it was a demand that he surrender.

"I don't understand a word," he called back.

The three northerners conversed for a moment; then one of them called tentatively, "You fight?"

"I'm not surrendering, if that's what you mean," Valder replied. Seeing the confusion that resulted, he decided this was obviously too much for the northerner's limited vocabulary and called his clarification. "Yes, I fight."

"Ah!" Three swords were drawn, and the northern leader advanced. Valder guessed him to be perhaps eighteen, the others younger.

Wirikidor seemed to drag him forward to meet his opponent. He did not bother to pretend that he was controlling his actions as steel clashed.

The other two hung back, and Valder quickly realized why. The lead northerner, despite his youth, was a superb swordsman, probably his divisional champion. His blade flickered like heat lightning in a summer sky. His companions could only have been in the way.

This obvious skill did not bother Wirikidor in the slightest. It countered each blow with supernatural speed and, when the northerner faltered in surprise, it swept past his guard and plunged into his throat.

Wirikidor, Valder thought, seemed to have a liking for throats. He wondered if that were in any way significant. He wrenched the blade away as soon as it had finished ripping open the northerner's neck.

The northerner collapsed in a lifeless heap, his sword rattling from a tree root.

His comrades stared at their fallen leader in astonished dismay. Valder stepped forward, waiting for Wirikidor to take on the next one.

Wirikidor did nothing; all Valder's advance did was to snap the nearer northerner out of his stunned inaction.

His sword swung for Valder's throat, and it was all the Ethsharite could do to bring Wirikidor up in time to parry.

Startled by his sword's failure to act on its own, Valder fell back several steps before the northerner's assault and took a small gash on his upper arm before regaining control. Fortunately, this second youth was far less skilled than the first, and the third northerner was still too disconcerted to join the battle.

"Damn you, Wirikidor!" Valder cried, "Why aren't you fighting?"

There was no response. The sword acted like any ordinary sword, utterly inanimate. Valder had passed the minimum competence tests in swordsmanship in order to acquire his rank of Scout First Class, but he was by no means an expert swordsman, nor even very good—however, luck was with him; the northerner was no better. He was faster than Valder, but less practiced—hardly surprising in a boy of sixteen or seventeen. The two were fairly evenly matched, so the duel continued—but only, Valder knew, until the other northerner got over his surprise.

Then his opponent stumbled, whether over a root or his companion's body Valder did not see. Valder seized the opportunity, and Wirikidor's magically sharp blade sank deep into the northerner's sword arm, cutting to the bone.

The northerner's sword dropped, and Valder brought Wirikidor back and around, striking at the soldier's neck. The man went down and stayed down.

The third northerner came out of his dumfoundment too late and chose not to take on, alone, the man who had slain his two compatriots. Instead, he turned and ran.

Valder did not pursue him. The young fellow was obviously faster, even without terror to aid him. Besides, a chase might lead directly into an enemy camp. Instead, he looked down at his fallen foes.

The second man was still breathing and had managed to clamp his left hand over his neck wound.

Valder stared down at him for a second or two, debating whether to kill him or to attend to his wounds. He quickly decided to do neither, but snatched the crossbow from the tree and, like his foe, turned and ran. He saw no need to kill a helpless man, enemy or not, particularly when there was another enemy who had gotten away and might return with reinforcements at any moment.

When he had put a little distance between himself and the scene of the battle, he paused to catch his breath. His feet, he noticed, had certainly been toughened by day after day of trudging barefoot through the woods; he had just dashed blindly across sticks, stones, and undergrowth without heeding what he stepped on.

He wondered whether he could risk going back after a pair of boots from one of his downed foes, but decided against it.

He found a rag in his belt pouch and wiped the blood from Wirikidor's blade. That done, he sank onto a mossy fallen tree, keeping a wary eye back along his trail.

The sword had been wonderful against the first northerner and had almost certainly saved his life—but then its magical animation had deserted him completely against his second foeman. Valder glared at the freshly wiped blade. Had the spell worn off already?

He had no way of knowing. When he had the metal clean, he slid the sword back into its scabbard; it went without protest.

Of course, that didn't prove anything. It had done that after he had killed the coastal sentry, too.

He threw a startled glance at the hilt as a thought struck him. Was *that* the explanation? Was the sword only good against single enemies? Did it need to be sheathed to recharge the spell before it would again act on its own?

That, he thought, could be very inconvenient. He tried to imagine fighting in a full-scale battle with such a sword. It would be marvelous until it had killed *one* enemy soldier and then would be no more than an ordinary blade—or rather, a blade with a spell of sharpness on it. That would certainly be better than nothing, but not by very much. One could scarcely sheathe it in the midst of a mêlée and then draw it again.

He realized that it still might get him home, but only if he was careful never to face more than one or perhaps two opponents at a time. One the sword would handle, and a second he would at least face on even terms, but beyond that he would be no better off than any ordinary fighter.

He wondered if the hermit had known how his spell would work—and if so, had he realized how limited its usefulness was?

This, he told himself, was all just guesswork. His one-foe-per-drawing theory did fit the observed facts, but so would any number of other explanations—a small magical charge that had been exhausted after two killings, for example. He could test that possibility by simply drawing the sword again and seeing whether it would allow itself to be sheathed, but he hesitated. Walking around with the sword drawn was an unbearable nuisance, one he did not care to burden himself with again. He left the sword in its scabbard and considered other aspects of his situation.

He was still lost behind enemy lines, but now the enemy knew he was here, thanks to the escape of the third northerner in the patrol he had just fought. Furthermore, in his hurry, he had left a discernible trail from the site of the battle. It was, he told himself, time to disappear.

He did not want to double back to the north. That would take him further from his goal, and eventually he would have to make up any lost ground. To the south, presumably, lay the enemy lines. To the west lay the ocean; he considered the possibility of returning to the coast and building or stealing a boat, but quickly abandoned it. He was no sailor. He had planned on boating before only because he had been unable to think of an alternative—but he always had alternatives, if he took the time to find them.

That left east—and that was almost certainly the direction the enemy would expect him to take, since they could eliminate the other three by the same means he had.

He reached a decision, not so much by conscious logic as because it *felt* right. He would head southeast. Pursuers would not expect him to head toward the enemy lines; and by angling over to the east he would, he hoped, be able to slip through at some point where he wasn't expected.

He would need to do his best to leave no tracks. That

could be very tricky if the enemy sent sorcerers or *shatra* trackers after him. One of his problems might become an advantage, as problems sometimes did—bare feet left less of a trail than boots.

He rose, checked to be sure that the scabbard was secure on his belt and Wirikidor secure in the scabbard, and then slipped off into the forest, moving as lightly and silently as he could.

That night he made no camp, lighted no fire; instead he climbed a tree and wedged himself into a fairly secure perch. He had seen no sign of pursuit, but, after fleeing for so long from the patrol that had chased him into the hermit's marsh, he was taking no unnecessary chances.

CHAPTER 7

Valder awoke at dawn, feeling very cramped and stiff.
He untangled his hands and feet, but, before lifting himself
up out of the tree crotch where he had slept, he glanced
down at the ground below.

He froze.

There was still no sign of enemy pursuit, but he would
almost have preferred that to what he saw instead. Looking up at him from the base of the tree was a small dragon
He stared down at it in dismay.

It was a glossy metallic green in color, and he estimated
its length at fifteen feet, counting the tail. It probably
could not talk yet; a small dragon was a young dragon,
and young dragons were notoriously stupid. It had its
wings folded down against its back, so that he couldn't
judge its wingspan, but he guessed that the mere fact that
it was down on the ground while he was up in the tree
meant it could not fly. Many, perhaps most, dragons
couldn't.

It glared up at him hungrily and hissed, a sound like
the dousing of a bonfire; that left little doubt of its inten-
tions.

Valder wondered whether it was a wild dragon from

birth, or whether it had been bred by the northerners and had escaped or been freed. If it had been raised as a military dragon, he might be able to control it.

"Ho, dragon!" he barked. "Rest!"

The dragon just stared up at him and hissed again. If it had been raised in captivity, its training hadn't taken— or perhaps it could tell Ethsharitic from the northern tongue. Valder had no idea what commands a northern dragon might obey; he had hoped tone alone would serve.

A fifteen-footer would be certain death for an unarmed man and more than a match for most fully equipped soldiers. Valder, however, reminded himself that he had a magic sword. He drew Wirikidor.

The sword looked and felt exactly as it always had. He hooked it on a tree branch near his side and tried to take his hand from the hilt.

The hilt adhered to his palm and would not come free. That meant that the sword *did* still have magic in it; this was more evidence for his one-foe-per-drawing theory.

Well, he told himself, a dragon is just one foe.

As he gripped the sword in his right hand, he suddenly realized that, surprised and still sleepy as he had been, he had done something very stupid. He should have used the crossbow first; a few well-placed quarrels might have sent the dragon in search of easier prey. He doubted that he would be able, while crouched in a treetop holding a sword, to cock, load, aim, and fire the crossbow.

He could, he thought, put the sword on his forehead or someplace while he loaded the bow—but even then, cocking it while wedged in a tree would not be easy, and he did have the sword ready here in his hand. A crossbow might seem more trustworthy than the mysterious enchantment on his blade, but he felt his nerve going as it was; better to attack while his courage held, with the weapon at hand. With that thought and no warning, he dove for the dragon's throat, plummeting from his perch.

The dragon saw him coming and reared back, startled. Valder's dive missed it entirely, and he landed on the forest floor. He managed to catch himself, turning his fall into a roll, so that he was not injured and was able to scramble up before the dragon could react.

The fall had knocked some of the wind out of him, however, and he was less than ideally steady on his feet. He could not organize his limbs and body sufficiently to attack, but instead held Wirikidor out before him, as if it were a magic talisman that would ward off the monster.

He had, in fact, hoped that the sword was exactly that, that it would defend him against the dragon of its own volition. His hopes were dashed. The dragon did not retreat, and Wirikidor did nothing in his defense. It wobbled in his unsteady hand as any other sword might, with no sign of the supernatural independence of movement it had displayed against two human foes.

Upon regaining its composure, the dragon stared at him for a moment, its long, arched neck bringing its golden eyes and needle-sharp fangs mere inches beyond Wirikidor's blade. Valder stared back, the realization sinking in that Wirikidor was not going to save him by itself. He slashed at the dragon, trying desperately to put some strength behind the blow.

Moving with incredible speed, the monster pulled its head back out of the blow's path, then struck at the blade with the full might of one of its huge foreclaws, obviously expecting to knock the sword out of Valder's hand.

Ordinarily, the dragon's blow would have done exactly that. This sword, however, was no ordinary one. This was Wirikidor. It was attached quite irremovably to Valder's hand by its magic. That meant that when struck by the dragon's irresistible blow it went flying off to one side, just as the dragon had intended—but that Valder's hand went with it, dragging the rest of him along. That was not at all what the dragon had had in mind; it had knocked its dinner well out of its own reach.

Valder realized what had happened in time to turn his unexpected sideways lunge into a roll that carried him still further away. When he was in control of his actions again, he scrambled to his feet and wasted no time in dashing away from the dragon, aiming for the thickest woods, where, with any luck, the beast would not fit between the trees. He did not have much of a lead, but the monster had expected him to stand and fight, not to flee, so that it did not immediately pursue him.

Valder did not worry about details, but simply ran, hoping that the dragon would not follow, or would tire of the chase. He was prepared to turn at bay if necessary; since dragons were never noted for their stealth, he was sure he would be able to tell from the sound of the beast's approach when the time had come to do so.

As it happened, it was several seconds, almost a full minute, before he heard the dragon crashing through the trees behind him. That gave him a significant head start. Furthermore, the underbrush slowed the monster far more than it slowed the man. Valder was able to maintain a diminishing lead for quite some distance, though he knew that the dragon's speed was much greater than his own. As he ran, he prayed that the dragon would lose interest, that a hiding place would present itself, or that some other miracle would save him, since his damnable magic sword would not.

Wirikidor flapped about in his hand. He did not need to worry about dropping it, but only about keeping it from becoming entangled in something and slowing or stopping his headlong flight.

The ground was uneven, and Valder found himself running up a sun-dappled hillside. The upgrade slowed him somewhat; he imagined he could feel the dragon drawing nearer, though he told himself that the sounds of its advance were not growing louder. Yet.

Then he reached the hilltop and abruptly ran out of forest. He was charging down into a virtually treeless river valley, and directly ahead of him was a camp. He knew that it had to be a northern outpost of some sort, but the hissing of the dragon behind him convinced him not to stop or swerve. Instead he ran straight toward the half-dozen large gray tents and the handful of black-clad people gathered around the remains of the previous night's cookfires.

He heard someone call an alarm, but not in time for anyone to block his path before he reached the first tent. He dodged around its far side, then turned and looked back.

The dragon had been charging after him, but now it

slowed as it saw the tents and the people standing among them. Valder could guess what it was thinking. Why pursue one difficult meal when here were a dozen that weren't running?

Indeed, the northerners were *not* running; instead soldiers were ducking into their tents after weapons, and the women—there were four or five women whom Valder took to be officers' wives or perhaps camp followers, since they were not wearing the black-and-gray northern uniforms—were clustering behind a smoldering firepit.

The dragon approached slowly, as if it hoped to avoid frightening away its prey, while northern soldiers began to appear with cocked and loaded crossbows. An officer barked a command, and quarrels flew.

Valder decided not to wait around to see the battle's outcome. So far the northerners had ignored him; he guessed that most had not even seen him, and others might not have realized he was an Ethsharite, despite his breastplate and green kilt. His luck could not last, however, once the dragon had been dealt with; he knew that. He began discreetly trotting past the tents, down toward the riverbank. He wished the sword were not naked in his hand, as it made him more conspicuous, but he could not spare the time to devise a means of hiding it.

Most of the first volley rattled off the dragon's scales, but bolts struck home in its mouth and one eye. Valder heard it scream and glanced back to see it fleeing back up the hillside. A few soldiers, those who were not reloading their crossbows, were pursuing it, apparently not willing to leave a wounded dragon roaming the countryside; they were hindered by the slope and the tall grass that covered it. Valder had not even noticed that the grass was there when he had come down the hillside; he had never been very observant when fleeing in terror.

Valder knew he would not have followed a wounded dragon, under any circumstances; he would have been satisfied with driving it off. He was not about to complain, however, as every man who pursued the dragon meant one fewer available to pursue *him*.

He stumbled down the riverbank and into the water. The stream was twenty yards across, but muddy and slow-moving; he hoped it was shallow enough to wade. He was not eager to try and teach himself to swim while carrying a sword and a crossbow and wearing a breastplate.

The bottom was soft mud; his feet sank in, so that the water reached his hips rather than his knees. He could feel small slimy things brushing against his bare feet and legs as he slogged forward. He concentrated on making his way out into the stream and ignored the shouting, hissing, and other noises from the camp. He held Wirikidor before him, up out of the water; annoying as its behavior could be, the enchanted sword was still a valuable weapon, and he preferred not to strain its resistance to rust.

He felt his way forward for half a dozen paces, then stopped; the bottom was dropping off suddenly beneath his feet. He stepped back, then worked his way a few yards upstream before trying again.

Someone shouted, so loudly it seemed in his ear. Almost immediately he heard someone splashing into the water behind him. He steadied himself, then whirled, Wirikidor flashing out in an unaimed blow.

It was his own hand, not the spell, that guided the sword; he could feel that. His hand swung the weapon faster than he could turn his head.

When his eyes did come around, he saw the tip of his blade slice open the cheek of a handsome young woman.

She was not armed, so far as he could see. She clapped her hand to her face as she felt the blade cut her and fell back, shocked.

Appalled, Valder waited for Wirikidor to move in for the kill, but the sword did nothing. After a second's hesitation, he turned and slogged out into midstream again.

The woman staggered back to shore and fell, her body on the bank and her feet still in the water. She stared after the Ethsharite, blood trickling between her fingers.

Valder reached the opposite bank without further hindrance and without actually swimming, though the water reached his throat at one point. A glance back when he was sure he could make it showed him that people had come to the aid of the woman he had struck; they stared out after him, but no one seemed inclined to pursue. Valder guessed that all the bolder warriors were still chasing the dragon.

Once safely across, he wasted no time in pushing himself up out of the river, water streaming from his tunic and kilt. He clambered up to the top of the grassy hillside.

He saw scattered trees, but the forest did not resume; instead, he saw before him an open, rolling plain. He had reached the vast central grasslands.

He did not pause to admire the scenery, but marched onward, leaving a clear trail of trampled grass. He had no idea of how to avoid leaving such a trail; he had been trained as a forest scout.

As he walked, he considered his experiences so far that morning. Wirikidor had done nothing against the dragon and had not insisted on killing the woman, yet it still retained at least part of its magic; he could not sheathe it or put it down. It had tasted blood from the woman's cheek, but was not satisfied; he still could not force it into the scabbard, though he tried as he trudged onward. That puzzled him.

He thought back over what he knew of the sword. In truth, he knew very little. He knew its name, but nothing else beyond his own observations since drawing it. The old hermit had said that Wirikidor meant "slayer of warriors." Did that tell him anything?

He stopped suddenly as a thought struck him. "Slayer of *warriors*," the old man had said. Not beasts and not unarmed women. *That* would explain its actions very nicely; it would only fight for him against warriors!

He frowned and began walking again. That, he told himself, could have drawbacks. Furthermore, how did it fit with his earlier one-foe-per-drawing theory? Had those other northern soldiers somehow not qualified as warriors by the sword's standards, or did it only kill one warrior per drawing?

His life might well depend on the answer to that question sometime; he had best, he thought, learn that answer as quickly as he could. He trudged onward through the grass, thinking hard.

CHAPTER 8

Late in the afternoon of the day after he passed through the northern camp, Valder realized he was being followed. The grasslands were not uniformly covered; large areas had been trampled by men or beasts, other areas had been grazed by various animals, and the height of the grasses varied with the soil conditions as well, so that there were places where the grass did not reach his knees, or even his ankles. Such areas provided no possibility of cover or concealment. As he passed through one such spot, at the top of a rise, he happened to glance back the way he had come and caught sight of a distant figure following his path.

At first he tried to convince himself that he had mistaken some beast for a man, or that the figure was some casual wanderer who happened to be behind him, but a few minutes later he looked back and saw the same figure, still on his tracks and significantly closer.

Not yet seriously concerned, he paused at the top of the next hill and again looked back, this time watching for several minutes, studying his pursuer. As he watched, his nonchalance vanished.

The approaching figure was gaining ground rapidly, though Valder had not been dawdling. Furthermore, it moved with a smooth, gliding motion that Valder tried to tell himself might be an illusion caused by the rippling grass that hid the figure's feet.

Before long, however, he had to admit to himself that the thing following him was either *shatra* or something very similar. He prayed to whatever grassland gods might hear him that it would not also prove to be a sorcerer; and while he prayed, he slid the crossbow from his shoulder and tried to set the cocking mechanism. The sword in his hand made him awkward, but he hooked the bow-string, then put his foot on the brace and pulled back.

The bowstring snapped.

He stared at the dangling remains in dismay, realizing that he had done nothing to care for it, even after fording the river. The string had almost certainly been soaked through. He doubted a day and a half would have been enough for it to rot badly, but the water would have softened it and helped along any previous damage. He had let the wet string dry in the hot sun of the plain, still on the bow, and that had apparently been enough to ruin it.

The captured crossbow, unfamiliar as it was, had been his best defense against *shatra*. At close range, even the slowest, weakest *shatra* was more than a match for any mere human. At long range, a sling did not have the accuracy or impact to stop one reliably. A crossbow had a good chance—though there were stories of *shatra* not merely dodging quarrels, but snatching them out of the air.

With his crossbow useless, the sling was the best he had. He pulled it from his belt and then realized that he had no stones, nor were any handy amid the tall grass. He had never bothered to keep any; in the forest he could always find stones or nuts or other small objects suitable for use as ammunition.

He had his bloodstone, but he could not bring himself to waste that on a long throw at a difficult target. Furthermore, loading and using the sling while he held a sword would not be easy.

He could stick the sword to his shin for the moment,

but he still had no ammunition. He cursed himself for his thoughtlessness in relying on the crossbow without bothering to care for it.

He looked at Wirikidor. *Shatra* were certainly warriors, but the sword had proved so unreliable that he could not imagine it being any use against one.

It was, however, the only chance he had. When he looked up at the approaching person, he saw that the pursuer was no longer simply following Valder's trail, but was instead dodging back and forth across the grassland, moving in fits and starts and generally making himself as difficult a target as possible. He was obviously aware that Valder had seen him. Even with ammunition other than the single gem, Valder would now have virtually no chance of harming him with the sling.

Valder looked around helplessly at the empty grassland, the few scattered trees—none near enough to be of any help—and the vacant blue sky overhead. Here he was, he thought, being stalked by a half-demon enemy, with no place to hide, nowhere to run, and only Wirikidor to protect him. He was as good as dead, he was certain. The sword might be enchanted, but it would need to be capable of miracles to save him.

He did not want to die. The air was sweet, the sun warm, and he had no desire whatsoever to perish and never again taste the wind or see the sky. No Ethsharitic soldier had ever killed a *shatra* in hand-to-hand combat, Valder knew—but he resolved to try. The sword's magic might possibly give him the edge he needed to do it.

He tried to think of anything else that might give him an advantage, however slight; whether any spot might be better than another. He could see nothing that would help. He was going to meet the *shatra* on open, rolling grassland, no matter what he did, and one part of it seemed very much like any other.

He was determined not to flee. He knew that demons and their kin had no compunctions about killing a man from behind; and if he were to die, he preferred to die facing his foe. He considered the possibility of a charge, a chance at taking the *shatra* by surprise, but dismissed it. In all honesty he could only believe that such an attack would get him killed that much sooner.

Instead he tried to relax, to enjoy his last few moments as best he could, and to save his strength for the coming fight, rather than wasting it by tensing up.

The sky was very blue, the only clouds thin, white streaks on the eastern horizon, the sun settling downward in the west. The grass was golden and rippling. When he had been walking, the day had seemed rather hot, but, now that he was standing still and letting the breeze cool him, the weather seemed ideal.

He was not particularly fond of grass nor of grasslands; he had grown up around forests and served most of his time in the army in forests, and the open country felt bare and unprotected by contrast. The best thing about it was the vast, uncluttered sky.

The *shatra* paused, perhaps two hundred yards away, and watched him; Valder could see the sun glinting on the demon's close-fitting black helmet. He suddenly realized that the *shatra* was well within the effective range of the sorcerous weapons that his kind sometimes used and might be debating whether to shoot now or draw closer. Against combat sorcery Valder knew he had no chance at all; he dropped flat, hiding in the grass. He had seen no wands or talismans, but his situation was quite bad enough without taking unnecessary risks.

He lay in the grass for what seemed like hours, halfway onto his left side, ready to thrust himself upward with the sword raised. He listened, but heard nothing but the grass rustling in the wind.

He looked, but from where he lay he could see nothing but the grass a few inches from his nose.

He debated crawling off into the grass, away from his trail, in hopes that the *shatra* would lose track of him, but gave up the idea after a trial poke at the surrounding plants. The grass in his immediate vicinity was not particularly tall and rustled quite audibly when he stirred it; the *shatra* would be able to locate him easily.

"Soldier!" a voice called, speaking Ethsharitic with a thick, unpleasant accent. "Soldier! Come out and we may talk!"

Valder lay still and said nothing.

"Soldier, you do not need to die. We treat prisoners well. Stand up and drop your weapons and you may live!"

Valder knew this was unusual, this attempt to coax a surrender. Ordinarily the northerners were no more eager to burden themselves with prisoners than the Ethsharites were; after all, prisoners had to be kept for life, since there were no provisions for exchange and the war had been going on since time immemorial and seemed likely to continue forever. The *shatra* had some reason for wanting Valder alive. Most probably, the Ethsharite guessed, the northerners wanted to find out how a lone enemy came to be wandering around behind their lines to begin with. They might also be wondering whether the dragon was a part of an Ethsharitic force.

As he thought back over what he had done, Valder realized that he had probably made quite an impression. He had appeared mysteriously out of nowhere, disposed of a coastal sentry, slain an expert swordsman in fair combat and then seriously wounded another man as well, and topped it all off by leading a hungry young dragon into a northern encampment that was presumably nowhere near the front.

He wondered how long he would live if he accepted the *shatra*'s offer of imprisonment and how long his dying would take. The northerners were said to be very ingenious in their use of torture. They were not likely to be gentle with someone who had caused them so much trouble. It seemed unreasonable to think that they might let him live out his natural span.

"Soldier, you are being very foolish. If you do not surrender by the time I count to five, I must kill you."

Valder noticed that the notherner's voice had come much closer. He had decided, without knowing it himself at first, that he was not going to buy himself a few days of life by surrendering, even though he had no important information that might be tortured out of him. He did not know where his unit was, or where the hermit had gone, or anything very useful about Wirikidor. He did not want to die—but he did not want to live in pain and disgrace, either. Besides, he could not drop Wirikidor if he tried; the sword would not allow it.

He listened carefully as the *shatra* began counting. "One!"

He judged the northerner to be no more than thirty feet away now.

"Two!"

He was somewhere ahead and to the left. Presumably he knew Valder's exact position and intended to take him from his bad side.

"Three!"

Valder adjusted his legs; he had changed his earlier decision and now intended to charge the *shatra*.

"Four!"

He launched himself upward, running through the knee-high grass toward the enemy, who stood roughly where Valder had expected him to be.

The *shatra* was not surprised. He smiled as Valder came toward him and raised his own drawn sword with leisurely grace.

Seeing the sword, Valder knew that the *shatra* either had no magical weaponry or preferred not to use it. He swung Wirikidor at the northerner's throat.

As he had expected, the *shatra*'s sword snapped up and deflected Wirikidor.

As he had not really expected, however, Wirikidor responded on its own, twisting around the intercepting blade and striking down diagonally, stabbing into the *shatra*'s shoulder. Something hissed strangely, and sparkles of yellow light spat from the wound before ordinary red blood appeared.

Valder stared in delight. He had drawn first blood from a *shatra*! Wirikidor would save him after all! He tried to relax and let the sword do his fighting for him.

Wirikidor, however, did not cooperate. It swung back from the shoulder wound as if forced back by a blow, though the *shatra*, as surprised as Valder, had reacted by stepping back and assuming a defensive posture, without making any attempt to knock Wirikidor away.

Startled, Valder looked at his blade, and the two of them stood, scarcely four feet apart, both warily watching Wirikidor.

Naturally, the *shatra* was the first to recover. He brought his blade darting down toward Valder's groin, apparently not troubled at all by his bleeding shoulder.

Wirikidor did nothing, but Valder managed to fall back out of the blade's path. He lost his balance as he did so and landed in a sitting position. As he struggled to regain his feet, the northerner's sword flashed toward his throat.

Wirikidor flashed up to meet it, then beat it back and slipped around the *shatra*'s hand and into the inside of his elbow.

There was no sound this time as the blade penetrated, but a single yellow flash preceded the first oozing blood. Wirikidor seemed to hesitate. It did not revert to lifeless metal but rather paused in mid-air, seeming to vibrate slightly.

The *shatra* was not so indecisive. The two wounds to his sword-arm, while scarcely more than pricks, nevertheless seemed to have affected his control; accordingly, he shifted his stance and tossed his sword from his right hand to his left before renewing the attack. This gave Valder time enough to rise to one knee.

For a moment Valder was unable to follow what happened, even though his own right hand was a part of it. At first the *shatra* was attacking, and then he was defending as Wirikidor met every attack and retaliated, pressing home its own assault, all in a blur of motion far too fast for a mere human like Valder to follow, never allowing so much as the fraction of a second the *shatra* would have needed to step back out of reach. Blood flowed redly down the northerner's black tunic and spattered the grass.

Then, abruptly, it was over, and Valder found himself still on one knee, not yet having managed to arise, but with his sword thrust through the northerner's heart. The northerner's own sword had fallen from his hand, the blade still gleaming and unstained.

Shatra, however, were not mere mortals, and the northerner was not dead. He looked down at the sword that had impaled him and reached for it with both hands. The right was unsteady.

Valder stared in horror. He had no doubt that Wirikidor had found the *shatra*'s heart; the blade was buried in the northerner's chest just left of center, yet he still lived.

Perhaps, Valder thought, he had no heart. He was *shatra*, not human, after all.

Valder tried to pull his sword free, but human reactions could not match *shatra*; the hands grabbed Wirikidor's blade.

Wirikidor writhed, ripping open the *shatra*'s chest, and that was the end of it; the hands fell away and the northerner toppled backward, sliding off the enchanted blade. He lay in a heap on the trampled grass.

Valder sank back to a sitting position and stared at the corpse, half-afraid that it would return to life. He could see the proof of its inhumanity in the gaping chest wound, where something smooth and slick and black gleamed, something that was definitely not human flesh or bone. He shuddered. On the outside the thing had seemed human enough—tall and pale and fair-haired, like most northerners.

Finally, he looked at Wirikidor, drooping in his hand. His wrist ached; his hand had been dragged along, willy-nilly, in the sword's movements, and, as a result of moving so much faster than it was meant to do, his wrist was now very sore indeed.

The sword had saved him. It had seemed hesitant at first, but it had saved him. He wiped the blade clean on a corner of the dead northerner's tunic, then sheathed it with a sigh of relief. It was good, very good indeed, to have it on his belt instead of naked in his hand.

He wondered why the sword had not immediately been enthusiastic. Surely, there could be no doubt that a *shatra* was a true warrior! The very name was said to be an old word for a great warrior—though apparently not in the same tongue as his sword's name.

The sword had seemed to hesitate after each of the first two wounds it had inflicted, he thought, as he stared at the body of his enemy. Those two wounds had almost seemed to strike sparks; perhaps the blade had encountered a demonic part of the *shatra* and had been daunted by it. *Shatra* were half man and half demon; perhaps Wirikidor was not up to handling demons.

Valder decided that that made a certain amount of sense.

As he sat gathering his wits and regaining his breath,

he heard a faint rustling and something that sounded like distant voices. His hand went to his sword hilt, but he resisted the temptation to draw; he did not want to be stuck carrying Wirikidor unsheathed again should he manage to avoid fighting. Carefully, he got to his feet and looked back along his tracks, expecting to see more northerners.

There were none.

The rustling continued, and the voices grew louder. Valder realized they were coming from the opposite direction. He turned around and saw half a dozen men advancing toward him through the grass; others were visible behind them, and still more on the horizon.

His hopes shriveled within him. Wirikidor would handle the first one without any difficulty; but if his one-warrior-per-drawing theory was correct, he would be on his own after that, and he knew he would stand no chance at all against so many. He must have come upon the entire northern army!

"You there!" one of the advancing men called, in good Ethsharitic. "Stay right where you are!"

Valder glanced at the corpse at his feet. At least, he told himself, he had killed a *shatra*. That was something that not very many could say. He sighed, trying to decide whether to surrender or go down fighting; he was sure that he would die in either case. He did not want to die, but he could accept it if he had to.

The sun was sinking in the west, and its light was reddening; the shadows were long, and he had been alone, surrounded by enemies, for months. Perhaps that was why it took him so long to realize the true situation. It was not until the six men of the advance party came within a hundred yards that he recognized their uniforms.

The new arrivals were not northerners; they were an advance guard of the Ethsharitic army.

He had made it. Wirikidor had brought him home.

PART TWO

The Reluctant Assassin

CHAPTER 9

They took away his weapons, of course. Despite the trouble it had caused him with its mysterious behavior, he found himself reluctant to let Wirikidor go; it was not so much an attachment because it had saved his life as it was a wordless feeling of unease at the thought of someone else handling it.

The soldier who confiscated his weapons seemed reluctant to handle the sword, but obeyed his orders and accepted it along with Valder's dagger, sling, and broken-stringed crossbow.

After a little discussion, someone located a pair of boots for Valder, which he pulled on gratefully. They even fitted him fairly well.

The brown-clad officer in charge of the party asked him a few questions—who he was, how he came to be where he had been found, and whether he knew anything about enemy positions. Not feeling up to long explanations, he briefly gave his name, rank, and unit, explained that he had been cut off months earlier, and said that the only enemy position he had seen was the small encampment he had passed through a day's walk to the northwest.

With that, the officer seemed to lose interest in him. Valder hesitated and then asked, "Sir, who are you people? What are you doing here? I thought I was still behind the northern lines."

The officer looked back at him. "I can't tell you anything," he said. "You might be a spy."

Valder had to admit that that would seem like a reasonable possibility. He said, "Oh."

Seeing his disappointment, the officer took pity on him. "I suppose it won't do any harm," he said, "to tell you that, as far as we know, there no longer are any northern lines around here to be behind."

Valder was not sure whether he was glad to have this tidbit of information or not, since it opened up vast areas of speculation. He lapsed into silence and stood waiting for instructions while the officer considered something.

A young soldier, one of the group that had found Valder, came up and saluted, the back of his hand tight to his shoulder in parade-ground style. "Sir," he said, "That dead northerner—he's *shatra*."

The officer looked up. "What?"

"The corpse we found this man standing over—it's *shatra*. No doubt of it. And the body's still warm."

The officer looked at Valder with renewed interest. "Care to explain that, scout?"

Valder shrugged and tried to look nonchalant. "He followed me, I think from that camp I mentioned. I killed him, just before you found me."

"You killed a *shatra*?"

"Yes."

"Single-handedly?"

"Yes."

"How?"

"With my sword; it's enchanted." He gestured in Wirikidor's direction.

The officer followed Valder's gesture, then turned back and eyed him carefully. "What's a scout doing with an enchanted sword?" he demanded.

"Oh, it wasn't enchanted when it was issued. I ran into a wizard in a marsh two sixnights or so north of here; he put a few spells on it to help me get back to my unit."

The officer did not bother to hide his disbelief, and Valder realized just how stupid his story must sound. Before he could say anything further, however, the officer said, "All right, your sword's enchanted. In that case you're not my problem; the general's magicians can decide what to do with you. Sergeant Karn! You and your detail will take this man and his belongings back to camp with you!"

That dealt with, he turned away and attended to other matters. Valder no longer concerned him.

Sergeant Karn was a black-haired giant of a man, well over six feet tall and heavily muscled; his detail consisted of five young soldiers, whom Valder guessed to be new recruits. Their green kilts were unworn, their breastplates still bright, and the oldest looked no more than eighteen. Valder greeted them, hoping to strike up a conversation, but the sergeant quickly stifled that. "He might be a spy," he reminded his men.

Within ten minutes of being given the order, Karn had Valder's weapons and belongings gathered together and added to the bundles his men already carried and was leading his little party southward along a newly made path through the tall grass. This path was merely the simplest and narrowest of trails at first, nothing more than the place a dozen or so men had trampled their way along; most of the advancing Ethsharitic line had been spaced out across the plain, but the commanding officer and his attendants had traveled in a tight little group, leaving the path behind them.

As Karn's party moved on to the south, however, they passed an assortment of people heading north—supply wagons, fresh troops, messengers, and even curious civilians. They passed captured northerners and wounded men traveling south more slowly than themselves and were passed in turn by hurrying messengers. By the time they had gone a league, the path had become a road, the grass trodden into the dirt. This was a welcome relief for Valder's tired feet after so long trampling his own paths—though any sort of walking was not something he welcomed. It did not help any that the soldier carrying

Wirikidor kept stumbling and bumping into him.

Shortly after that they passed the smoking ruins of a small northern outpost; Valder stared in fascination, but the others, obviously not interested, hurried him on.

The sun was down and the light fading when Karn called a halt. "All right, boys," he said. "We'll take a break and see if we can hitch a ride on a supply wagon going back empty. Once the men at the front have had their dinner, there should be a few."

"We aren't stopping here for the night?" Valder asked.

Karn looked at him scornfully, the expression plain even in the gathering dusk. "No, we're not stopping for the night. We're on campaign, soldier!"

"*I'm* not," Valder protested. "I've been barefoot for two sixnights or more and walking for three months, and I need my rest!"

"Rest in the wagon, then." Karn turned away.

As he had predicted, an empty wagon came trundling southward perhaps half an hour later, as Karn was showing his men how to make torches of the tall grass. Valder had refused to help with the instruction, so that he was the first to see the wagon's own torches.

Once they were aboard the wagon, the rest of the journey was almost pleasant; the road was smooth enough that even a springless ox-drawn cart did not jolt excessively, and Valder was able to sleep off and on until dawn.

They reached the camp early in the afternoon. The first sight of it, as they topped a final hill, was impressive indeed; lines of dull green tents reached to the horizon in three directions amid hundreds of streamers of smoke from cooking fires, broken here and there by an open space. Of course, the camp lay in a narrow depression, so that the horizon was not as far away as it might have been, but Valder was impressed nonetheless. Certainly the encampment was far larger than any he had seen before; he judged that it must hold more than fifty thousand men, and at least one of the open spaces held a tethered dragon. Some of the others held horses or oxen.

He had several minutes to look it over as the wagon made its way up over the hill and paused, while the sentries at the perimeter met them with a perfunctory challenge. They were quickly allowed through and moved on down the slope past the outermost line of tents. At the third row, Sergeant Karn signaled the driver, who slowed the oxen to a halt and allowed his passengers to disembark.

After that, the party split up; besides escorting their prisoner, the detail had brought an assortment of papers and captured materials that were to be delivered to various places. Three of the soldiers were selected to take Valder and an assortment of magical or possibly magical devices to the magicians' section, while Karn and the others went elsewhere.

Valder was led back into the depths of the camp, up over another hill, and around a corner, where he found himself looking, not at yet more straight lines of identical military-issue green, but at a circle of bright tents in a wide variety of shapes, sizes, and colors, clustered around a large area of open ground.

His escort stopped at a chalked line a dozen paces from the outer edge of the circle; Valder stopped as well, though he saw no reason to. The four of them stood and waited for several minutes. Valder was growing restless when a middle-aged woman in a blue gown came hurrying over to them.

"Stuff from the front," one of the soldiers said before the woman could speak.

"I'll take care of it," she replied.

One of the others grabbed Valder by the arm and pushed him forward. "We found this man up there, too. He claims he got cut off from his unit and got back by using a magic sword. Tell your people to check him out. Here's the sword." He indicated Wirikidor, thrust into a sack with the rest of Valder's possessions.

The woman looked at Valder with mild interest. "I'll take care of it," she repeated.

"Where do we put everything?"

She turned and pointed to a small pink tent. "On the table in there, as usual—the wards aren't up, so you can go right in. And I'll take care of this fellow and his sword myself, for now."

"Right." A soldier handed her the bag containing Valder's belongings, Wirikidor protruding gracelessly from the top. "He's all yours."

"Come on, then," she said as she led the way toward a red-and-white striped pavilion. Valder followed obediently.

CHAPTER 10

*H**e had been in camp for two days before he was* allowed outside the magicians' section. During that time he was passed from hand to hand and subjected to various interrogations, magical inspections, analyses, and divinations, verifying that he was indeed who he claimed to be and had not been possessed by demons nor placed under any sort of sorcerous control—at least, no sorcery that the latest in modern wizardry and witchcraft could detect, as the camp did not have a competent sorcerer on hand.

Valder wondered anew at this omission; surely Ethshar had a few good sorcerers somewhere, enough to supply one to a camp of this size!

Other than these constant investigations, he was not mistreated. The blue-robed woman turned out to be a sort of clerk who acted as a general helper and liaison between the community of magicians and the rest of the world, but was not a magician herself. She found Valder a bunk in a gold-trimmed white tent otherwise occupied by an old man who did not stir out of his trance at any time during Valder's stay, and it was she who scheduled his appointments with the various wizards and witches who were to study his case.

Shortly after his arrival, as he was checked out by a nervous young wizard who had been put in charge of his case for the moment, another wizard contacted his old unit—or what was left of it. A plump theurgist let slip shortly after contact was made that the unit had caught the brunt of the enemy's drive to the sea and been badly mauled—in fact, it effectively no longer existed, the survivors having been distributed elsewhere. Fortunately, the survivors included men who knew Valder, such as his bunkmate Tandellin, and his identity was confirmed through dream images the night after his arrival in camp.

In what seemed an excessive precaution to Valder, they even double-checked the wizardly dreams by witchcraft, lest some unknown enemy wizard's trick interfere.

Every test bore out his story, of course, since his every word was the truth, and eventually his interrogators were convinced of his honesty and accuracy. He had not realized until he had tried to explain himself to his rescuers—or perhaps captors—just how unlikely his story sounded. Surviving, lost and alone, behind enemy lines for two months, then being rescued from an enemy patrol that had him hopelessly outclassed by a mysterious hermit wizard nobody had ever heard of ... Valder had to admit that, stated simply, it did sound unlikely, even before bringing Wirikidor into it. And then, to top it off, he had killed a *shatra* in single combat. Nobody would ever have believed that at all, had he not been found standing alone over the fresh corpse. He suspected that a great many people still did not believe it, even with witnesses and magical verifications.

Eventually, though, after two days of continuous probing, the whole thing was officially accepted, and he was allowed the run of the camp. That done, the various wizards turned their attention to Wirikidor. Until his identity was established, he had not been permitted weapons, naturally; and furthermore, no one had touched Wirikidor, lest it be booby-trapped. The sword had remained on the

table in the pink tent with other unknown magical items.
It still looked like any ordinary, standard-issue sword, but,
when it was brought out into the open circle, Valder could
somehow sense, beyond question, that this was Wirikidor
and no other.

He was currently in the hands of a red-haired young
wizard in a dull green robe who had refused to give her
name and a man called Darrend of Calimor, dark haired
and middle-sized, of indeterminate age, wearing a standard military tunic and kilt, but with no breastplate and
carrying no sword. Instead of the usual simple soldier's
dagger he bore an ornate ceremonial knife and wore a
soft green cap instead of a helmet. Valder assumed him
to be a wizard, though he had not actually seen the man
perform any spells. These two stood on either side of him
as the clerk brought out the sword.

"That's it, is it?" Darrend asked.

"Yes," Valder answered without hesitation. "That's
Wirikidor."

Darrend glanced at him, then took the sword from the
clerk. "We've heard your story, of course, so we know a
little about how this sword behaves, but how is it you
can be so certain that this is in fact your sword and not
another?"

Valder shrugged. "I don't know, but I *am* sure."

"It's inactive as long as it's sheathed; we tested that
right after you were delivered here. Do you know anything
about what it's likely to do when someone draws it?"

"Ah . . . not really," Valder said unhappily. "But each
time I drew it, I was unable to sheathe it again until it
had killed a man."

"Was it in any great hurry to kill someone?"

Valder's unhappiness grew. "I don't know," he con-
fessed. "Each time I drew it, the next person I saw was
an enemy, and each time I killed him as quickly as I
could—or the sword did."

"That doesn't help much. Perhaps we had best assume
that it will demand a victim immediately."

"It might," Valder agreed.

"We need to draw it in order to examine it, so I think

we had best find ourselves a prospective victim."

"How are you going to do that?" Valder asked. He quickly wished he hadn't, as he remembered the northern prisoners he had seen on the road south.

"I'll have to talk to General Karannin," Darrend replied. "Until then, I think perhaps you should carry the sword again; you'd look out of place around camp without it, and if it does carry an ownership spell, as I suspect, keeping you apart for much longer might be dangerous." He handed Valder the scabbarded weapon.

Valder accepted it gravely and restored it to its accustomed place on his belt.

"Until we find a prisoner, I don't think we'll be needing you," Darrend said. "You're free to go where you please, so long as you don't leave the camp, but be back here at dusk."

"Thank you," Valder said. Darrend nodded a farewell and then strolled away. The clerk and the other wizard, after a moment's hesitation, also moved off, leaving him alone in the magicians' circle.

For a moment he was not sure what to do. He had no friends in this camp; although his old unit was scattered, none had wound up this far inland, and he had not had time since arriving to meet anyone but his interrogators. It was faintly possible, though highly unlikely, that a cousin or other kin could be in the camp, but he had no idea where any such relatives might be found.

That meant there were no people he wanted to see, but that did not leave him utterly without purpose; after three months of near-total isolation, more than anything else he wanted news—and he would have no objection to wine and women—song would be strictly optional, as he had never been particularly musical. He had picked up a few bits of information in conversation with the wizards and witches, but only enough to whet his appetite for real news. His meals had included only water or weak beer, and the idea of a good drunk, on wine or something stronger, was appealing. The various female magicians or magicians' helpers he had encountered had been unavailable, unattractive, or both.

If this camp followed the pattern of every other camp he had ever been in, he knew exactly where to go for what he wanted—but it was not technically in the camp, nor was he likely to return by nightfall.

What the hell, he told himself; he deserved a little relaxation. He had been cooperative enough since his capture. He turned south and headed for the rear of the encampment, where the camp followers and hangers-on were sure to have a camp of their own.

Sure enough, as he had expected, the tents and shacks of the camp followers were strewn across the plains south of the main camp; and, as he had expected, the largest structures were all either bars or brothels. The others catered to different interests; some even sheltered soldiers' families, which was the official reason such camptowns were tolerated. Valder ignored the freelance seers, officers' wives, and other respectable or semirespectable people and headed directly for a large, tan-colored tent hung with red lanterns.

News, he decided, came first, since it was still only mid-afternoon. He suspected he might not remember the evening and he did not want to forget anything important. With that in mind he settled at a table in the half-empty, improvised tavern in the front of the tent, ignoring what lay beyond the bead curtain. He ordered a mild wine, since he intended to start off slowly.

As he had hoped, there were a few other people in the place; and as might be expected so early in the day, they included some serious drinkers. It was not difficult to get one of them started talking. Valder asked questions whenever the stream of words seemed to be slowing and sipped at his wine every so often to keep the taverner happy.

He started the conversation off with the usual banter about how miserable military life was, but quickly brought up the fact that he had been cut off for months.

"Did I miss anything?" he asked, half-jokingly. "Any generals drop dead, or anything?"

"Nope," his drinking companion, a lieutenant by the name of Sidor, replied, "It's still Gor and Terrek and Anaran and Azrad running everything—them and their flunkies, like our own dear General Karannin, sitting here in the middle of nowhere because he doesn't want to cause trouble."

That sounded interesting; Valder prompted the lieutenant, asking, "How do you mean that?"

The resulting tirade was not always clear, but the gist of it seemed to be that the enemy was in a state of near-collapse and General Karannin was failing to take advantage of it. The northerners' drive to the sea, which had cut Valder off from his unit in the first place, had apparently been a desperate gamble that had not paid off; the Empire had put everything it could muster into a high-speed attack that had supposedly been intended to sweep around the western end of the Ethsharitic army, down the coast and back across toward Old Ethshar itself—or at least toward Admiral Azrad's home base. The attack had failed; the Ethsharitic resistance had been enough to wear away the northern assault force until, by the time it ran up against General Gor's coastal fortress, there was almost nothing left of it.

Naturally, realizing the enemy's weakness, Ethshar had counterattacked along a broad front, advancing up across the plains and meeting virtually no resistance. The few scattered northerners they did encounter appeared to be simply scouts, sentries, and remnants of the assault force's supply line that had been left behind when the attack collapsed.

It was obvious to anyone with any wits, the lieutenant said repeatedly, that the Empire had finally run out of troops and launched their last attack while they still had men to do their fighting. Everyone had seen that the northern soldiers had gotten younger and younger of late. All Ethshar's army had to do to end the war was march straight on into the Empire's capital and take over.

The generals, of course, would not do that. Sidor got quite sarcastic on that point. The generals, he claimed, were afraid the whole thing was a trap or trick of some sort, when anybody could see that it was nothing of the kind. General Karannin, in particular, had insisted on advancing with what Sidor considered truly absurd cau-

tion. The very fact that his camp had stayed in one place
for the two days Valder had been in it was, to Sidor, proof
that Karannin was wasting a golden opportunity to put
an end to the interminable conflict.

For his own part, Valder had some doubts. The Empire
still appeared, from what he had seen, to have a good
many sorcerers and *shatra* on hand, even if they were
running short of regular infantry; furthermore, nobody
knew what other surprises the northerners' tutelary
demons might provide, should *shatra* prove inadequate.

Besides, the war had been going on for centuries. It
seemed unlikely to Valder that, of all the generations that
had fought in his family, he should happen to be the one
lucky enough to have it end during his lifetime.

Of course, he was the first in his family to own a magic
sword—but that was a minor thing, really, where the end
of the Great War would mean an entirely different world.

He had managed to nurse his single cup of wine for
over an hour of Sidor's diatribes and gossip, but it was
gone at last, and he decided it was time to move on to
more serious drinking. He ordered a mug of *oushka* and
took a sip as Sidor raved about why the war should have
already been won.

The drink burned going down; he coughed. It had been
a long time since he had drunk *oushka*, and, he realized,
he had lost his taste for the stuff. That took most of the
fun out of the prospect of getting drunk—and now that
he thought about it, he did not really want to get drunk
in the first place. That had been what he always did in
the evening when he had nothing better to do, but most
of the fun of it had been in the company he kept—friends
who were not here, many of whom were apparently dead.
He had come here out of habit. Sidor was a poor substitute
for the comrades he had spent years with.

He looked at the bead curtain, unsure whether he
wanted what it hid; his hand fell to his purse, and he
decided the point was moot. He had forgotten that he had
almost no money—in fact, his only money was the single
silver bit every scout carried. The magicians might have
established his identity, but so far nobody had given him

his back pay, and all his belongings left behind had presumably been lost when his unit was overrun. The lone coin was probably not even enough to pay for his two drinks.

He glanced around, trying to seem casual, and saw that the taverner was not looking in his direction. He dropped the silver bit on the table and sauntered out, his heart beating a little faster than he liked.

No one called after him. The sun was reddening in the west; he decided to obey orders after all and return to the magicians' circle.

CHAPTER 11

*G*eneral Karannin's tent was no more luxurious, inside or out, than that of any of his officers. Even the number of cots was the same, as he had his secretary and two aides sharing his quarters, to be available when he wanted them. It was, however, somewhat larger, and the extra space was occupied by a table jammed into one end, with an assortment of gear stowed underneath.

Valder was slightly surprised by the lack of ostentation. He was unsure whether to credit it to practicality on the general's part or a show of egalitarianism. He waited for perhaps five minutes, guarded by two soldiers, before the general arrived. The wizards who had brought him slipped quietly away out of the tent after making their delivery. Valder waited, looking around with unconcealed interest; he had not expected to be brought directly to the general himself.

Karannin was a short, balding man, brown-haired and green-eyed, wearing an ordinary green kilt and brown tunic; he moved quickly and energetically when he moved at all and swept into the tent like a breaking wave. "You're

95

Valder," he said as he slapped aside the tent flap.

Valder saluted, open palm at his shoulder. "Valder of Kardoret, Scout First Class, Western Command, Coastal Division, Third Regiment, detached, sir."

"Right. Sit down."

Valder obeyed, seating himself on the edge of the nearest cot. The general remained standing throughout the conversation, taking a few paces back and forth, then pausing for a moment, then pacing again.

"The wizards have been telling me about you, trying to convince me to let them have a condemned prisoner. You got cut off by the enemy's drive to the coast?"

"Yes, sir."

"Has anybody told you what happened, how the attack went?"

"No, sir, not really," Valder replied; he had not officially been told anything and did not care to explain his chat with the drunken lieutenant.

"Good; not all of my men are blabbermouths. So you survived and escaped northward, where you encountered a wizard—or at least a hermit you took to be a wizard— who enchanted your sword. Correct?"

"Yes, sir." Valder knew better than to point out that he knew beyond any possible doubt that the hermit had been a wizard.

"Just what sort of an enchantment is it supposed to be? Did he say? I'm not asking you to remember any details, son, just whether he said."

"No, sir, he made a point of not telling me, it seemed. I'm afraid that we weren't on very good terms by that time."

"You're absolutely sure he didn't say anything about the nature of the spell, or mention any names?"

"He told me that he had put every spell he could manage without his supplies on it, sir—or at least every one he thought would be of use. He mentioned some kind of ownership spell, I think. And he told me the sword's name was Wirikidor and that I mustn't draw it until I was well out of sight of him."

"You told my people this when they asked you?"

"Yes, sir."

"My wizards heard this?"

"Yes, sir."

"That's your sword there, right? The one that was enchanted?" He paused in his pacing and pointed at Valder's belt.

"I believe so, sir."

"And you used this sword? Killed a sentry or two, fought a dragon, and an enemy you thought was *shatra*?"

Valder suppressed his urge to take offense at the doubting way his killing a *shatra* was mentioned. Karannin was not Gor or Azrad or Anaran or Terrek, but he was still a general, whatever Sidor might think of him. One did not argue with generals. "Yes, sir."

"My wizards tell me that it might be dangerous to draw the thing."

"Yes, sir, it might. Every time it's been drawn since it was enchanted, it has killed a man at the first opportunity."

Karannin stared at him. "Tell me about it," he said.

"Sir, once I draw the sword, I won't be able to sheathe it or put it down until I've killed a man with it. Furthermore, I don't know for certain whether I can choose *which* man I kill. Remember, the hermit would not let me unsheathe it in his presence. So far, I have never drawn it in the presence of anyone not an enemy, so it hasn't been put to the test."

The general looked at him shrewdly. "The sword can act on its own? You don't need to direct it?"

"Yes, sir, that's right. That's how I survived against the *shatra*; if I had been controlling the sword I'd be dead now."

"I've heard of such things, but the spells aren't reliable."

"Yes, sir."

Karannin contemplated him for perhaps three seconds before barking at one of his guards, "You, there, sergeant, go fetch the wizards, and then ask Captain Dar to bring that prisoner."

The soldier bowed in acknowledgment and slipped out through the flap. Karannin began pacing again, but did not resume his questioning.

A moment later the guard returned and stepped aside to allow Darrend and the young red-haired wizard to enter. Behind them came a burly black-haired man in a captain's uniform, hauling by one arm a young soldier who was extraordinarily unkempt and, to judge by his odor, long unwashed, his hands tied behind him. To Valder's surprise, this prisoner was an Ethsharite, not a northerner.

"Well, Captain Dar?" the general said.

"Yes, sir," the brawny captain replied. "This is Felder Venger's son. He was caught robbing the corpses of his comrades and stripping their jewelry. When spotted, he ran; when apprehended two days later, he stabbed the arresting officer in the belly. He was sentenced to be flogged, as it was a first offense and the officer survived, but three days ago, while awaiting punishment, he attempted escape and brained one of his guards. We were waiting to see whether the guard died before deciding what to do with him; the guard died this morning. Will he do?"

"I think so, Captain. Wizards? Valder? Will he do?"

Valder shrugged, the redhead stammered, and Darrend said, "I would think so." The prisoner himself was staring at the lot of them, trying to figure out what was happening.

"Good enough, then. I want to see this. Scout, give Darrend your sword."

Reluctantly, Valder removed Wirikidor from his belt and handed it over. The wizard accepted it cautiously, then held the scabbard in his left hand and put his right to the hilt, preparing to draw the sword.

Staring at Darrend's hands with morbid fascination, Valder said, "Sir, need I remain here? I would prefer not to watch."

The general peered at him. "You expect danger?"

"No, sir, I just don't want to watch."

"Squeamish?"

"Yes, sir."

"All right, then, you may go—but don't leave camp."

"Yes, sir." Gratefully, Valder slipped out the tent flap and looked about, glad to be outside, away from the impending killing. He tried to decide which way to go.

Somewhere, he knew, there must be a paymaster—and he was due three months' back pay. This was not his unit, so some argument would probably be required, but he thought he ought to be able to get at least part of what he was owed. A guard stood nearby, in addition to those inside the tent—but Valder suddenly decided, upon hearing voices from inside the tent, that he wanted to get out of earshot as well as out of sight of what he was sure would be the execution of Felder Venger's son. He had no quarrel with sentencing such a criminal to die, but he was also not fond of watching or listening to anyone's death. He turned left, choosing his direction at random, and started walking.

He turned left again a few tents down and began working his way toward camptown. Maybe, he thought, someone would treat him to a drink. Despite his earlier experience with the *oushka* he thought he could use one now.

He had gotten perhaps halfway when he heard someone calling his name. Surprised, he turned and saw a young soldier waving at him.

He waited while the soldier came up to him. "Are you Valder of Kardoret?" he was asked.

"Yes," he replied, mystified; the soldier was a complete stranger.

"The general wants to see you immediately in his tent."

Still mystified, Valder followed the soldier back to the general's tent.

The instant he stepped through the flap, Karannin stopped pacing and barked at him, "You said you used this infernal sword?"

"Yes, sir," Valder answered, still puzzled.

"Then why in Hell can't anyone here draw it for the wizards to study?"

The question startled Valder. "I don't know, sir." It had not occurred to him that anyone would have any difficulty in drawing it. He never had.

The general had not resumed his pacing and was now staring at him as if expecting him to say more. Valder stared back for a few seconds, not feeling particularly cooperative—after all, he had not been treated very pleasantly—but then remembered the penalties for insolence.

"I never had any difficulty in *drawing* the sword, sir," he said. "At times I found it impossible to *sheathe* it, but I never had any trouble *drawing* it. Ah . . . the hermit told me that the sword's name means 'slayer of warriors,' and I suspect it has a certain affinity for soldiers; perhaps the people who tried to draw it did not meet its standards."

The general stared at him for another second before snapping, "One of these wizards who tried to draw it is Darrend of Calimor, thrice commended for bravery in action. When caught without the tools of his trade, he once fought and killed an enemy sorcerer with only his ceremonial dagger. Furthermore, I tried to draw it myself. If your sword doesn't consider any one of us to be a warrior, I would like to know just whom it *would* accept!"

Taken aback, Valder replied, "I don't know, sir." He glanced at Darrend with renewed interest and wondered how old the wizard was; he looked no more than thirty, which was young to have the sort of respect the general gave him. He did not have the appearance of a man who had often been in combat.

"Well, then, let's find out, shall we? There's the sword, Scout First Class; let us see if you can draw it where Darrend could not."

"Ah . . . sir . . . if I might say something?"

"Speak, damn it, that's what you're here for."

"Sir, I would really prefer not to draw the sword. While I have no love for this prisoner, I would rather not kill him. Killing an enemy in battle is one thing—I've done that a few times—but killing a defenseless man in the same uniform I wear is something entirely different."

"I am sure your scruples do you credit," the general replied. "However, I believe that if we're going to have a demonstration of the sword's magic, you will have to be the one who draws it. Assuming, that is, that anyone can draw it."

Delaying in hopes of a miracle, Valder asked Darrend, "You tried to draw Wirikidor?"

Darrend nodded. "It was like trying to pull apart a steel

bar. A highly polished one, at that; it kept slipping out of my hands."

"I tried it, too," the other wizard remarked. "Felt as if I nearly broke my fingers."

"Really?" Valder stared at the sword in the general's hand. "I never had any trouble."

"Well, we all did," Karannin said. "Slippery thing, isn't it?" He handed it to Valder, hilt-first.

It did not feel slippery to him. His hand closed firmly on the familiar grip, and he looked unwillingly at the waiting prisoner. The man was sweating profusely, his mouth tight shut, his eyes fixed on the tent's ridgepole.

Of course, Valder told himself, no one was *sure* that Wirikidor would insist on a killing. It was all just guesswork and inference. Reluctantly, he drew the sword.

It slid easily from the sheath, as it always had done for him; this time, however, it seemed to be trembling in anticipation as soon as it left the scabbard.

"There it is," he said, displaying the bared blade to the general and the wizards.

"Can you sheathe it again?" Darrend asked.

Valder made the attempt, but Wirikidor not only refused to return to its scabbard, it actively fought against him. It was, he realized, struggling to get into a position where it might strike out at one of the people in the tent.

The general was the closest; Valder found his hand being dragged in Karannin's direction. Realizing he had little choice now that the sword was free of the sheath, he turned and took a step toward Felder.

Wirikidor flashed out and cut the prisoner's neck open, half severing his head. Felder died with only a dry croak, his eyes and mouth suddenly wide with surprise. As he fell to the floor, Valder felt the tension vanish from the sword; the trembling ceased completely, leaving him holding what seemed an ordinary blade.

"Don't sheathe it!" Darrend called.

"I wasn't going to," Valder replied. "You wanted to study it, didn't you? Here, then; you take it!" He turned the weapon and passed it to Darrend hilt-first, then passed the scabbard along as well.

The wizard accepted both gravely, and Valder smiled

beneath an overwhelming wave of relief as it left his hand. The smile vanished an instant later as he again caught sight of the corpse on the dirt floor of the tent. Disgust seeped up his throat.

He was, he assured himself, glad to be free of the sword responsible for such a killing. He wished he were also free of the general who had arranged it and the wizards who had requested it.

CHAPTER 12

The wizards kept Wirikidor, but bed space in the magicians' circle was at a premium, so the day after Felder's death, Valder was transferred and assigned to share the quarters of three lieutenants. The previous fourth occupant of their tent was missing in action as a result of a brief and inconclusive skirmish between the advancing Ethsharites and a small party of northerners that had included at least one sorcerer.

The lieutenants were less than delighted with his presence. They had hoped for the return of their comrade, or else for the greater space a vacancy would allow; to have a stranger thrust upon them, a soldier from an entirely different part of the army, and not even an officer, was not welcome. Another regular lieutenant would have been someone with whom they might talk shop, exchange stories and perhaps duties—but instead, they found themselves with a battered scout, nominally below them in rank but with considerably more experience of the world and the enemy and with no assigned duties at all.

Valder, understanding their position, did everything he could to accommodate them. He had no belongings to take up precious space, and his lack of duties allowed him to keep whatever hours suited their mutual convenience. He was perfectly willing to stay awake until all hours talking, or to stay quiet, or even to go elsewhere for a time, if his tentmates so desired.

He was also a willing listener in his eagerness to catch up on everything he had missed, not just while lost in the north, but even before, as his unit had been an isolated one. For that matter, just the sound of human voices, regardless of what was being said, was comforting.

Everyone liked a good listener. After a few hours, his affability and open interest in what his new companions had to say had worn down the initial strain, and one of the three, a gangling young man of twenty-two, freshly arrived from a training camp near the port of Shan on the Sea, got talking.

The lieutenant's name was Radler Dathet's son, and, although he was only a year or so younger than Valder, he seemed to the scout little more than a boy.

Radler agreed, in general, with Sidor's assessment of the strategic situation, but attributed the slow advance to the lack of roads and adequate means of supply, rather than to timidity on the part of the Ethsharitic commanders. General Gor's Western Command and General Anaran's Central Command were both advancing, chewing up the scattered enemy units they encountered. In the interior, Azrad was doing his best to provide the necessary logistical support, but supplies and men were both becoming scarce. General Terrek's Eastern Command was still stalemated, as no foolhardy attack had been made on that front—and Terrek, suspecting a ruse, was not willing to send anything to his compatriots.

General Karannin was one of Gor's subordinates, as Valder had thought—though the possibility that he was one of Anaran's, somehow strayed west, had occurred to him. Gor himself was reportedly still in his coastal fortress, coordinating, rather than leading the advance personally.

Losses had been fairly heavy on both sides, Radler thought, despite the small numbers of the northerners, because a disproportionate number of the enemy were either sorcerers or *shatra*. Nonetheless, like Sidor, he thought the long war was finally nearing an end.

Valder still didn't believe that, but, not wanting to antagonize Radler, he said nothing of his doubts.

After that topic was exhausted, Valder picked up assorted camp gossip—none of it, unfortunately, mentioning anyone he had met. He asked about Darrend, but none of his tentmates knew anything about the wizard.

As the afternoon wore on, the three lieutenants, one by one, departed on various errands. Radler was on duty, commanding a supply detail; the others, Korl and Tesra, mentioned no destination. Valder thought they might be headed for the brothels of camptown. Having no money and therefore nothing better to do—it was far too late to find the paymaster—Valder settled back for a nap.

He was awakened by the sound of the tent flap opening.

"Excuse me, sir," a soldier said, standing in the light so that Valder could not see his face, "but I believe this is yours." He held out an unsheathed sword, hilt-first.

Valder took it without thinking, then started to protest. He stopped suddenly before the first word was finished, when he realized that the sword he held was indeed his own.

That made no sense. The wizards were supposed to be studying Wirikidor. Surely they weren't done with it already? And if they were, would they hand it back so casually? And where was the scabbard? He turned back toward the flap, but the soldier had gone.

He sat up, and his foot struck something. He reached down. As he had half expected, he found Wirikidor's sheath lying on the dirt floor. He picked it up and stared at it, sword in one hand and scabbard in the other.

Puzzled, he arose and peered out of the tent. Nobody was in the immediate area; nobody was looking at him. Still confused, he emerged into the late afternoon sun and gazed about.

The camp was going about its business; men were sharpening blades, talking, eating, hurrying back and forth.

He saw no sign of the soldier who had delivered the sword.

With a shrug, Valder turned toward the magician's circle. He was not sure whether he was meant to have the sword back or not, and the wizards were obviously the people who would know.

As he approached the chalked line where the warding spells began, someone caught sight of him and called out. Figures emerged from the polychrome tents and faces turned toward him.

He stopped at the line until a wizard beckoned him on; a moment later he was in the circle, surrounded by magicians.

Darrend was among them. "So there you are," he remarked.

"Here I am," Valder replied. "Where *should* I be?"

"I really couldn't say soldier, but that sword of yours is supposed to be right here. No one was authorized to move it, yet the first time we took a break—just for a moment—it vanished. Not magically vanished; someone walked off with it. And while we were looking for the sword, the same thing happened to the scabbard. Now here you are, with both of them. Odd, isn't it?"

"Perhaps so, sir," Valder replied. He had the impression that Darrend ranked as an officer. "It was none of *my* doing, though, or I wouldn't be here bringing them back, would I? Someone just handed the sword to me, and I found the scabbard on the floor of the tent, as if someone had tossed it there while I was taking a nap."

Various magicians exchanged glances. "The Spell of True Ownership, I'd say—or at any rate, a close variant," one remarked.

Darrend frowned. "I tested for that and got ambiguous results. It isn't the standard form, but it could be something close."

"But," the redhead said, "that's why no one else could draw it, of course. And now it's found its way back to Valder as if by chance—that's the Spell of True Ownership, if I ever saw it!"

"It's an odd form, though," Darrend insisted. "There's something unhealthy about it."

"There's *always* something unhealthy about True Ownership to my mind," someone new answered.

"No, it's different. I tested for it, of course—when no one else could draw the sword, True Ownership was the first thing I thought of. But there's no trace of a gold ring's use, and how can you work the Spell of True Ownership without a gold ring?"

Valder had no idea what Darrend was talking about. Only recently awakened from his nap and still not entirely recovered from his adventures, he was not very much interested in anything but once more disposing of the sword. "True Owner or not, I'd prefer you take the sword and finish your tests, if you're going to," he said testily. "Sir," he added belatedly.

"Yes, of course," Darrend said, accepting the weapon's hilt.

Valder relinquished the sword and scabbard and then paused. "How long will the tests take?" he asked.

Darrend shrugged. "I have no idea. It depends on just what was done to it. With luck, we'll finish by midnight; without it, we may never figure it out completely."

"Oh." Valder looked at the sword. "Well, good luck, sir." He turned and marched back toward his tent.

He was fairly certain that sooner or later either the sword would again find its way back to him or he would be drawn to the sword. He wondered how much of his future would be tied to Wirikidor and whether the enchantment might be broken, or perhaps just the Spell of True Ownership removed, so that anyone could use the sword.

Darrend watched him go, fighting down a sudden urge to follow. He found himself thinking of urgent errands to be run in the vicinity of Valder's tent.

Annoyed, he recognized the action of the Spell of True Ownership, trying to return the sword to its master—or perhaps its slave. One could never be sure with magic swords. He worked a simple counterspell against compulsions and stalked back toward the laboratory tent.

CHAPTER 13

After four days of study, days during which more than half the camp had been packed up and sent north while Valder did nothing of any use other than finally obtaining his accumulated pay, the wizards had finished their investigation of Wirikidor's properties. Shortly after the noon meal, a messenger fetched Valder and brought him to the magicians' circle.

Darrend was waiting for him in a blue-and-gold tent, where Wirikidor and its sheath lay on one of the two cots. Valder took the seat he was offered on the other cot and listened as Darrend spoke.

"We have finished our studies of the sword you call Wirikidor, despite its resistance to being handled by anyone but you and despite its constant attempts to get back to you. There are several details of its enchantment we can't make out by any means currently at our disposal, but we have the basic characteristics figured out."

Valder nodded, listening attentively.

"I've discussed it with the general. I don't know if he has any use for it in mind yet, but he told me that, as the sword's owner, you should be informed."

"Very kind of him," Valder remarked with mild sarcasm.

"Yes. Well, firstly, we were right about the Spell of True Ownership. The sword *does* have a variant of that spell on it, a deteriorating and unhealthy form. The Spell of True Ownership can be bad enough in any case, since nobody has yet established whether the person owns the enchanted object or the object owns the person, but in your case it seems to be especially bad, due to the spell's decaying nature. The link between the sword and yourself is quite strong and will stay that way for ... well, for a time. Before I can explain that, let me explain some of the other things."

He paused, as if uncertain what to say, and Valder prodded him, asking, "What other things?"

"Other spells—there are several other spells here, all woven together. I've never encountered anything like it. There's Ellran's Immortal Animation, for example—that's a nasty, awkward spell, and your crazy hermit had no right to use it, if you ask me. It's irreversible, completely irreversible—and what's worse, it makes any spell linked to it irreversible, too. It's the Animation that allows your sword to move of its own volition, as you've seen it do. Furthermore, the Animation makes the other spells on the sword permanent and unbreakable—unless one were to use *really* powerful counterspells, and, even then, it would be incredibly dangerous. The combination of the Animation and the True Ownership has the effect of linking you and your life to the sword—breaking the spells would kill you, at the very least, as well as destroying the sword."

Valder stared at the sword on the cot opposite him. This was not anything he had expected. What it would mean to him was still unclear, but it appeared that Wirikidor's existence was not going to be a mere passing episode in his career.

"This has its good side, of course," Darrend went on. "The sword is virtually indestructible now, and there's a curious benefit for you in that, as nearly as we can determine, you can no longer be killed by any ordinary means. Since your life is now bound up *in* the sword, you see, you can't be destroyed by anything *outside* the sword.

If the sword is destroyed, you'll die, very definitely—but it's almost impossible for anyone, even a very high-powered wizard, to damage the sword, let alone destroy it. Ellran's Immortal Animation is indeed very close to the immortality it claims. The sword itself can kill you, under certain circumstances—I'll speak of that in a moment—but to the best of my knowledge, after intensive study by myself and my comrades, there is nothing else in the world that can."

"What?" Valder blinked. He did not believe he had heard Darrend correctly. He was shocked out of the torpor that had beset him since Kelder's death.

"You can't be killed, Valder; you can't die by any means whatsoever, except to die on Wirikidor's blade, or if someone should find a way to destroy the sword."

"What?" Valder stared, still not comprehending.

"No one is going to destroy the sword; doing so would almost certainly cause a catastrophe. Valder, you are going to live until you die on Wirikidor's blade. There is no other way you can die, not since you first drew the sword."

Valder stared in mute astonishment.

"This doesn't mean you're invulnerable. You can still be injured—you just can't die. You can be maimed, tortured, blinded, deafened, driven mad, crippled, dismembered, even cut into pieces—but you won't actually die until Wirikidor kills you. That's part of what's so nasty about the Immortal Animation."

Valder struggled to assimilate this information. "I can't die?"

"Not from any ordinary means. However, there is a catch, and this is where that deteriorating spell comes into it. Your hermit substituted something else for the ring of drawn gold that's supposed to be a part of the Spell of True Ownership, and the resulting enchantment is corrupt. You became the true owner of the sword when you first drew it; whoever drew it would have owned it. However, because of the flaw, you won't *stay* the true owner forever—only gold never tarnishes, not whatever substitute was used here. You'll be able to draw the sword and use it one hundred times, give or take one or two—

and that's all. After that, the sword will renounce you. The next time the sword is drawn after that—and you, Valder of Kardoret, will be the only man in all Ethshar *not* able to draw the sword then—whoever draws the sword will be its new owner, and you will be the first man to die on Wirikidor's blade when that happens. The new owner will be able to draw and wield it ninety-nine times, give or take—one fewer than you, at any rate—and then it will turn on *him*. After that the third owner will be allowed ninety-eight, and so on, until some poor fool, centuries from now, will draw it and have it turn on him immediately. That will use up the spell completely, and there will be no true owner thereafter."

"Wait a minute—nothing else can kill me, but Wirikidor is going to turn on me and kill me?"

"That's more or less correct."

Valder was outraged. "That's insane! What sort of an enchantment is that?"

Darrend shrugged. "Hermits often *are* insane. I suspect this one didn't like you."

"How long will this take, then? How long do I have to live?"

"Who knows? That doesn't seem to be built in anywhere. There isn't any compulsion to draw the sword; leave it undrawn and in theory you could live forever."

Valder stared first at the wizard and then at the sword. He was still having trouble taking this in. As a soldier, he had long lived, albeit reluctantly, with the idea that he might be killed at any moment. Now that was no longer true. How could the hermit have wreaked such havoc on his life?

He could still be harmed, though. "I'm not sure I want that," he said slowly. "Can the spell be removed?"

Darrend sighed. "Not by me. I don't think anyone could do it. Your hermit was either very lucky or an incredibly talented wizard. It would take a spell more powerful than all the ones he used put together to remove the enchantment, the way he has everything linked up, and I doubt that any wizard alive could handle such a spell. *I* certainly can't. Ellran's Immortal Animation is usually rated as an eighth-order spell, and that's just *one* of the charms he used. Only one wizard in a hundred or so makes it past fourth-order enchantments alive. On a good day, I can handle one eighth-order spell, but not a tangle like that; nobody I ever heard of short of Fendel the Great could undo that mess." He paused, a startled look on his face. "I just thought of something," he said. "Nobody really knows what happened to Fendel; do you think he might be your hermit?"

Valder shrugged. "I suppose he could be."

"Oh, probably not." Darrend waved the possibility away.

"Isn't there any other way of getting the enchantment off, other than this impossible counterspell?"

"Not that I know of. There are legends about ways of canceling out wizardry entirely, like snuffing a candle, but I've never believed in them. If they existed, the northerners would have found them by now and used them against us."

Valder knew enough to dismiss such scare stories.

"Why worry about it, though?" Darrend said. "You don't need to remove the spell; it won't be that hard to live with, if you're careful about drawing and not drawing the sword. You'll have to keep Wirikidor with you, of course—leaving a Truly Owned object around can be dangerous. If it takes a tidal wave or an earthquake to bring it to you when the spell has built up enough potential, you'll *get* a tidal wave or an earthquake and all the damage that would cause. It's a ruthless sort of spell."

"Oh," Valder said. He had been thinking of quietly burying Wirikidor somewhere to keep it from being drawn that hundred-and-first time—or ninety-ninth or one-hundred-and-third or whatever.

"I think that covers the ownership angle," Darrend said. "Now, about the sword's name and what it does. The hermit told you that 'Wirikidor' means 'slayer of warriors,' but that's a bad translation. 'Mankiller' is closer. It doesn't care if its victims are warriors, so long as they're human, male, and past puberty."

"Oh," Valder said again. That explained why the sword had not killed the dragon or the woman and why it had hesitated against the half-human *shatra*.

"Furthermore, as you have discovered, it's 'man killer,' not 'men killer.' It's only interested in taking one life each time it's drawn."

"I had noticed that," Valder agreed.

"Yes, I'm sure you have. Each time it's drawn it will kill a man as quickly as you can provide it with a victim. You'll want to be careful about that. I think you can control which man of several it kills, but I doubt you can hold it back entirely—it needs to kill *someone*. You saw that with that convict. Against its proper foe—a single man—it's as close to unbeatable as wizardry can make it. You'll never need to worry about being outmatched. Besides the Animation that lets it all work, it's got three separate blessings—one of which I never encountered before—and the Spell of Perpetual Sharpness and a few other little charms and cantrips. This hermit may have been mad, but he knew an amazing amount of magic and he didn't stint in using it. If he could do something like this after most of his supplies were destroyed, he'd certainly be an asset to the war effort."

"He said he had already served."

"If he did, he either kept his talents hidden, or has developed them since—or maybe he was kept secret. Ordinarily, I'm sure I'd have heard of anyone with his abilities."

"He seemed quite old," Valder said. "Maybe he was before your time. Maybe he *is* this Fendel the Great you mentioned. I don't know."

"Well, whoever he is, you've got an impressive weapon here. Not flashy, but powerful. I'm returning it to you—no point in letting the Spell of Ownership get dangerous—but I want to warn you to be extremely cautious with it." He reached out and pulled the sword and scabbard from the table, then handed them to Valder, who accepted both, then slid the blade into its sheath and hung it on his belt.

"Get to know it," Darrend said. "You and Wirikidor are going to be together for the rest of your life, so you had better become accustomed to its behavior. Be grateful that it hasn't got a mind of its own—reflexes, yes, but no mind that I can detect, no whims, no personality. It's a very powerful and valuable item—and a very dangerous one as well, both to you and to others."

"Yes, sir." Valder was not absolutely certain that Darrend was technically a superior officer, but he spoke like one and obviously commanded considerable respect, so that the "sir" seemed natural.

"Remember that it will keep you *alive* but not *safe*. Don't get overconfident, or you might wind up so badly crippled or maimed that death would be mercy. And don't forget that you're destined to die on its blade. That sword is both friend and enemy; remember that."

"Yes, sir." Valder did not think he was likely to forget anything of such vital personal importance.

"I've passed on a complete report, and your superiors are considering just what to do with you. Since your old unit is disbanded, you'll be given a position here, I understand. I think they'll probably find some special use for you and Wirikidor—it would be a shame to waste such a sword's talents."

"Yes, sir." Valder was still too busy absorbing what he had been told to wonder about what special duties he might be given.

"I believe the general had hoped we might produce more swords like Wirikidor—after all, a weapon that can kill *shatra* at close range is impressive. Unfortunately, though we have identified most of the spells on it, we can't figure out how to reproduce most of them without killing half a dozen people in doing it, so it looks as if you, Valder of Kardoret, are going to remain unique."

Valder could think of no sensible reply to that. After a moment's pause he simply said again, "Yes, sir."

"That's all," Darrend said, motioning toward the tent flap. Valder got to his feet.

"Yes, sir," he repeated, as he stepped out into the sunlight.

CHAPTER 14

Valder settled quietly on his cot, Wirikidor on his hip, and mulled over what Darrend had told him.

The wizard had seemed very sure of his findings. Valder saw no reason to dispute them, but had vague recollections of once hearing that magical analysis of enchanted weaponry was not always reliable. He glanced down at the sword in the dimness of the tent. It looked like an ordinary sword, just as it always had, yet its power had supposedly made him virtually immortal—so long as he did not draw the sword too often. About a hundred times, the wizard had said. Since leaving the marsh he had drawn it three—no, four times. He had killed the coast-watcher, the swordsman, the *shatra*, and the prisoner. That left him with a minimum of ninety-four and a maximum of ninety-eight more drawings, which seemed like a safe enough margin. Very few soldiers actually confronted a hundred enemy soldiers at close range in their whole careers, let alone killed that many. He himself had served six years before Wirikidor's enchantment without ever being sure he had killed anyone.

Of course, there was the mention of possible special duty. That prospect might prove troublesome. He was a scout and preferred to remain a scout if he was to be a soldier at all. He tried to think what unusual service Wirikidor's characteristics would be suited to.

He certainly wasn't going to be a fencing instructor, or anything else where he might need to draw his sword for any reason other than battle to the death. That eliminated sentry duty and guarding prisoners, as well, unless he were to carry a second sword, which would be awkward, to say the least.

He could be a fine executioner, but that seemed a waste of the sword's power. Besides, he violently disliked the idea. He did not like killing anything, especially not people, most particularly Ethsharites. The fact that they would be helpless prisoners made it even worse. Not, he reminded himself, that the army had beheaded anyone in centuries or that they used a professional executioner in the first place. Murderers and deserters and so forth were usually hanged by whoever was handy. The poor fool he had killed in the general's tent had been an exception; dying by the sword usually happened only in battle.

He tried to approach the question logically. Wirikidor's magic was directed toward keeping him alive and killing other men one at a time, if the wizards had analyzed it correctly. The men that his superiors would presumably most like to kill would be the enemy's soldiers. Therefore, it followed that Valder would be sent to kill enemy soldiers.

How was that a special duty? And would it be practical to send him into battle when he would need to sheathe his sword after each killing before its power would serve again?

He sighed and gave up. Whatever the special duty might be, it was likely to be dangerous and unpleasant, and there was no point in making life unpleasant by worrying about it sooner than necessary. He would have plenty of time to worry when he knew what was to happen. Whatever the duty, he could live with it—or if not, he would find some way out. There was always a way out.

With that thought, he rolled over and went to sleep.

He found himself in a dream—very obviously a dream, as huge runes on the wall in front of him spelled out, "This dream is being provided by Sharassin of Shan." He supposed such runes might be drawn on a real wall somewhere, but he had no reason to doubt what they said in this instance; he felt as if he were dreaming. As soon as he had read them, the runes writhed about and reformed to say, "Dreams and communication wizardry of all sorts at reasonable rates."

That seemed to complete the advertisements; the runes faded away, leaving him staring at a blank stone wall.

"Hello, Valder," a familiar voice called from behind. He turned.

He was in a library; the walls of rough gray stone were mostly hidden by shelves of books and scrolls. The ceiling was coffered wood, the floor polished flags. In the center of the chamber stood a large oaken table, and sitting atop the table was a handsome young man in his late teens, wearing military tunic and kilt but no breastplate or helmet. His curly black hair was in disarray, his eyes bright, and a broad grin covered his face. Valder recognized him immediately as his former bunkmate, Tandellin Landin's son.

"They told me you were still alive, but I wanted to see for myself," Tandellin said.

Valder grinned back. "And they told *me* that *you* were still alive, and I figured I had best leave well enough alone. What's this spell costing you?"

"Oh, not all that much; Sharassin's a friend of mine. All I had to do was buy her the ingredients and provide her with a few vials of blood—but one of the ingredients was a pan of beaten silver, so you better appreciate this!"

"Oh, I do!" Valder hastened to reply. "How long do we have?"

Tandellin shrugged. "I'm not sure—I think until you wake up."

"Plenty of time, then—I just went to sleep." He hesitated. "At least, I *think* I just went to sleep, but you know how dreams are."

"Well, let's not waste it, then. Tell me what happened—we all thought the northerners got you when they first came charging down out of the woods at us."

Valder related his adventures, glad to be able to do so at his own speed and without being completely serious about everything. Even though he had told the story several times, this was the first chance he had had to tell it to a friend rather than an interrogator.

When he had finished he asked, "And what about you?"

"Oh, I was just sitting in camp when the attack came. At first I was out there with my bow and sword, like everybody else, but, when we saw that we didn't stand a chance, Captain Lorret sent half a dozen men south to see if we could find reinforcements. He picked the youngest, I suppose because he thought we could run fastest—I was the last one he chose, and he told me to head straight for General Gor's fortress. I did—and I'm still here, because I was too tired to go back out and fight after I got here. I was up on the ramparts with a bow when the enemy finally got this far, though; don't think I hit anything. And I may have been spending some time with wizards, but I haven't gotten my sword enchanted—just my heart. Or maybe somewhere lower down. You'll have to see Sharassin some time; she's really . . . well, you'll have to see her."

Valder laughed. Even though it was only a dream, it felt good; he had not laughed much in recent months. It was indescribably good to know that someone, somewhere, still cared about him. He had lost contact with his family years earlier, and friends had come and gone; of them all, only Tandellin had taken the trouble to find him again.

He asked after other friends and was dismayed by how many had died or vanished. After that, the conversation rambled on, largely taken up with the gossip of the Fortress.

Tandellin was making a lewd suggestion as to why General Gor hadn't yet married when Valder suddenly felt himself seized and shaken. The library walls wavered and dimmed around him. "I must be waking up," he called. "Stay in touch!" Then Tandellin and the library were gone, and he was lying on his cot in General Karannin's camp, looking up at two hard-faced guardsmen, their features eerily lighted by a single shaded lantern.

He glanced around the tent. Radler and Korl were watching silently from their beds; Tesra slept on, oblivious.

"Come on," one of the guardsmen demanded, in a voice like stone scraping stone.

Valder made a vague noise of agreement and rolled off the cot onto his feet, somehow managing not to snag Wirikidor on anything. He started to smooth down his hair and adjust his clothing, but the guardsmen politely convinced him not to bother by grabbing his arms and moving him gently but irresistibly out of the tent.

Valder went along without further argument or delay. Apparently, he thought, he was about to find out what special duty had been chosen for him.

The guardsmen said nothing further but merely escorted him to an undistinguished tent near the dragon pens. They thrust him inside and then vanished into the night.

Inside he found himself facing two men, a tall, brown-haired officer and a short, pale man in civilian attire but wearing a sword on his belt like a soldier.

"I'm Captain Endarim," the officer said. "You're Valder of Kardoret?"

Valder acknowledged his identity.

"Good. I think we've figured out what to do with you."

No answer seemed to be called for, so Valder said nothing. He looked politely interested and glanced at the other man, inviting an introduction. None came.

"Darrend and the rest have explained something of the workings of your sword to me," the officer said. "They have also sworn, under oath to a good theurgist, that they have no chance of duplicating it. That means that you're unique and a resource not to be wasted." He rose up onto his toes for a moment, then dropped back, as if emphasizing his point.

"Yes, sir," Valder answered noncommitally. He did not particularly care to be called a resource. This was a rude contrast to his warming magical chat with Tandellin.

"We've been giving the matter considerable thought as to how best to employ you. Putting you in open combat seems wasteful. You would need to be constantly sheathing and unsheathing your sword to be really effective, and you might get yourself killed in between."

"Yes, sir," Valder said again, noting to himself that this pompous captain seemed to be unaware of the semi-immortality the sword theoretically provided. Even if he could not be killed, however, he had no desire to be cut up, so the point was essentially correct.

"You've been trained in reconnaissance and have demonstrated over the past few months that you can take care of yourself and survive alone behind the enemy lines. You can, as I understand it, kill any man with ease and with great speed—that should allow you to deal with sentries. I'm told the sword provides a certain measure of protection, though I'm not clear on that. And you're ideally suited to fighting individuals, rather than groups. It seems to us, therefore, that there is one job exactly right for a man with your talents. We want to send you after not just enemy soldiers, but the really important men among the enemy—generals, sorcerers, members of the government, and so forth. Each such man you remove is worth dozens, maybe hundreds, of enemy soldiers. Do you follow me?"

Valder followed him all too well. "You want me to be an assassin?"

"That's an ugly word, but you do have the right idea."

"I'm not sure . . ."

Endarim cut him off. "Before you go any further, let me say that the pay for such work is excellent. You would rate as a captain to start and go up from there. You would have no other duties; when not working, your time would be your own."

"It's not that," Valder said. "I'm just not sure that I could do the job. I don't know how to find these men you want me to kill, for example, and I really don't like the idea of killing . . ."

"Of course you don't like the idea of killing," Endarim interrupted him. "But this is war, soldier. The more damage we do to the northerners, by whatever method, the less they'll be able to do to us. If you can kill one enemy sorcerer, you might be saving the lives of a dozen or more of your own comrades in arms! As for the technical problems, our wizards will help you with those. We have used assassins before. Finding targets and delivering our men to the right area has never been very difficult. The problem has always been getting through the personal defenses and getting our man out alive—and your sword should make that part much easier."

"I . . ."

"Listen, Valder, we prefer to have volunteers for this sort of work, but you're a special case. I can order you to take on assassination duty if I have to, because you are, without a doubt, one of the most promising candidates we've ever had, thanks to that sword, and we need a good assassin right now. We would prefer that you go willingly, because that would greatly improve your chances of survival, but we don't insist on it. If you refuse an order, we may even resort to a geas."

"Are you ordering me, then, sir?"

"No, I'm not—not yet. Listen, try it once and see what you think. If it's that much worse than regular combat for you, maybe we can put you somewhere else—but that magic sword you've stumbled onto doesn't entitle you to any more pampering than any other man in the Ethsharitic army, soldier, and, one way or another, you're going to fight and you're going to kill."

"Yes, sir." Valder was not happy, but he saw that his only options were obedience or desertion—and he was not a deserter. He knew, firsthand, that the northerners were ruthless and were out to destroy Ethshar. He loved his homeland and its people, even if he had never actually seen very much of either. All he knew was the army, since that was all he had seen since turning sixteen, and a healthy young man wasn't welcome anywhere else. He had no choice. He liked to believe that there was always a way out of everything, but he could not see one here.

"Good," the captain said. "Very good. I'll have your formal orders drawn up tomorrow, and you'll start drawing pay at your new rank."

"Yes, sir."

"And Valder—I wouldn't tell anyone what you're doing. It wouldn't do any good for everyone to know we use assassins, and I'm sure it wouldn't do you, personally, any good. It may seem dashing and romantic at first, but assassins are never really popular. They make people nervous."

"Yes, sir." Valder had wondered vaguely why he had been brought here in the middle of the night and now guessed that it was to maintain the secrecy of the assassination project.

"If anyone asks, you're a wizard's assistant now."

"Yes, sir."

"Good. You'll start immediately. Kelder, here, will tell you what to do." The captain waved at the civilian. Valder looked at him, openly curious now.

"Come on," the man called Kelder said, speaking for the first time. He had a high, thin voice.

Valder looked him over. He was short, of medium build, with an unusually scraggly beard and mustache. His skin was unhealthily pale, his hair a nondescript brown and thinning. His clothes were of undistinguished cut and material, though better than peasants wore. The sword on his belt was standard military issue, very like Wirikidor in appearance.

After this brief appraisal, Valder glanced back at the captain, who was already turning his attention elsewhere, looking at a stack of papers on his cot. With a mental shrug, Valder turned and followed the civilian out of the tent.

They headed directly toward the back of the camp, past the dragon pens and the last few rows of tents and into camptown, where the vintners and whores, undaunted by the late hour, still plied their trades. The main camp was mostly dark, but here about half the tents were still brightly lighted, often with multicolored lanterns. Valder heard singing somewhere and nearly tripped over two soldiers lying semiconscious in the dirt, obviously very drunk.

Kelder led the way past the rowdiest area, past the bright lanterns and thinly clad women, almost to the edge of the circle of wives' tents that served as a market. He ducked suddenly into a small tent, the abrupt change in course catching Valder by surprise.

He started, the followed.

Once settled on the dirt floor of the little tent—there was no furniture nor room for any; a quilted mat served as a bed—Valder demanded, "Who in Hell are you, anyway?"

"I'm called Kelder," the other replied. "No parentage, no birthplace, no eponym—just Kelder. I'm a spy." He smiled, as if he had just made a joke. Valder stared at him uncertainly, not sure whether he was joking or not.

"Seriously," the little man went on, "I'm a spy. In fact, I'm in charge of espionage for this entire front, which, unfortunately, doesn't mean much, because we haven't *got* any espionage to speak of here. General Gor sent me to fix that, and I happened to arrive in time to hear about you and your sword. You may be interested to know that we have seven wizards and two witches searching for your mysterious hermit with all the magic at their disposal, and a relay of theurgists praying for information about him. We take this very seriously. A scouting party will be sent up the coast to look for him, as well. So far we haven't found anything, but a wizard who can casually throw around eighth-order spells is worth a little effort. We don't have very many of them. Whether we find him or not, though, we have you and Wirikidor."

Valder could think of nothing to say; he stared at the man in the dimness; the only light was what seeped through the tent's canvas.

"I suppose you're feeling overwhelmed by all this. You've gone from being an ordinary scout to an unimportant bit of coastline to being involved in all sorts of strange things, tangled up with wizards and spies and assassins. Life can be like that. I'd like to give you time to sort it all out, but I'm afraid we can't spare any. I'm to train you, and then you'll start work. Ten days from now, with any luck, you'll kill the Northern Empire's chief sorcerer on the western front."

Valder started to protest.

"Let me rephrase that," Kelder said. "Within the next ten days you'll give Wirikidor the opportunity to kill the enemy's chief sorcerer on the western front." He smiled. "You're going to be very useful, Valder."

Valder was not at all sure of that, but he did not argue.

If assassination proved unbearable, he could botch it, and they would reassign him. He found it impossible to believe that he was going to kill any sorcerers.

Nine nights later, as he stood over the body of a dead sorcerer, he still found it hard to believe.

CHAPTER 15

His first five assassinations were made in fairly quick succession, at two- or three-day intervals; each time Kelder told him how to find and identify his target, each time a wizard or two got him into the general area, and each time he managed to get in and out without serious injury. Two of the five were sorcerers; he was never told just who the other three were.

Wirikidor disposed of all of them in short order, in addition to dealing with assorted guards and other interference. Valder had been pleasantly surprised to discover that sorcerers died as easily as anybody else, once the blade reached them; he had expected them to be at least as bad as the *shatra* had been, reaching for the sword or doing other eerie, discomforting things after they should have been dead. His fears proved unfounded; sorcerers folded up and died just like anybody else when their throats were cut.

This was not to say he had no trouble; one sorcerer had had an ugly metal talisman that spat magical fire at him and gashed his left arm rather badly. Valder had brought the talisman back with him after killing the man but turned it over to Darrend for study and never saw it again.

After the fifth mission, he was left alone for a full sixnight, giving him time to recover—and time to think.

At midevening of the sixth day he lay sprawled on his cot, staring at the dark canvas overhead. His left arm still ached dully where the sorcerous wound had been, despite a prompt and mostly effective healing spell; that ache combined with the lingering effects of an inadequate dinner washed down with *oushka* made it difficult to concentrate.

It had not been good *oushka*, either; Valder suspected it was made locally and was quite certain it was watered. Watered *oushka* was replacing wine as the standard tipple, because wine was becoming impossibly expensive, due to short supply.

Several supplies were running low, which was why his dinner had been rather skimpy. The army was relying ever more heavily on forage rather than proper supply caravans, and grasslands and forests did not provide very much in the way of forage. Sustenance spells were being left intact when men came in from patrol in order to save food—and because fewer wizards were available to renew them when the men were sent out again.

In fact, it seemed to Valder that *every* resource was being stretched thin. The magical assistance provided for his assassinations varied from night to night, according to what was available, and there was no longer a single witch in the entire camp. He had heard from his tentmates that entire regiments were going into battle with no magical support at all. No more troops were coming up from the rear, and the camp had been stripped, leaving Valder wondering whether any replacements were being sent to the front. He was not sure what had become of the men and material, but they did seem to be far less plentiful than in times past.

Could it be, he asked himself through a thin haze of pain and alcohol, that the war really was drawing to a close? It didn't seem possible—yet it didn't seem possible that the army could stretch itself much further, either.

What would happen, he wondered, if the war *did* end? What would become of him? What did he want to do with his life? What did one do with a life that might last forever if he could avoid drawing his sword?

Valder supposed that one did very much the same thing one did with *any* life. No one ever knew how long he would live, after all; Valder did not know how long he would live—merely that the rules were different for him.

But then, what did he want to do with himself, whether for a normal span or all eternity?

He knew what he did *not* want. He did not want to kill anybody else. Counting the various guards and others, as well as his intended targets, and adding in the four he had killed before reaching camp, he had drawn Wirikidor seventeen times, and seventeen men had died on its blade. That was too many. If peace actually came, he did not intend to draw Wirikidor again.

He did not want any sort of adventure any more. He had had quite enough of that, first with his three months in the wilderness and then with his five assassinations. He wanted to settle down quietly somewhere, with a place of his own and perhaps a family. Not a farm—he had no interest in working the soil and was not fond of tending animals. A shop, perhaps—he knew nothing of the mercantile trades, but they seemed appealing.

His head hurt. He reminded himself that he was still a soldier and that the war was still going on, as it always had. The war would probably be going long after he was dead, even if he lived to a ripe old age. The promise of living forever was still too new and too incredible to accept, after living all his life in the sure knowledge of his own mortality, so he ignored it for the present.

He would be a soldier until he had served his full thirty years if the war went on. He would be forty-six when he was finally discharged, just over twice his present age. That was hard to imagine. Some men were still strong and healthy at that age—General Anaran was fifty or so, but was said to be still in perfect condition. Valder might be equally lucky and emerge still vigorous, ready to start a new career. The army usually offered such men promotions or other incentives to re-enlist, but Valder told himself that he would never be so foolish as to be swayed by such blandishments. He would go and open a shop somewhere, dealing in wines, perhaps. He could leave Wirikidor in a back room and forget about it. Even just working for some wealthy merchant might be enjoyable; every civilian business was always short of men, since the army got first pick.

He had been taking orders all his life—first from his parents and then from his officers. Taking orders from a merchant could be no worse, and he would have none of the risks or responsibilities of running his own business.

On the other hand, he was getting tired of taking orders from anybody and he still had two dozen years to serve. There was no knowing what he would be like at forty-six. People change, he decided, including himself.

He had just reached this profound conclusion when the tent flap swung open and Kelder entered.

Startled, Valder swung his feet to the floor and sat up. Before he could rise, Kelder said, "Don't get up yet."

Valder stopped where he was, looking up at the self-proclaimed spy.

"May I sit?" Kelder asked politely.

Valder gestured at the empty cot opposite, and Kelder settled on it. Valder was puzzled; he had assumed when he first saw Kelder that his rest was over and he was going to be sent out to kill another northerner, but in that case, he would ordinarily have been summoned either to Kelder's tent in Camptown or Captain Endarim's near the dragon pens for a briefing. He was not sure what to think now; this change in the pattern might mean anything. He tried to decide whether he dared protest again that he did not want to be an assassin; after he had been successful on his missions no one had taken his claim seriously any more.

They had no idea what it was like, alone and terrified in the enemy's camps and cities, knowing that the only way he would be brought back was if he either completed his task or was seriously injured. He was no hero; he hated the thought of pain and carried out his assassinations as quickly and efficiently as he could so that he could go home that much faster.

Kelder knew his views, but had still sent him out repeatedly. He decided there was no point in rehashing the matter.

"I was beginning to wonder what had happened to you," he said instead.

"I was away," Kelder replied. "But now I'm back. I have your new orders."

"*What* new orders?"

"From General Gor. I told him about you, and he thinks you're being wasted here, killing sorcerers and administrators."

Valder was unsure whether that was good or bad. Much as he hated what he had been doing, it was always possible that what General Gor had in mind for him would be even worse.

He suppressed a slight shiver at the thought of General Gor thinking about him at all. Gor commanded the entire land-based Ethsharitic military west of the Great River's basin, after all; he was one of the four or five most powerful men in Ethshar, along with General Anaran and General Terrek and Admiral Azrad, and perhaps whoever was the current civilian head of state.

"What," Valder said at last, "does General Gor have in mind?"

"I wouldn't presume to guess General Gor's thoughts, Valder—and I wouldn't say, even if I did. However, your orders state that you're to be transferred from General Karannin's command to General Gor's personal staff, effective immediately, with the same title and position. It seems to me—though this is strictly a guess, and I'll deny ever saying it—that our illustrious commander has no objection to your current services other than the choice of targets."

"More assassinations, then?"

"I would think so."

"What if I refuse?"

"Don't be silly, Valder. That would be treason; you know that."

"But damn it, Kelder, I don't *want* to be an assassin! It scares me half to death, and I hate killing people—I get sick to my stomach."

"There are times when I don't like being a spy."

"I wouldn't mind spying as much, I don't think. Couldn't I do that?"

"Oh, maybe you will; I can't say. I'm just here to give you your orders and get you safely to Gor's headquarters on the coast. It's too late tonight; we leave at dawn."

"But . . ." Valder's objections trailed off.

Kelder smiled ruefully. "I sympathize, Valder, honestly. You have no choice, though. That hermit trapped you for life when he enchanted your sword; we can't possibly allow something like that to remain unexploited."

Valder glared resentfully at Wirikidor where it hung at the foot of his bed.

Kelder stood up and pulled the tent flap open. "We leave at dawn," he said.

Valder watched him go, then lay back, hoping that somehow dawn would not come.

Dawn came on schedule, however, and they departed.

Valder was startled by the transportation provided. They rode no horses, used no levitation spells; instead, Kelder led him to a small lavender tent in the magicians' circle, empty save for a rich tapestry that seemed stupendously out of place in a military camp. It hung from a crossbar nailed to the rear tentpole, its ornately fringed lower edge dragging in the dirt, and depicted a seascape seen from a stone rampart.

Kelder calmly walked directly *into* the tapestry, pulling Valder in after him.

To his astonishment, he found himself standing on the seaward battlement of General Gor's coastal fortress, Kelder at his side. The salt air washed into his nostrils, and he realized for the first time how accustomed he had become to the stench of General Karannin's camp, compounded largely of sweat, dust, and cattle. The sun was rising behind him and pouring out across the sea, lighting the wave crests with gold.

He turned around, expecting to see an opening back into the little tent, but instead he saw the upper court of the Fortress.

"Now, that tapestry," Kelder remarked. "That's a twelfth-order spell, and it took a very good wizard a year to produce it, but it does come in handy. They carefully avoid changing this section of the ramparts so that it will keep working. It has its drawbacks—you'll notice that it only works one way and that we had to leave the tapestry behind. It will be shipped wherever it's needed next. I wanted to get you here immediately, and there simply isn't anything faster, so I requisitioned the tapestry; nobody else was using it just now, so I was able to get it."

Valder was still staring about in amazement at the solid stone of the Fortress, trying to convince himself it was not a dream or illusion. "Oh," he said. Then a thought struck him. "Why did you wait until dawn, if the tapestry works instantly?"

"Because the tapestry depicts this spot just after dawn, of course. We'd arrive at dawn regardless of when we left, and I prefer a good night's sleep to several hours in some wizardly limbo. We could have entered the tapestry at any hour, true enough, but we would not arrive here until the hour the tapestry showed, regardless of how long a wait that might require. We wouldn't have noticed anything; to us the trip would still be instantaneous, but we would actually have lost those nighttime hours. I did that once; it messed up my sleeping schedule for days. And the weather can affect it, too—in fact, we *may* have missed a day or two if the weather was bad, but the prognostications were all favorable, so I don't think we have."

"I never heard of anything like that before."

"Of course not; it's a military secret, like almost any useful magic. Only the Wizards' Guild and important officers know anything about most of the more powerful wizardry. You'd be amazed what wizardry can do; there are spells for any number of things you would never have thought possible."

"Could they make more tapestries?"

"There are others, but right now no wizard can be spared for long enough to make more."

Valder was over his shock and beginning to think again. "Couldn't they use them to dump assassins, or whole regiments, behind enemy lines, maybe right in the enemy's capital?"

Kelder sighed. "It's a lovely theory, isn't it? But it

won't work. The wizard making the tapestry needs to see the scene he's weaving very, very clearly. If it isn't absolutely perfect, right down to the smallest detail, the tapestry won't work—or at least won't work properly. We don't have any way of seeing clearly enough behind enemy lines; our scrying spells are good enough for most needs, but not for making these tapestries."

After a moment's pause he added, "Yet."

Valder decided against pursuing the matter; instead he looked around the battlements. He had seen this fortress from a distance, assuming that it was indeed General Gor's headquarters, but he had never before been inside its walls. Tandellin was here somewhere, he remembered.

The place was impressive. The stone walls appeared to be several feet thick, and the outer faces were steep enough that he could see nothing of them from where he stood. He did not care to lean very far out over the seaward parapet; the height was dizzying.

From where he stood, he could see nothing beyond the fortress walls but the sea, the sky, a few gulls, and, very far off in the northeastern distance, a line of dark green hills. The citadel was built atop the highest ground in the area, a jagged cliff that towered above broken rocks right at the ocean's edge—Valder remembered that from his previous visit.

The wall he stood upon stretched for almost a hundred yards in either direction; behind it, the courtyard was more than a hundred feet across, but long enough that that seemed disproportionately narrow. Dozens, perhaps hundreds of people were going about their business there. Men were sharpening swords or practicing their use, women were hanging clothes out to dry, and members of both sexes were sitting or standing in pairs or groups, talking. Off at the northern corner, two sentries peered out over the ocean; to the south, a bend in the wall and a small guardhouse hid the next pair from Valder.

"Well," Kelder said, "if you've finished admiring the view, we have an appointment with one of General Gor's staff, a Captain Dumery, who is to get you settled in and tell you your next assignment."

"Oh," Valder said unenthusiastically. He had no interest in any assignments, and the mere mention of one had ruined his enjoyment of his surroundings.

Kelder ignored the soldier's tone and led the way to one of the staircases down into the court. They descended and, from the foot of the steps, proceeded across the court, through a vestibule into a corridor, down a flight of stairs, back along another corridor, across a large hall, along still another corridor, down another flight, across yet another corridor into a smaller hall, from there into an antechamber, and finally into a small room lined with tightly packed shelves. Valder was startled to see a small window slit with a view of the ocean; he had gotten turned around and would have guessed that they were deep in the interior of the Fortress, facing south toward the shipyards, and nowhere near the seaward side.

The room was inhabited by a small, white-haired man who invited them to sit down. He himself was perched on a stool, so that, when Valder and Kelder took the two low chairs provided, he could, short as he was, still look down on his visitors.

"You're Valder?" he asked. His voice was thin but steady.

Valder nodded.

"That's Wirikidor?"

"Yes," Valder said.

"It works the way Darrend says it does?"

"It seems to."

"Good. Then we want you to kill the Northern Emperor."

Valder stared up at the old man in silent astonishment. Kelder started and said, "You're not serious!"

The white-haired man shrugged. "Oh, well, maybe I'm not. If we can locate him, however, I think this man might be our best shot. After all, that sword is like nothing anyone has ever had before, so far as I know, and they probably have no defense against it. They can defend against just about everything else we throw at them!" He sighed. "Unfortunately, we can't locate him. Never could. So we'll be sending you against anyone important we *can* locate, Valder. Any problem with that?"

"Ah," Valder said, trying to give himself time to think.

"You know, I assume, that the sword is going to turn on me eventually, after a certain number of drawings."

"Yes, of course—but you have a long way yet to go. Darrend told me that it would take a hundred or so deaths before it could kill you, and you've only used up what, maybe five?"

"Seventeen," Valder corrected him.

"So many? Ah, well, that still leaves us with eighty-three, give or take a couple."

Valder was desperately unhappy at the sound of this, but could not think how to phrase a protest. Before he could work out what to say, the white-haired man raised a hand in dismissal. "I'll call you when we need you," he said. "My secretary will tell you where to go."

Valder started to speak, but Kelder shushed him and hurried him out of the room.

CHAPTER 16

While Valder remained inside the fortress walls, life as General Gor's assassin was not unpleasant. The food was good and plentiful, where the meals in General Karannin's camp had not been, although a far larger portion of it was seafood than Valder might have liked. The floors were dry stone, rather than dirt or mud, and most of them had some sort of covering, whether carpets, rush matting, or at least strewn straw, so that they were not unpleasantly cold and hard underfoot. He had been assigned his own little room deep in the bowels of the stronghold, with a tiny slit of window letting in air and, for a few hours a day when the sun was in the right part of the sky, light. He could not see out of the opening, which was eight or nine feet from the floor, but he judged it to be facing southwest.

To keep him from being called upon for menial duties, he had been issued new clothing. His worn and weathered old uniform was disposed of, and he was instructed that from now on he was to wear the gray-and-black tunic and black kilt that indicated the wearer to be performing some special service for General Gor. This outfit was more practical for sneaking about at night and had a certain drastic elegance, but Valder thought it uncomfortably reminiscent of northern uniforms; he was reluctant to be seen in it until he had observed other people in the Fortress, including Kelder, similarly attired.

He quickly discovered that the new uniform had one very definite advantage: it attracted women. Valder, unsure just what special services Gor was in the habit of demanding, was not sure why this was so, but it was undeniable that women who had scarcely glanced at him in his old green kilt and battered breastplate now stared at him with hungry eyes and looked for excuses to speak with him. Since he did not know when he might be sent off on a mission that could easily end in capture or mutilation, he refused to make any sort of long-term arrangements, but did spare an hour now and then to accompany a particularly eager or attractive young woman back to her quarters.

He hoped that such women were not disappointed, that the black-and-gray uniform had not led them to expect something more than an ordinary man.

He had been in the Fortress for almost a day before he managed to find Tandellin. The youth's barracks was nowhere near the areas Valder found himself frequenting; but once he had taken care of the minimal necessities of settling in, he took the time to track down his former bunkmate.

Tandellin had been permanently posted to the Fortress as part of the garrison; he stood a watch on the ramparts for six hours a day and was on call as a messenger and errand boy for six more. Calls came frequently. Still, he was able to find time for a quiet drink and conversation with Valder in a seldom-used storeroom on the evening of the day following Valder's arrival.

When they had exchanged a few polite phrases, Valder asked, "How are things going? Still running errands for that wizard?"

"Sharassin? No."

The answer seemed uncharacteristically brief. "What happened?" Valder asked.

Tandellin grinned crookedly. "If you must know, she found out where I had been spending some of my time when I was off duty and she wasn't. She didn't take it well. Just as well; she was transferred out a few days ago, anyway."

Valder grinned back. "So where were you spending that time—or wasn't it always the same place?"

"Oh, it was the same place all right. Her name is Sarai of the Green Eyes."

Valder waited, but Tandellin did not continue. "What's this?" he asked. "No description? No suggestion that I really must meet her? Could there be something special about Sarai of the Green Eyes?"

Tandellin's grin turned sheepish. "Maybe there is."

"Ah, well, congratulations, my boy, if it's true." Valder was genuinely pleased. He was a great believer in love and marriage, or so he had always said—though he had, as yet, no particular inclination in that direction for himself. It delighted him to see Tandellin showing signs of settling down, giving up the wildness of youth. The world needed more quietly settled people, he was convinced, something to provide stability and offset the chaos of the eternal war.

That thought brought to mind his own part in the war, systematically trying to produce chaos among the enemy by killing the men who kept order. He wondered whether any northerners were attempting similar missions in Ethshar. If so, they did not appear to be very successful, since the approximate whereabouts of the commanders, Azrad, Gor, Terrek, and Anaran, were common knowledge, yet no assassins had killed any of them.

Given a choice, Valder decided, he would much have preferred to be maintaining order in Ethshar, rather than creating chaos in the Empire—but since acquiring Wirikidor he had had no choice. Wirikidor was very much an agent of chaos, it seemed, and his superiors would not allow him to keep the blade sheathed and ignore it, as he wanted to. Some time soon, when they had found a target worthy of him, he would once again be sent out to wield Wirikidor. That took a great deal of the pleasure out of life in the Fortress.

It was three days after his arrival that Captain Dumery's secretary found him and led him to his first briefing.

That first mission went well; he was able to kill the enemy general they had chosen quickly and without killing anyone else. That brought his total to eighteen.

The next, three days later, was disastrous; Valder managed his part well enough, but it was a joint mission, involving himself, a wizard who provided magical transportation, and a cocky young thief, and the thief botched his part. Valder and the wizard made it back alive, though the wizard had a long scar to show for it and Wirikidor's total was up to twenty-five, which did not include the intended target.

Twenty-five down, seventy-five to go—or seventy-three or seventy-seven. Valder almost began looking forward to his next task; if he kept on using Wirikidor at that rate, he would be forced to give up assassination in a matter of months. Dumery could not order him to draw the sword once the possibility of it turning on him became imminent. He would still be a soldier, but no longer an assassin; he could leave Wirikidor safely in its scabbard and fight with more ordinary weapons.

He had been resting up from that errand for a day or so when he was summoned, not to Captain Dumery's little office, but to meet General Gor himself. With some trepidation, he went.

Gor of the Rocks was of medium height, but heavy, broad at shoulder and hip, with thick black hair and beard. He stood with his feet planted well apart, as if bracing himself, and wore the standard brown tunic and green kilt of the Ethsharitic army, his badges of rank hung in a bunch on a chain around his neck.

"Valder, is it?" he said.

"Yes, sir," Valder answered.

"From now on you take orders from me and nobody else; not Captain Dumery, not Kelder, not Azrad or Anaran or Terrek. You understand that? If I want you, I'll send for you, but you take your orders for where to go and what to do when you're outside this fortress from me and me alone. I don't want you wasted on any more messes like that last one Dumery thought up. You did well enough—brought back Cardel, and the gods all know we need every wizard we can get at this point—but you shouldn't have been there in the first place. Wasted seven out of a hundred!"

"Yes, sir," Valder said with calm resignation.

"Good. You're getting your food and pay on time?"

"Yes, sir."

"Good. This war is finally getting somewhere, Valder, and we need all the help we can get, even swords with curses put on them by deranged hermits we can't find, if they can be useful. You may not like what you're doing, and I wouldn't blame you. It's not exactly glorious, sneaking in and killing people with an unbeatable magic sword— more like butchery than soldering, in a way. Still, remember, it's useful. You're doing something that may turn out to be essential."

"Yes, sir." He admired Gor's estimate of his own thoughts and attempt to answer them. He did not agree with it; his objections were not rational but emotional and had nothing to do with glory or its lack. Still, the general was at least trying to help him accept his role, which was more personal attention than he had expected.

"Good luck, then. I'll send someone when I need you."

Valder nodded, bowed, and withdrew.

He was somewhat overwhelmed by General Gor, who had managed to cover everything essential within three minutes, including his little speech of encouragement. On consideration, though, assassination was not so much like butchery as like burglary, save that, rather than jewelry, Valder stole lives.

With Wirikidor's talents and habits, it did seem very much like stealing.

It was ten days after that that Gor sent for him and gave him another assignment.

This one was planned very neatly and went off smoothly. That, Valder discovered, was to be the standard in his work for Gor. The general did not plan the assassinations himself, but he did review the plans and modify or reject them, if they were in any way flawed or incomplete.

From then on, it was a rare and difficult mission when

Wirikidor was drawn more than once. The missions came less often, but seemed more important. Valder disposed of the Empire's minister of transportation, assorted generals, and even a prince, as well as unidentified targets. Assignments came, on the average, one every three sixnights.

In between, he was free to roam the Fortress, spending Tandellin's off-duty hours drinking and gaming with his old friend and spending most of the rest of the time either with women or alone in his bed, staring unhappily at the ceiling.

Winter came and went, and Valder continued his duties ever more reluctantly. The count of his victims mounted. He was horrified, after one exceptionally complex errand involving three related targets he took to be the entire family of a northern nobleman, to realize that he was no longer absolutely sure what the correct count was.

Occasionally, one of his brief liaisons developed into something more; the first was with a girl named Hinda, a few years younger than himself, who stayed in his room for almost a month before finding a more cheerful companion. She was followed by someone who called herself Alir; Valder suspected that that was not her real name, though the only reason for his suspicion was her excessively romantic nature. She seemed to be convinced that Valder was doing something very exciting and glorious whenever he was out of the Fortress; she finally departed when, even in bed, he refused to say just what it was that he did for General Gor.

He acquired friends of both sexes as well as lovers, though none were especially close. He grew to like Sarai of the Green Eyes, a vivacious girl of eighteen or so, and was glad when Tandellin included her in their evenings together. He encountered Kelder occasionally and found that, once the little man was no longer telling him who to kill, he was pleasant company. He came actively to dislike Captain Dumery, who seemed to resent having Valder removed from his authority. In this latter opinion he was joined wholeheartedly by several of the men in Tandellin's barracks, but few agreed with his assessment of Kelder, who was generally considered to be a fool.

The summer of the year 4997 arrived, and, by the fourteenth of Summerheat, Valder's count had hit eighty, give or take one. He lay alone in his room for a long time, staring at the vaulted ceiling and considering this.

He had killed eighty men. With the connivance of the old hermit and his enchanted sword, he had ended fourscore lives. Most soldiers never actually managed to kill anybody. In his six years of regular service, he had never been certain he had killed anyone. He had drawn blood on occasion in skirmishes or with his bow, but he had never known whether anyone he had struck had died.

Wirikidor, on the other hand, never left any room for doubt. He had killed eighty men and sent eighty souls to wherever northerners' souls went—Hell, presumably. Those men might have been anything—good, evil, or somewhere between. He had no way of knowing anything but that they had been the enemies of the Holy Kingdom of Ethshar.

Why, he wondered, was it called a kingdom? So far as he knew, there had never been an actual king. He had never been very clear on just how the civilian government *did* operate, having spent his entire life under martial law in the lands outside the traditional boundaries where there was only the military, but he thought he would have heard of a king if one existed.

What would the gods think of a man who had killed eighty men? Would they condemn him as a murderer or praise him for doing so much to rid the World of the demon-guided enemy? Everyone agreed that the gods favored Ethshar over the Empire, but not all agreed on why they did not directly intervene in the war, even when petitioned. One school of thought maintained that they were, in fact, waging war on an entirely different level, but were being countered so exactly by the demons aiding the Northern Empire that no sign of this conflict penetrated to the World. Another school argued that the gods were so pure that they could not take, were actually incapable of taking, any aggressive action; that they found violence so repugnant that they could not bear to help even their chosen people in the violence of war. There were dozens of variations. If the gods were repulsed by violence, though, then had Valder damned himself by wielding Wirikidor?

If he had, it was far too late to do anything about it now. He wished that he had never drawn the sword or that he had never told anyone how he had come to kill the *shatra* on the plain that day.

His thoughts were interrupted by someone shouting in the corridor outside his room; the words were unintelligible, and he tried to ignore the noise.

He was, he told himself, a young man, scarcely twenty-three. He owned a magic sword that would, supposedly, prevent him from dying indefinitely. Yet, less than a year after acquiring this wonderful weapon, less than a fourth of the way through his term of service in the military, he had used up *four-fifths* of his ownership of the sword.

That, he told himself, was stupid. It was idiotic to go on squandering his life in this manner. His life was tied to his ownership of the sword; with each killing a part of his life slipped away. His superiors were forcing him to throw it away.

He would refuse, he promised himself, to continue doing so. As politely as he could, he would tell General Gor at the first opportunity that he, Valder of Kardoret, had done his duty, contributed his fair share to the war effort, and would no longer be available for assassinations. After all, they could not kill him; only Wirikidor could do that.

The shouting in the corridor was still going on, and now someone was pounding on his door. Annoyed, he rose and lifted the latch.

Tandellin tumbled in, panting. "Valder, have you heard?"

"Heard what?"

"The enemy has broken through on the eastern front, clear into the homeland! Old Ethshar itself is under attack by demons, they say, *real* demons, not just *shatra*! General Terrek is dead, and the Kingdom is in retreat. Everyone is to be ready to leave on a moment's notice; the wizards are getting spells ready, and we expect to be sent to the new front at any time."

"Demons?"

"Oh, there are hundreds of stories about them! There's definitely something new happening!"

"Demons." Wirikidor would be of no use against demons. He knew of nothing that would be—but then, he did not know what *wouldn't* be, other than his own sword with its insistence on killing men. Nobody, so far as he knew, had ever actually fought a demon before. Even the very few Ethsharitic demonologists, or the theurgists who worked both sides, never directly fought the demons they conjured up, but instead controlled them through complex magical restraints and elaborate prayers that only the original summoner could use. If the northerners had really unleashed demons on Ethshar, the war might well end very soon—perhaps with no victor at all.

This, he thought, would be a good time for the gods to intervene if, by some chance, they had been waiting for the right moment, like the magicians in the songs who always appeared in the last stanza to rescue the doomed heroes.

He strapped on his sword and headed for General Gor's office to see if he had any orders. This was not, he knew, a good time to try resigning from his job as an assassin.

CHAPTER 17

Valder sat in the bare stone antechamber feeling stupid.
Naturally, Gor had been besieged with questions, advice,
requests, demands, and information; he had no time to
spare just now for an assassin. Valder knew that, had he
given it any thought, he would have realized as much.
What could an assassin do in a battle against demons?

Having come to offer his services, however, he was
not about to slink back to his room. Instead he sat and
waited while officers and messengers ran in and out, so
that he might be ready if summoned and so he might catch
a few bits of information in passing. All the magicians in
the Fortress and some brought from elsewhere were busily gathering information—the wizards by various spells,
the theurgists by prayer, the witches and the lone sorcerer
by arcane methods Valder did not understand. Gor's two
demonologists had utterly failed to make contact with
anything, or so rumor had it, which seemed to confirm
that quite literally all the demons of Hell were loose in
the east.

As people hurried in and out, Valder could catch snatches of conversation, and every so often someone would pause to rest, or be asked to wait, and might be willing to answer a hurried question. Nobody seemed very sure of what was happening. A steady babble poured out through the door of the inner chamber, but Valder could make sense of none of it.

Then, abruptly, the babble died. In the sudden silence as the echoes from the stone walls faded, Valder heard a single voice exclaim, "Gods!"

He heard questioning voices raised, and the silence was washed away as quickly as it had come by officers and men demanding to know what had silenced the magicians.

Valder could not make out the reply and was astonished by an outburst of wild cheering. He could stand it no longer. He rose and marched up to the door.

"What's happening?" he demanded of the guard posted there.

"I'm not sure, sir," the soldier said, deferring to Valder's special uniform.

"You couldn't hear what was said, what started the cheering?"

"I'm not sure, sir—I *think* he said something about a counterattack, that the gods themselves had counterattacked. I don't really know. The gods couldn't do that, though, could they?" The soldier's voice was pleading and uncertain, though he struggled to maintain the properly stolid expression a sentry was expected to have.

"I don't know," Valder said. "I'm no theologian." The whole affair seemed unreal. He knew very well that gods and demons existed, had always existed, but, aside from the halfbreed *shatra*, they had always been aloof from human affairs, intervening in the World only when summoned by elaborate invocations, and even then usually offering little more than advice and the occasional petty miracle. Had this somehow changed? The whole universe seemed to be turning topsy-turvy around him.

Valder found himself wondering whether perhaps he wasn't lying delirious in a coastal marsh in the summer of 4996, imagining it all. He had led an ordinary life for twenty-two years, boring and predictable—born to a soldier and his woman of the moment, raised in an assortment of camps and villages, signed up at sixteen and trained as a scout, and assigned to the western coast where nothing of importance ever happened. Then, suddenly, everything had shifted. The enemy had attacked, seemingly out of nowhere, destroying his home unit and driving him into the wilderness, where he found an old hermit who had enchanted his sword and thereby granted him the possibility of eternal life—or of a rather nasty doom. That enchantment had made him an assassin, prowling the streets of northern cities and camps that most of his former comrades never knew existed. *Former* comrades, because his work as an assassin set him apart.

All that, however, seemed logical and coherent compared with the news that demons were attacking eastern Ethshar and the gods themselves counterattacking. The World had always been fraught with magic, controlled by unseen forces, but those forces had been predictable unless manipulated by men and women. The gods had never been prone to whims.

What would this superhuman conflict mean to the World, to the war—to Ethshar and to Valder?

The cheering in the inner room had spread, become universal, and then died down again. Now Valder heard the unmistakable tones of orders being given, and a stream of men and women began pouring out past him. Among them was Kelder, who spotted Valder and paused, stepping out of the onrushing human current for a moment.

"Go get some rest," he said. "None of us can do anything right now; it's all in the hands of the gods. That's not just a pious saying anymore, but the literal truth. Go back to your room and get some sleep, so you'll be well rested if we need to move quickly. Everyone is getting this same order—wait and be ready. Go on."

Reluctantly, Valder got to his feet and went. He was not in need of sleep, but he sank back on his cot again nonetheless, one hand slipping down the side of the mattress to grip the rope webbing beneath. He lay there, staring at the ceiling, until he knew every joint in the vaulting and the shape of every stone.

The universe was coming apart in the east, and there was nothing he could do about it.

Eventually he must have dozed off, because he was awakened by a knock on the door.

"What?" he managed to say in reply.

"Everybody in the upper court—General Gor has an announcement. Everybody up!"

Whoever the messenger was, he had a voice like an avalanche. He roared off down the corridor, rousing all and sundry.

Valder was still fully dressed and, at this point, cared not at all about his appearance, so that he rose immediately and without ceremony headed for the upper court, hoping to find a spot where he could hear the general directly, rather than needing to rely on relays.

That hope did not last long once he reached the top of the stairs; his corridor, not surprisingly, given its out-of-the-way location, must have been among the last to be called. Men, women, and even children jammed the courtyard, and some were standing on the surrounding ramparts as well. He squeezed to one side to allow the people behind him to emerge and looked about for General Gor, hoping that he would be able to follow the proceedings from where he was. The din was unbelievable, even under the open sky, as everyone present seemed to be trying to guess what Gor was going to say.

Valder saw no point in that particular game, since a brief wait would tell all. He was more interested in trying to figure out who all the hundreds of people were. There seemed to be far more present than he had thought the Fortress housed; had some been summoned in from elsewhere?

Before he could pursue this line of thought, he was pushed back by guards emerging from the stairway door; to his surprise, immediately behind them came the general himself. Once out in the sun—for the first time Valder noticed that it was late morning; he was unsure of what day—Gor turned and ascended one of the emergency ladders to the battlements. To his surprise, Valder found himself standing almost directly below, in the front row of the entire mob. He had expected General Gor to appear elsewhere, as had, apparently, almost everyone else; it took several minutes for the noise to fade as people gradually noticed Gor's arrival.

When at last the roar of conversation had died to a dull muttering of breath, shifting feet, and rustling garments, Gor took a deep breath and announced in a powerful, carrying bellow, "I am Gor of the Rocks, heretofore High Commander, Field Marshal, and General Commanding the Western Forces of the Holy Kingdom of Ancient Ethshar."

Valder wondered at this formality. Surely all present knew who Gor was!

"I have come here today to tell you several things. The World in which we now live is not the one we have all known for so long—and the time has come to reveal that most of you did not know the old World as well as you thought you did." He paused to catch his breath and a low murmur swirled through the crowd.

He looked about and hesitated, then shouted, "The war is over!"

If he had intended to say anything more right away, he never had a chance; the wave of cheering battered at him like a storm wind. He grinned and looked out at the sea of faces and flailing arms, mopped perspiration from his brow with his sleeve, then folded his arms and waited for the noise to abate.

The noise did not abate for several seconds, during which time Gor said, apparently to himself but loudly enough that Valder, almost beneath his feet, managed to catch it, "Oh, gods, I have always wanted to live to say that!"

Finally, after a solid minute, the cheering subsided; Gor raised his arms for quiet and, when satisfied with the lessened sound level, he said, "I'm sure that most of you have heard that our ancient enemy, the Northern Empire, unleashed the demons of Hell itself upon the eastern marches of our nation. This is true, and I'm sorry to say that at first the attack was a great success—if any of you had family or friends to the east of the southern mountains, I'm afraid that they are almost certainly gone, as what fragmentary reports our magicians can provide indicate that *all* the eastern lands, from the Empire's borders right to the southern edge of the World, are now a burning waste. General Terrek is dead, and his armies destroyed."

He paused to allow that to sink in; shocked murmurs arose and died. The earlier elation was gone, and Valder was sure that many of the people were now wondering whether the war had ended in victory or defeat. For his own part he was sure, from Gor's face and the fact that the Fortress itself still survived undamaged, that at worst a truce had been arranged.

Gor continued, "The fact that our vile foes resorted to demonic aid, despite the horrible price such aid always demands, shows us that, as we had thought, their situation had become desperate and their cause hopeless by any other means."

He paused again, then continued, "Many of you may also have heard rumors about divine intervention, and I am pleased to say that these stories, too, are true! The gods themselves, in all their glory, intervened on behalf of their chosen people! The theurgists tell me that an ancient compact prevented both gods and demons from interfering directly in human affairs and that, once that compact was broken by the northerners and their demonic mentors, the gods were free to unleash divine retribution for centuries of injustice and evil. We have established this divine intervention by every means at our disposal: divination, clairvoyance, oneiromancy, and every variety of verification we could devise. There can be no doubt at all of the effects, but we will probably never know the details—only the inhabitants of the Northern Empire were witnesses to the final conflagration, and in the past day the Northern Empire has ceased to exist!"

He paused there for the inevitable renewed cheering. When the crowd had calmed down sufficiently to allow him to continue, Gor said, "The gods have achieved in a single day what we could not in all these centuries of war! The Black City, capital of the Empire, has been blotted from the face of the World as if it had never been, and the other northern cities lie in ruins or worse. The Imperial Army is broken and scattered. The demons have been forced back into the Netherworld—and, that being done, the gods in turn have retreated into Heaven, swearing never again to interfere so directly in human affairs. The openings from the World into both Heaven and Hell have been permanently sealed; there can be no more prophets, no more *shatra*, no more night-roving demons, no divine messengers, no unsought miracles. Let us all offer a prayer of gratitude to the beings that forsook their nonviolent principles to defend us against evil!"

That roused a cheer, followed by a moment of confused muttering. When Gor judged that the faces turned expectantly toward him made up most of the crowd, he spoke again.

"Now, I fear I have some unpleasant news."

The crowd sobered; an uneasy hush fell.

"Oh, it's not all bad. The war is over, and with the help of the gods we won. A few northern stragglers remain to be mopped up but nothing significant. However, the World may not be quite as you have imagined it to be at the war's end—those of you who have thought about it at all.

"Firstly, due to the withdrawal of the gods, some of the laws of magic may have changed. I'm no magician, I can't say anything very definite about it, but my advisors tell me that magic we have taken for granted may no longer work. What this means remains to be seen.

"For most of you, that's a minor detail, though. Far more important for all of you is that, whatever you may have expected, the end of the war does *not* mean that you will all be going home to our motherland of Old Ethshar. You can't."

Gor apparently had not intended to stop there, but the hubbub was such that he had no choice. He held out his arms and waited for the crowd to quiet somewhat before continuing.

"There are two reasons that Azrad, Anaran, and myself will not be leading you home. Firstly, there is simply no room for the three million men and women who now occupy the camps and battlefields. The eastern half of Ethshar—yes, fully half—was destroyed by the demonic invasion and is now uninhabitable. In the remainder—

well, you all know that this war has dragged on for generation after generation and that our defenses were sound. Despite the ravages of war, the population of our old homeland has increased steadily, and there is simply no room for more."

He paused; the crowd waited expectantly.

"That's the first reason. The second has been carefully kept secret for years, lest it damage morale and aid the enemy. Now that that enemy is destroyed, the time has come to reveal the truth. Ethshar is no more."

Gor paused again, as if expecting a loud response, but received only a puzzled silence.

He said, "Or rather, I should say, *Old* Ethshar is no more. The government collapsed almost a hundred years ago, and where the Holy Kingdom of Ancient Ethshar once was—or at least the western half of it—there are now dozens of squabbling little fiefdoms, each claiming to be the rightful government of the country, and therefore our superiors. We in the military have refused to acknowledge any of these factions and, instead, have been operating independently—Azrad, Anaran, myself, and, until his death, Terrek have answered to no one but ourselves. We four were chosen, not by the civilian government as we led you to believe, but by the commanders who came before us. We have traded with the small kingdoms that were once Old Ethshar for the supplies we need and have defended them against the northerners, but have never heeded their authority. *We* are the government of Ethshar—not of the Old Ethshar that was once our people's homeland, but of the *new* Ethshar, the Hegemony of Ethshar, all the lands that have been taken and held by our victorious armies. All the lands that lie outside the old borders—*all* the lands outside the borders now that the Empire is destroyed—are ours. Are *yours*! Captured with your strength and your blood and your courage, they belong to *you*, not to the cowards who stayed behind and couldn't even hold their own nation together!"

This was apparently intended to evoke a cheer, but the response was feeble and quick to die, as each individual in the crowd tried to absorb what had been said, evaluate it, and guess what it meant for him or her, what place he or she might hold in the new order.

Valder wondered if it actually *was* a new order, when in fact the generals had been running everything for centuries anyway.

"There is much to be done," Gor went on, hiding any disconcertment he might feel at the lukewarm response. "This stronghold is to become our new northwestern capital, one of three, to be called Ethshar of the Rocks. I fully expect that in our lifetimes, now that the demands of the war are gone, it will grow into a great and beautiful city."

An uneasy murmur seemed to be bubbling up here and there in the crowd.

"Of course, the army will be disbanded as quickly as possible, save for a small contingent to keep the peace and defend against any marauding northern survivors. My staff will remain in authority temporarily, but will be converted from a military establishment to a civilian government. The rest of you will be discharged as fast as you can be—with full pay, of course! After that, you will be free to do as you please, to stay here and help build our new city or to go where you like and do what you will. For those who wish to take up farming or other settled tasks, all the lands in the Hegemony not already privately owned, all the plains that reach from this ocean to the Great River, will be free to any family that wants them. You need merely find your new home, claim it, and use it—only claims by those who actually work the land will be recognized, as we need no landlords or other parasites."

Valder tried to digest this. How did one go about becoming a wine merchant? Would he need to claim a vineyard somewhere? He was not interested in growing the grapes and making the wine, merely in selling it. Would he be free to do that under the revamped regime?

And what would he do with Wirikidor? A merchant did not need a sword.

That was nothing to worry about, he told himself. He could just put Wirikidor away somewhere and forget about it, live a normal life—a normal life that would go on indefinitely. He would never be called upon to kill twenty more men, not in peacetime.

He was so involved with consideration of his own future that he paid no attention to the crowd around him, which was restive and uneasy.

"That's all," Gor announced. "I've said what I came to say. If you have any questions, ask your superiors. We aren't keeping any more secrets. And as quickly as the change can be made, we will no longer be the Western Command of the Holy Kingdom of Ethshar, but an integral part of the new Hegemony of Ethshar, and I will no longer be a general, but rather overlord of the city of Ethshar of the Rocks. After centuries, peace has come! The war is over, and victory is ours!"

Even Valder, lost as he was in his own musings, noticed that the crowd was still so unsettled and confused by the news that this surefire applause line received only a brief, half-hearted cheer.

CHAPTER 18

For three days after the self-proclaimed overlord's speech, the busiest man in the Fortress was the paymaster. Hundreds of soldiers took Gor at his word and mustered out as fast as they could get through the red tape, each one collecting his back pay—less a fee for early discharge, of course, a fee carefully calculated to keep the treasury solvent without letting anyone feel seriously cheated. It came to a single silver piece, which Valder had to admit was reasonable enough, and the cash settlements were reportedly being made promptly and honestly.

When Valder attempted to collect his pay and go, however, he was refused. Enlisted men were free to go, but as yet officers and special services people were being asked to wait.

Valder thought about just packing up and leaving anyway. He doubted that anyone, in this chaotic new peace, would care about a deserter. However, he had a goodly sum owed to him; whatever its other drawbacks, assassination paid well. He knew he would need money to set himself up in the wine business, and so he waited.

In doing so he was operating on the assumption that

he actually intended to become a wine merchant, but now that the prospect was an immediate reality, rather than a vague plan for the distant future, he was having second thoughts. What did he know about being a merchant?

Whatever he might do, however, he would almost certainly want money and he saw no harm in waiting a few more days to collect it. Tandellin, too, was staying, for the moment; he had not yet decided what to do with himself; as he explained it, "Why give up free room and board?" Sarai, too, was staying, and somehow, with the arrival of peace, it became implicitly accepted that Tandellin and Sarai would be married when they got around to it.

Valder remained uneasy about staying in the Fortress, however. He tried to reassure himself as he watched the men and women trickling away down the hillside, leaving the inner corridors ever less crowded. He caught glimpses of their faces—some as they turned back for a last look at the Fortress, others as they turned to face new directions. Some were smiling, full of life and hope, ready to conquer a piece of the World for themselves. Others seemed worried and uncertain as they left behind the only life they had ever known.

For three days, new-made civilians walked away down the hillside, and for three days, at irregular intervals, soldiers would march up into the Fortress, alone or in patrols or squads or entire regiments, to be made into civilians and join the outward stream. A few were determined to remain soldiers, of course, and the barracks population fluctuated, rather than decreasing steadily.

As yet Gor had done nothing about his announced intention of building a city around the Fortress and its adjoining shipyards, but a ramshackle city was growing up anyway, a city of tents and crude huts. People were arriving faster than they could be dealt with and sent away, and no one wanted to bother finding places inside the walls for all the newcomers. Furthermore, many of the new civilians who descended the hill went no further than the impromptu camps.

Valder had not ventured outside the Fortress for fear he would have difficulty getting back in; his tall, narrow room with its inaccessible window was not much, but he had become accustomed to it and greatly preferred stone floors to dirt. He suspected that, when someone found the time to update accommodations, it would be given to someone more useful in peacetime than himself, but he intended to use it while he still could.

He did find himself spending hours on end standing on the ramparts above the largest landward gate, watching the departing figures and trying to decide whether he actually envied them or not. He made no secret of his time at this post, so he was not surprised when, on the third day after the overlord's speech, someone called his name.

He turned to see a messenger boy, perhaps twelve or thirteen, standing at the top of the nearest ladder. "Are you Valder of Kardoret, sir?" he called.

Valder nodded.

"I've been looking all over for you! The general—I mean, the overlord—wants to see you immediately!"

"General Gor, you mean?" Valder was puzzled. He could think of no reason that Gor would want to see him, now that the war was really over. There were no more enemy officials to assassinate.

Or were there? Perhaps he was to be sent against the stragglers. Stories had come in of encounters with northern forces who were still fighting.

Of course, those who *didn't* fight were often butchered by overenthusiastic Ethsharites, even after they surrendered, so Valder hardly blamed those who resisted. Still, he had not thought that Wirikidor's special talents were called for. Wizards and ordinary soldiers were more practical for such work than assassins.

Perhaps he was to take care of a lingering *shatra* the wizards could not handle.

"Yes, General Gor," the boy was saying. "Except he's an overlord now. Didn't you hear the speech?"

"Yes, I heard the speech," Valder admitted as he crossed to the ladder. He wondered what the correct form of address might be for speaking to an overlord.

He followed the boy down the ladder and into the Fortress, through the maze of rooms and passageways, until he found himself in Gor's office, unchanged by the switch from military to civilian authority.

A secretary leaned over and whispered through his beard, "Address him as 'my lord,'" answering Valder's unasked question. Apparently the point had come up before.

Gor looked up and said, "Ah, Valder. I would like to speak to you in private." He rose, crossed the room, and opened a small door in the rear wall, a door Valder had never really noticed before. He gestured, and Valder reluctantly came and stepped through the door into the tiny room beyond. A glance behind him showed him that some of the half-dozen secretaries and aides in the office were at least as surprised as he was at this unexpected secrecy.

Once inside the bare stone chamber, Gor carefully closed and locked the door. The room was small, perhaps eight feet wide and ten feet long, with two simple wooden chairs the only furnishings; Gor seated himself on one and indicated that Valder was to take the other.

Wary, Valder obeyed.

Once both men were seated, Gor wasted no time on preliminaries. "Valder, I don't know what you had planned to do now that peace has come, but I'd like you to stay on here."

Confused, Valder stammered in asking, "As a soldier, you mean?"

"As a member of my staff—soldier or civilian, it doesn't matter. Take your choice."

"Why? What would I do?"

"Why? Because I think I might find an assassin very useful."

"An assassin? In peacetime?" Valder was shocked and made no attempt to hide that fact.

"Yes, in peacetime—perhaps more than ever. When somebody gives me trouble now, I can't just order him hanged, you know; not anymore. I know that there are people who aren't happy with this triumvirate that Azrad and Anaran and I have set up; by the gods, there are times when we aren't very happy with it ourselves! Still, it's better than chaos, and that's what there would be if we stepped down. That's what happened in Old Ethshar when it wasn't clear who was in charge, and it's not pretty at all—all the small kingdoms fighting over the bones of the old one. I don't want to see that happen out here in the Hegemony. I'll use whatever methods I need, whatever methods I can find, to prevent it, and that includes assassination. Wizards can handle some of it, but magic leaves traces, and most magic can be guarded against—just as the northerners tried to guard against it. That sword of yours seems to be an exception, though—you got through in the north where wizards couldn't, and it would be no different here. Besides, I may need to eliminate a wizard or two, and they have a guild—they're more loyal to their guild than to anything else, including me or any other mortal, so I can't often get them to attack each other. I think Wikridor, or whatever its name is, could be just what I need to keep the Wizards' Guild in line."

"Wirikidor," Valder corrected absently.

"Wirikidor, then."

"Um."

"Well, man, what do you say? The job will pay well, I can promise you that."

"Sir—ah, I mean, my lord—I don't think I can do it. The day you told us the war was over I had been planning to come to you and resign and ask for different duties. I don't like being an assassin. I can't take any more of it. It isn't in me to do this sort of killing. If I hadn't stumbled into owning this sword, I wouldn't... well, I wouldn't have been assassin, certainly."

"Why not?"

"I don't like killing! I don't like danger, or sneaking about, and I don't like killing. I don't like blood. When the war was going on, it wasn't too bad—everybody was doing it, after all, killing or being killed, and there was a reason for it. We were defending ourselves. Now, though, I wouldn't be killing the enemy, but our own people, just to protect *you*. I..." Valder suddenly realized that not only was he expressing himself badly, but he was on the verge of saying something irretrievably tactless. He changed direction abruptly. "And besides, the sword is cursed, you know, and is due to turn on me soon if I keep using it. I couldn't serve you for very long in any case. All I want to do, sir—my lord—is to collect my pay and retire quietly, perhaps set myself up in business somewhere. I'm not interested in fighting or killing or government or politics. I never was. Please, my lord, don't misunderstand me, but do just let me go."

He stared hopefully at Gor. The overlord, obviously irritated, had gone from leaning back in his chair to leaning forward, elbows on knees. Now he rose, his hand falling naturally to the hilt of his sword. "You're sure of your decision?"

Valder rose, but pointedly kept his own hand well away from Wirikidor. "I'm quite sure, my lord. I will not be your assassin." An odd feeling of confidence seeped into him as he stood facing Gor. Here he was, defying one of the three most powerful men in the world—and he had nothing to fear! Gor could not kill him; Wirikidor would make sure of that. Nor could Valder be demoted or court-martialed, now that the war was over; he was sure that an attempt at military justice against a man who had tried to leave the army peacefully would result in a public outcry Gor could ill afford, and what would demotion matter any more?

Gor seemed to sense Valder's changed attitude; his own became less certain, less belligerent, and he glanced at Wirikidor. "You won't speak of this conversation with anyone, I hope," he said. "I would not appreciate that. Unpleasant things might happen. I can allow you to go in peace, Valder of the Magic Sword, but I cannot allow you to work against me. I know the sword guards you against death, but there are other unpleasant things that can happen. Remember that and say nothing."

"I'll remember."

"Good." Gor turned to open the door. "That's all, then."

"Not quite, my lord." Valder stayed where he was and allowed his hand to drop nearer Wirikidor's hilt. In this room he had the upper hand; if he drew Wirikidor there could be no doubt that Gor would die. Of course, there would also be no doubt about who killed him, but Valder could claim it was an accident; given Wirikidor's untrustworthy nature, he might be believed.

He had no intention of drawing the sword, but it made a very effective threat indeed.

"Oh?" Gor was wary and, Valder sensed, very dangerous. He might hope to wound Valder and delay him long enough to slip out and allow the sword a choice of victims.

"I realize it's an imposition, but if you could send a message to the paymaster to release the money owed me, I would like to be discharged and go about my business. You don't need me around here anymore, talking to people."

"Oh, is that all?" Gor relaxed visibly. He turned and opened the door, then leaned through and called to the people waiting in the main office. "Bragen! Inform the paymaster that Valder of Kardoret has been discharged without prejudice and is to be paid the full amount due him upon request!"

"Yes, my lord," replied the secretary who had told Valder the appropriate form of address.

"Thank you," Valder said as he made his way past Gor and out of the little room.

Gor did not answer; he was already bellowing for some other officer to pay attention.

Valder and Bragen marched side by side down the corridor, not speaking. Valder was thinking and planning intently, as he had not really done for months.

Gor was not a man prone to making empty threats; he undoubtedly really did have wizards working for him who would not balk at an assassination or two. He might well decide that Valder was simply too dangerous to have running around loose, particularly in his own home. That was why Valder had insisted on his immediate discharge and full pay; he did not care to stay in the Fortress where Gor might stumble across him and be reminded that Wirikidor was a real threat and where Valder could easily be found, if the overlord decided to do something about him. It was time to go—and quickly—as he had no desire to be blinded or hamstrung or imprisoned.

In his first rush of worry, he was not even certain he should take the time to collect his few personal belongings and make his farewells to Tandellin and other friends, but he decided, while the paymaster was counting out his coins, that Gor would be too busy to worry about him for at least a few hours yet. He would have time, once his pay was all securely in hand, to gather his things and stop by the barracks briefly.

That settled, the next question was where to go. Since the ocean lay to the west and an almost-empty wilderness to the north, his choices were limited. To the east was the former Central Command, under Anaran of the Sands; beyond that, he was not sure, since the demonic attack had wiped out the old Eastern Command. Somewhere to the southeast was Azrad's Coastal Command, which had always been concerned with supply and communication rather than combat, and beyond that, across the Gulf, lay the small kingdoms that had once been the Ethsharitic homeland.

He had no interest in wandering about in the wilds, nor in being alone. If he were to hide from Gor, as it seemed he might need to, it would be easier to lose himself in a crowd than somewhere in the wilderness. Any decent wizard could locate the general area an individual was in with a few simple spells, and if he were living by himself somewhere he would be easily found by such methods—but the spells could not pick one man out of a camp.

The Fortress and the surrounding area were certainly crowded enough, but he did not care to stay so close. What of the other two headquarters, then?

Anaran was based on the south coast, well on the other side of the major western peninsula, and Azrad's home port, reputed to be an actual city rather than a camp, was far beyond, on the northeastern corner of the eastern peninsula, not far from the mouth of the Great River and almost at the borders of the small kingdoms—after all, Azrad had been in charge of ports and coasts throughout the World, and his command had been the link between the other three and the old homeland.

Azrad's base sounded promising; it was on the far side of Anaran's, making it that much less accessible to Gor; and furthermore, Valder judged that there would be far more business opportunities there, where trade was already established. He might not wind up a wine merchant, but, by all the gods, he would find something and not wind up a farmer!

When he stopped in and told Tandellin he was leaving, Tandellin naturally asked where he would go.

"Oh, I don't know," he muttered.

"Yes, you do, Valder; you wouldn't just leave this suddenly if you hadn't picked a destination."

Sheepishly, Valder admitted, "Well, I was thinking of Azrad's home port—should be plenty of work there."

"So there should. Good luck, then, in finding it!" With that, Tandellin embraced him and then turned away.

Valder was slightly startled; he had expected Tandellin to try and extend the conversation, not cut it short. Unsure whether to be relieved or hurt, he headed for the gate. Just an hour after the end of his interview with the overlord, he was marching down the hillside with a full purse on his belt, bound for Azrad's headquarters.

CHAPTER 19

Valder was no sailor, nor was he particularly fond of the sea, though he did think its scent freshened the air nicely. Still, he decided after due consideration to travel by ship, rather than overland. He estimated the distance to Azrad's home base at more than a hundred leagues, a long and weary walk under the best of circumstances. Nor did such circumstances exist, as the roads, he knew, were not good. Much of the route had been disputed territory at one time or another in the past few decades, and although roads had been built to accommodate troop movements, they had been intended as temporary and had not been maintained. A few had been torn up by actual battles.

And a walk it would have had to be, as no horses or other beasts of burden were available. The hundreds of people who had left the Fortress before him had bought or stolen every one to be found in a two-league radius.

Once this became clear, Valder took the first shipboard vacancy he could find. Fortunately, ships were coming in steadily, so that this caused no delay.

He was surprised to learn that these ships were bringing people in from further south and east, people who hoped to find greater opportunities in this most northerly of the three new capitals. Less startling was the observation that dozens of others were following his own course, leaving the Fortress for places closer to the old homeland.

He wondered how things stood elsewhere. Was all the Hegemony as unsettled as this? The sudden end of the war had apparently left hundreds or thousands of people unsure where they might fit in.

As he stood at the ship's rail and watched Gor's demesne fade in the distance, he assured himself that he had done the right thing. True, all his living friends were still in or near the Fortress, but his departure meant a clean break with his past as an assassin and with all the rest of his former life. Nobody would know him in Azrad's city; nobody would know that Wirikidor was anything more than an ordinary sword such as any veteran might carry. He would make new friends in time, friends who would not care what he had done during the war, and he would live peacefully as long as he kept Wirikidor sheathed.

If he kept it sheathed long enough, he could just outlive everyone who knew of its existence.

He wondered if that was really a good thing. He enjoyed life, or at least he usually had enjoyed it, but might it get wearing eventually? Living on indefinitely while everyone around him grew old and died might be depressing. Of course, he would presumably be growing older, too.

That thought brought him up with a start. Just how would that work? Would the sword keep him young, or merely alive? It would not protect him from injury—his left arm still ached sometimes where that sorcerer had wounded him—so why should it protect him from aging?

In that case, would it really prevent him from dying of old age? Darrend had said the *only* way he could die without breaking the spell was on Wirikidor's blade, so presumably it would keep him alive somehow.

Living for several centuries and aging normally all the time might be worse than death—if anything could be. He had seen men who were worn out at sixty, others who still enjoyed life at eighty; but after a century or two, surely no life would still be worth living.

Well, maybe the sword *would* keep him young. He had plenty of time left before he had to worry about it, and there was always a way out of anything—though not always an easy or pleasant one. He turned away from the rail and went below. His stomach was uneasy.

The ship stopped briefly at a town called Shan on the Sea at the tip of the southwestern peninsula, but Valder paid little attention. He was too seasick just then to rise from his hammock.

The second stop was at Anaran's vast walled camp, now called Ethshar of the Sands; by then Valder was well enough to stagger up on deck and lean heavily against the rail. He debated with himself as to whether he should disembark and put an end to the internal discomfort he felt by returning to dry land, but finally decided to continue. He was recovering and knew that he would be safer in Azrad's city.

In any case, the maze of tents and temporary buildings that covered the flat, sandy ground was not particularly encouraging. A large building of polished stone was under construction in the center, its immense unfinished dome half-hidden by scaffolding. An extensive system of lighthouses, port facilities, and coastal defenses lined the waterfront. In the distance he could see an impressive city wall. Everywhere else, however, Ethshar of the Sands was a tangle of narrow unpaved streets, lined with mismatched tents and crude houses, apparently thrown together from driftwood and wreckage. People were jammed into these structures in incredible numbers, even more than in Gor's Ethshar of the Rocks.

All this was plainly visible as the ship inched in toward the docks, and, seasick or not, Valder thought it best to stay on board and sail for Azrad's port—Azrad's Ethshar, the crew called it.

Within a day or two of leaving Ethshar of the Sands, that decision seemed wise indeed, as his stomach had finally adapted to the ship's motions, and he was able to stroll the deck casually, watching the progressively greener and lusher coastline slip by. When they had rounded the headlands at the tip of the peninsula that separated the Great Ocean from the Gulf of the East the countryside seemed even more beautiful, the loveliest Valder had ever seen.

Finally, two sixnights after leaving the Fortress, Valder caught sight of Azrad's Ethshar.

At first it was nothing but a gray line on the horizon, a gray line amid the green that grew and grew until it covered the entire shoreline. By the time the ship crept up one of the canals to its own dock, Valder had had a chance to readjust his thinking.

This was no camp, in any sense of the word; even calling it a city seemed an understatement, as it was far larger than any he had ever seen, larger than he had imagined any city could be. The waterfront extended for miles, every inch of it lined with docks and warehouses, piers and tenements. Two large canals cut their way inland and were likewise lined with docks and warehouses. No mere tents or shacks were anywhere to be seen; these buildings were mostly stone or brick, and not particularly new.

That was reasonable, of course, since this had been the headquarters for the navy, not the army, and for the extensive supply system that had kept both branches of the military fed and equipped. Although technically outside the borders of Old Ethshar, the enemy had never claimed the area, never approached it or threatened it in any way, so there had been no reason *not* to build it up, and the navy had not had much else to do in the war against a landlocked enemy.

Valder's consideration of the subject was rudely interrupted by a gang of blue-kilted sailors, marching arm in arm along the deck bellowing, "All ashore! All ashore!"

He managed to get back to his tiny shared cabin long enough to snatch up his bundled belongings and then found himself, with the rest of the passengers, herded down the gangplank onto the dock, where they were left to their own devices.

Almost immediately, some of the new arrivals turned around and clamored for passage elsewhere—Ethshar of the Rocks, Ethshar of the Sands, Shan on the Sea, anywhere but this strange, forbidding place of stone and brick. None of them had ever seen a real city before; after all, this was the only one in the Hegemony at present, though two more were building, and travel to the Small Kingdoms had been carefully restricted for a century or so.

Valder was an exception. He had visited three different northern cities in the course of his assassinations, so the endless rows of buildings, the stark bare walls and streets, did not seem completely alien and unfamiliar. The northern cities had been smaller and half-empty, almost abandoned, and Azrad's Ethshar teemed with life, which seemed a good sign. Such a place was surely far more promising than the other two Ethshars; he marched down the dock to where it met the waterfront and turned left, inland, onto the street there.

This street paralleled the canal; as might be expected so near the docks, it was lined with buildings that had shops on the ground floor and brothels or warehouse space upstairs. He saw no inns, which seemed a bit odd, but the shops did include shipfitters, ropemakers, coopers, carpenters, sailmakers, chandlers—and a distressing number of wineshops. The market here, Valder realized, was already full. If he were going to go into the wine business, he would need to go elsewhere; if he were going to stay here, he would need to choose another occupation.

He noticed all this while fighting his way through crowds. The streets were jammed with people, going in both directions at varying speeds, clad in a fantastic variety of dress. The tangle at one intersection was such that he had to fight his way into the thick of the crowd simply to avoid being forced over the ankle-high parapet and into the canal. He was grateful that all the traffic was on foot, as horses or oxen would have made the tangle impassable.

A few hundred feet from the dock where he had disembarked, the canalside street was joined diagonally by another, and where they met was a good-sized triangular marketplace, where farmers and fishermen were hawking their wares. At the near end three men stood on a raised platform, one of them shouting numbers to a small crowd, another wearing chains. Valder realized with a start that this was a slave auction in progress.

He had known that such things existed; the few northern prisoners who survived had presumably wound up as slaves somewhere, and certain crimes were punishable by enslavement, but this was the first time he personally had come into direct contact with the institution of slavery.

He wondered where the man being auctioned off had come from and how he had arrived in his present state—and just what a healthy slave was worth. He had no intention of buying one—he had no use for a slave and did not want the added responsibility—but he was intensely curious all the same to learn what a man's life was worth in silver. He pressed forward to listen.

He was too late; the auctioneer called out, "Sold!" just as Valder came close enough to make out what was said. He waited for a moment to see if any more slaves were to be sold, but this one had apparently been the last in the lot. The auctioneer stepped down from the platform, and the other free man led the slave away.

Mildly disappointed, but also thrilled with the exoticism of this strange city, Valder shrugged and turned away—and nearly stepped on the tail of a tiny golden dragon, scarcely three feet long, that was being led past him on a chain held by a plump woman in red velvet. Valder stared after it; he had not realized that even newborn dragons could be so small.

When the little monster had vanished in the throng, Valder resumed his former route, pushing his way southward through the crowd toward the inland end of the market. He had reached the midpoint of the plaza when he suddenly realized that he had no idea where he was going. He was in Azrad's Ethshar, and that was as far as he had planned. His hope of setting himself up as a wine merchant was best abandoned, as the competition was too fierce and too well established. He was alone in a strange city, with a few clothes and personal items, a full money-pouch, a magic sword, and nothing else.

Obviously, the first order of business was to find food

and shelter. A city would have inns, certainly; he need
only find them. Once he had a room and a meal he could
take his time in deciding what to do. He had his whole
life before him—and a very long life it might be, at that—
to do with as he would and as he could. He was free,
unfettered, and uncertain, with no obligations and no plans.

He had rather expected to find inns near the docks,
but none were evident. The next logical place would be
near the city gates. That left the question of where the
nearest gate might be.

He reached the narrow end of the market and found
himself with a choice of two streets, one heading east
across the head of the canal and the other angling off to
the southwest. He chose southwest and struggled onward.
The crowds were somewhat thinner here, but seemed to
move faster, though still exclusively pedestrians.

Roughly five hundred feet from the intersection, the
street he had chosen ended in a T, offering him northwest
or southeast. He stood for a moment at the corner, puzzled, then stopped a passerby in a pale yellow tunic and
asked, "Which way to the city gate?"

The man glanced at him. "Westgate?"

"If that's nearest."

The man pointed southeast and said, "You follow this
to Bridge Street, turn right, follow that until it merges
into West Street, follow that to Shipwright Street, and
that goes to Westgate Market." Before Valder could thank
him or ask for more detail, the man had pulled away and
vanished in the crowd, leaving Valder wondering if he
might have asked the wrong question. There might well
be inns closer at hand.

Still, he had directions and he followed them as best
he could. The street leading southeast ended at a broad
avenue after a single block; although Valder saw no sign
of a bridge nor any indication of the avenue's name, he
assumed he had the correct street and turned right.

Bride Street, if that was what it was, seemed interminable and was as crowded as the other streets. After
he had gone roughly half a mile, elbowing his way along,
he reached an intersection where the avenue did not con-

tinue directly across but turned at an oblique angle. He hesitated, but guessed that this must be the junction with West Street and turned right. A glance at the sun convinced him that he was now heading due west.

As he progressed, the nature of his surroundings altered somewhat. The shipfitters and ropemakers had vanished when he left the canal behind, replaced by wheelwrights and metalworkers, and to some extent the brothels and warehouses had given way to residences. This new street was lined with weavers and cloth merchants, tinkers and blacksmiths, carters and tanners. Valder had never seen so many businesses gathered together before; any street in this city put to shame the traveling markets that had serviced military camps.

The buildings in this area also appeared to be newer than those right on the canal, favoring the modern half-timbered style for upper floors rather than the older custom of solid stone from foundation to ridgepole. That made sense, of course; naturally the city would have started out clustered around the port and only gradually grown inland.

West Street, if that was in fact the street he was on, ended eventually at a diagonal cross-street; Valder chose the left turn, to the southwest, without hesitation. Quite aside from any more abstract considerations, he could hear and smell a market and, from the corner of West Street, he glimpsed the top of a stone tower that he took to be a gate tower.

Sure enough, as he rounded the next curve he found himself looking down a straight street at a market square, a very crowded market square, in the shadow of two immense towers.

He wanted to hurry forward, as the long walk had made him impatient, but was unable to do so. The street was too populous, and it seemed that a significant part of the crowd was not moving. A good many people were just standing, not walking in any particular direction.

He managed to force his way into a stream of people that was moving steadily toward the market, marveling at the endless throngs as he did so. He had not realized there were so many people in all the World as he had seen in Azrad's Ethshar.

A hand thrust itself in front of him and a voice demanded, "Alms for a crippled veteran!"

Valder thrust the hand aside with a shudder and marched on. Beggars! He had somehow not expected beggars in this vast, overwhelming city. Of course, it made sense that they would be here. They would naturally want to go where there was money to be had, and Azrad's Ethshar certainly had money.

A signboard caught his attention. It depicted a huge, golden goblet with purple wine slopping over the rim, and a line of runes across the bottom read, "Food & Lodging." Valder turned his steps in that direction, back out of the flow of traffic.

A good many people, mostly scowling, stood around the door of the inn, but they did not interfere as Valder shoved his way through. He stepped over the threshold into the dim interior and stopped dead.

The inside of the inn was almost as crowded as the street. The main public room, just inside the front door, was more than twenty feet on a side, but, except for a narrow path that led from the door to one end, across the hearth, down along the row of barrels, and then to the back corner where a stair and two doors led to other rooms, the floor was completely covered with blankets, displacing all the expected tavern furnishings. These blankets were neatly laid out in rectangles about two feet wide and six feet long, and on each one a man or woman sat or stood or lay, each with his or her personal possessions stacked at one end. Some had nothing but a spare tunic, while others had large, unwieldy bundles. Virtually all wore the green and brown of the Ethsharitic armies.

Startled and confused, Valder followed the path across the hearth and paused at the first barrel. The innkeeper emerged from one of the doors.

"What can I do for you?" he asked.

"Ah...a pint of ale, for now."

"That'll be four bits in silver," the innkeeper warned. Valder stared at him in astonishment, forgetting the crowded floor for the moment in the face of this greater shock. "What?"

"Four silver bits, I said. We've only got half a keg left, and no more due for a sixnight."

"Forget it, then. What about water?"

"A copper a pint—no change for silver, either."

"That's mad! You're selling ale for the price of a fine southern vintage and water for the price of the best ale!"

"True enough, sir, I am indeed. That's what the market will bear, and I'd be a fool not to get what I can while these poor souls still have their pay to spend."

"It's theft!"

"No, sir, it's honest trade. The gate and the market are so jammed, and the roads so full, and the ships so busy with passengers, that I can't get supplies in. We have a good well out back, but it's not bottomless and yields only so much in a day. I understand that the taverns nearest the gate are only accepting gold now."

"And your rooms?"

"All taken, sir, and the floor here as well. I'm an honest man and I won't lie about it; there is nowhere left to put you that won't block my path. They're sleeping four to a bed upstairs, with six on each floor, and a blanket and a space down here would cost you a full silver piece, if I had any left."

"It's all mad. Where are all these people coming from?"

"It *is* mad, sir, I won't argue that. It seems as if the entire army of Ethshar is jammed into Westgate. I've never seen anything like it. It's the end of the war that's done it, of course, and I'm sure we'll never see anything like it again. If prices come back down, I'll retire a wealthy man at the end of the year—but who's to say what prices will do when once they've started changing? The army doesn't set them any more, so I need to charge what I can get."

"I have money, innkeeper, but I'll be damned to a northerner's hell before I'll pay a silver bit just for water."

"A copper piece will do."

"I don't intend to pay that, either."

The innkeeper shrugged. "Please yourself. I have all the trade I need without you."

"Isn't there anywhere in the city that still charges honest prices?"

"I have no idea, really. There might be some poor fool somewhere. If so, he's surely drained his every barrel dry by now."

"Well, we'll just see about that," Valder said, knowing even as the words left his lips that they sounded foolish. He turned and, in a petty display of temper, marched directly across the array of blankets and back out into the street, ignoring the angry protests from those he stepped over.

CHAPTER 20

*T*o Valder's surprise, he found the situation to be exactly as the proprietor of the Overflowing Chalice had described it. In fact, each door closer to the Westgate Market brought another jump in prices. The inns and taverns that actually faced on the market were indeed accepting nothing smaller than a gold bit, even for water, let alone bread, cheese, or ale. Valder estimated that his entire accumulated pay, which he had thought ample to live on for two years or more, would scarcely buy a good dinner and a night's lodging at the Gatehouse Inn—which was, oddly, not in the actual gatehouse or even adjoining it. The gatehouse itself was in the base of one of the two towers and was still manned by the army, as were the rest of both towers and the wall. Taverns and inns faced the gate from across the broad market square, and the Gatehouse Inn was at their center.

Strangely, the north and south sides of the market were completely open, marked only by a drop in the level of the ground, and Valder could see the city wall stretching off into the distance. Paralleling it, but a hundred feet or so in, was a broad, smooth street, also stretching off out of sight. In the rough depression between the wall and the street were no buildings, no structure of any sort, but more blankets like those in the Overflowing Chalice—hundreds upon hundreds of them, each with its occupant. These, Valder realized, were the veterans too poor—or too frugal—to pay for space in an inn or tavern. Several, he noticed, were crippled or wounded, and most were ragged and dirty.

After he had inquired at a dozen or so inns without finding food, drink, or lodging at a price he was willing to pay, Valder found himself standing in the middle of the market square, surrounded by the milling crowds. To the north and south were the homeless veterans on their pitiful blankets; to the east were the incredibly priced inns; to the west was the gate itself, fifty feet wide and at least as tall, but dwarfed by its two huge towers. He suddenly felt the need to talk to someone—not a greedy innkeeper nor a wandering, aimless veteran, but somebody secure and sensible. Without knowing exactly why, he headed for the gatehouse.

The towers, of course, were manned by proper soldiers, still in full uniform, and Valder found himself irrationally comforted by the sight of their polished breastplates and erect carriage. Three men were busily directing the flood of traffic in and out of the gate, answering shouted questions and turning back everything but people on foot, but a fourth was obviously off duty for the moment. He was seated comfortably on a folding canvas chair, leaning up against the stone wall of the gatehouse.

Valder made his way over and leaned up against the wall beside the soldier. The man glanced up at him but said nothing, and Valder inferred from this that his presence was not unwelcome.

"Has it been like this for very long?" Valder asked, after the silence stretched from sociable to the verge of strain.

"You mean the crowds? It's been going on for two or three sixnights, since they announced the war was over.

Nobody knows what to do without orders, so they all come here, hoping somebody will tell them."

"It can't keep up like this, can it?"

"Oh, I don't think so—sooner or later everyone will have come here, seen what a mess it is, and given up and left again."

"I expect a good many will stay; I'd say this is going to be a very large city from now on, even more than before."

"Oh, no doubt of that; they're already laying out new streets wherever they can find room inside the walls."

"Is anybody doing anything about all these people?"

"Not really—what can they do? We have orders to keep out horses and oxen, to reduce the crowding in the streets, and Azrad did have free blankets issued, so that nobody would have to sleep in the mud, but that's about it. There just isn't anything *to* do with them. There's plenty of land outside the walls if they want to go farm it, and I suppose there will be work for builders and the like, but beyond that, I don't know what's going to happen to them all. I stayed in uniform for a reason, you know; the army may be rough at times, but it's secure, even in peacetime. Someone's got to watch the gates and patrol the borders and keep order."

"You said the overlord gave out those blankets?"

"That's right; that was intended to be the entire supply for the whole Ethsharitic army for the next three years, and they've been given away to whoever asked for them. Need one? We've got about twenty left, I think."

"I might, at that, unless you can tell me where I can find lodging at a reasonable price."

"Friend, there isn't a place in this whole city where you can find cheap lodging except the Hundred-Foot Field and the barracks, and the word is that the penalty for civilians sleeping in the barracks is a hundred lashes—*and* you re-enlist. And not as an officer, either, regardless of what you were in wartime."

"Seems severe, but I know better than to argue. What's the Hundred-Foot Field?"

"You walked right past it." He gestured vaguely toward the market. "That's the space between Wall Street and the wall. The law says you can't build there, ever, in case the army needs the space to maneuver or move siege machines—but the law doesn't say anything about sleeping there on a blanket or two in warm weather. Even during the war, we usually had a few beggars and cripples who slept there, and now it's jammed full of these damned veterans, all the way around the city—or so I'm told, I haven't checked. I never go south of Westwark, nor more than a few blocks into Shiphaven."

"I don't know my way around the city, but I take it those are neighborhoods?"

"That's right; even without these veterans, the city was already too big, and it's more like a dozen little cities put together—Shiphaven and Westgate and Westwark and Spicetown and Fishertown and the Old City and the Merchants' Quarter and so forth."

"I hadn't realized it was so big." Valder glanced back at the mobbed marketplace. The crowd seemed to be thinning somewhat—or perhaps the fading light just made it appear to be. He realized with some surprise that the sun was below the western horizon, and the shadow of the city wall covered everything in sight. He still had not eaten, and had nowhere to stay the night.

"Ah—how many gates are there?"

"Three, though they're planning to put in a fourth one to the southwest."

"Are there inns at all of them?"

"I suppose so, but Westgate gets the most traffic. This is the main highway here, going through this gate, the road to Ethshar and Anaran and Gor and the northern lands, while the other gates just go to the local farms on the peninsula. I think most of the inns must be here."

"How far is it to the next gate?"

The soldier leaned back in his chair and considered that for a moment. "I'd guess two miles or more," he said. "It's a big city."

Valder glanced at the thinning crowds, then at the dimming sky. Torches were being lighted in front of some of the taverns and shops, but the streets would still be dark.

Walking two miles through an unfamiliar city at night on
the slim chance that the other gates would be preferable
when he was already tired was not an attractive prospect.
"Let me have one of those blankets," he said. "It looks
as if I'll be spending the night in the Hundred-Foot Field."

The soldier grinned. "Right. Got to make that back pay
last, don't you?" He sat up and let the chair's front legs
down, then got to his feet. With a nod, he vanished through
the gatehouse door, to emerge a moment later with a
brown bundle. "It's all yours," he said, tossing the blanket
to Valder.

Valder decided against replying; he nodded politely and
slipped away into the crowd.

As he made his way southward on Wall Street looking
for a blanket-sized opening in the Hundred-Foot Field,
he kept a steady eye on the field's inhabitants. The further
from the market square he went, the less savory his view
became; by the time he had gone six blocks, he had the
blanket tucked securely under one arm in order to keep
his hands free, his right resting on his sword hilt and his
left clutching his purse.

The wall, and Wall Street with it, jogged three times
before he found himself a spot. He judged the distance
from Westgate Market at roughly a mile and briefly considered continuing on toward the second gate.

He quickly dismissed the notion, however. Night had
fallen, and the light from the scattered torches and lanterns did not amount to much. He did not care to travel
further by such uncertain illumination, particularly with
a full purse. Furthermore, if the crowd from Westgate
extended this far, might not the crowd from the next gate
extend as far in the opposite direction, so that he would
be walking into a throng similar to the one he had just
departed? Westgate might be the most active gate, but the
others would surely be almost as busy and expensive.

It was quite obvious that he was not going to get anywhere in Azrad's Ethshar; far too many people had gotten
here before him, and every available opportunity must
certainly have already been taken. He would have to get
out into the countryside, at least temporarily. He still had

no interest in becoming a farmer, but surely something, some sort of an opportunity, would present itself.

He had not eaten since leaving the ship, and his stomach was growling persistently as he smoothed his blanket on the hard-packed, bare dirt of the field. He promised himself that he would buy something to eat in the morning, no matter what the cost.

With a wary glance at his neighbors, he settled down, keeping his right hand on Wirikidor's hilt, his left still securely gripping his purse. He did not intend to be robbed. He fell asleep, finally, and awoke at dawn to find sword and purse still intact. Any thieves who might have been around had presumably found easier pickings.

He was stiff and cramped from sleeping curled up in his blanket. He struggled to his feet and stretched vigorously. All around him, men and a few scattered women were still sleeping. A few were awake, some of them moving, some just sitting and gazing about sleepily. Valder found himself becoming depressed just looking at them—all this potential going to waste! He was determined that he, at least, would not sit and rot in the Hundred-Foot Field. He would get out of the city and find himself a career. He had not seen the horrendous inflation in prices anywhere but Azrad's Ethshar—which was, of course, far more crowded than anywhere else—so he hoped his savings would tide him over.

He had wanted to lose himself in a crowd, where Gor would be unable to find him, should he decide ex-assassins were dangerous, but the crowding in this city was more than Valder had imagined possible, so much so that now he was eager to leave it behind. Rolling up his blanket, he picked his way carefully across his neighbors to Wall Street, where he turned left and headed for Westgate.

No one took any special note of him as he marched out the gate onto the highway. The guard he had spoken with was nowhere in sight.

By noon he was almost four leagues from the city wall.

As the day progressed, the traffic grew from virtually nothing moving to a steady stream in both directions. People were still drifting in toward the city from the disbanding armies, while others who had already seen the situation and given up on finding a place in Azrad's Ethshar were heading back out to look for someplace better.

This struck him as futile, and he tried stopping a party heading toward the city to tell them that there was nothing for them there. They ignored his warning.

"Maybe there's nothing there for you, fellow, but perhaps we aren't as picky," the leader said, glancing significantly at Valder's black-and-gray uniform. Like most people, the man wore green and brown; very few people had bothered to acquire civilian clothes yet, though insignia and marks of rank were now rare, and only those that remained soldiers were permitted to keep their breastplates.

"I'm not picky," Valder insisted. "The whole place is mobbed. Food is running low, and lodging costs more for a night than it should for a year."

"Well, we'll just have to see this for ourselves. We don't know you; why should we believe you?"

Valder shrugged. "I'm just trying to help," he said.

"We don't need your help," the spokesman said, turning away. Valder watched helplessly as they trudged on toward the gates. When they were lost in the streaming traffic, he turned and headed onward.

The highway had left the city running due west, but quickly curved around to the north, leading from the peninsula to the mainland. Valder knew a little basic geography, enough to know that the only land routes from Azrad's Ethshar to anywhere worth mentioning would have to run northward across the isthmus to the mainland; there simply wasn't anything except open countryside surrounded by sea to the south, east, or west. He supposed that some of that land might be suitable for farming—though he had an impression it was too sandy to be much use, even for that—but he was not willing to try farming it.

That meant he had to head north, and that was what he was doing, but once he reached the mainland he had more of a choice. He could head back west along the coast to Ethshar of the Sands, perhaps—but that would take him closer to Gor, and though Ethshar of the Sands was less crowded than Azrad's Ethshar, it was more primitive, and he was not at all sure it would be any real improvement. Somewhere far to the north were the mines and mountains taken from the Northern Empire in the course of the last century or so, and beyond them lay the ruins of the Empire itself. He had no interest in mining and knew that it was never the common miners who got rich from the jewels and metals they found, but those who owned the mines, or bought from the miners, or sold to the miners. A wine merchant might do well in the mining country, but first he would need stock, and as yet Valder had no stock and no idea where he might find any.

In all the wide arc of land between the mines and Ethshar of the Sands, there was only wilderness, forests and grasslands, and a few scattered farms that had been established to help feed the armies fighting in that wilderness. Those armies had once had camps dotting the plains and forests in every direction, but were now disbanded. A few camps might survive as villages and towns, but Valder doubted any would have much to offer him.

That covered the compass from south sunwise through northeast, leaving only the east and southeast. That was where the old homeland had been. It had never actually been his home, of course; he had been born in the camptown at Kardoret, a base on the line between the western and central commands, and had never seen Old Ethshar. The official story, which he had no reason to doubt, was that it was now fragmented into dozens of pretty states, warring with one another. Valder had had his fill of war, certainly, but he wondered whether there might not be opportunities to be found there. Certainly, Gor of the Rocks had no authority there and so could not pursue him; the Hegemony of Ethshar claimed only the lands *outside* the old borders.

His worries about the overlord might be unfounded, he knew; but even so, the prospect of actually seeing the land he had fought for so long, a land that had history extending back before the war, had a certain charm to it. Most of the veterans were unimaginative enough to accept the official line and stay in the Hegemony, he was sure, so the competition for work would not be as fierce in the Small Kingdoms.

That decided him. He would head for the Small Kingdoms, where Old Ethshar used to be. That meant he must bear right at every major fork, following the highways around the northern end of the Gulf of the East.

So far, however, he had seen no forks; the highway rolled on, indivisible, across the isthmus.

He marched on through the afternoon, despite mounting weariness. He was not accustomed to long walks any more, after his enforced inactivity at sea and his long stint as an assassin, where speed and stealth had been far more important than stamina. Furthemore, he had realized he had broken his promise to himself in his rush to get out of the city and had not eaten anything since his last meal aboard ship, which had been a large breakfast the day before. He had found water at several small streams that crossed the highway, but no food.

For that matter, he had not encountered a stream recently, and, although the day was no more than pleasantly warm, he was again growing thirsty. He cursed himself for not having planned more carefully and brought adequate supplies.

Of course, he had expected to find everything he needed in Azrad's Ethshar. The impossibly high prices had been a complete surprise and had shocked him so badly that he had forgotten how essential food and drink could be. He had refused to buy anything at all, despite his sizeable store of cash, and was now paying for his miserliness. He wished he had somehow wangled a Spell of Sustenance somewhere along the line, but he no longer even had a bloodstone; he had turned his in after his last assassination, in accordance with his orders.

If mere food and drink were so outrageously expensive in the city, he wondered what astronomical sum might be required to buy an enchanted bloodstone.

Somewhere along the highway, he told himself, there would surely be an inn or a tavern, or at least a farmhouse, where he might buy bread and ale, or find water. With that in mind, he kept marching and even managed to pick up his pace a trifle.

The sun was reddening in the west when he reached the fork. As he had decided, he bore right. Some of his fellow travelers were already settling by the roadside for the night, some with elaborate camps, others with just a blanket. Virtually all the traffic that was still moving was using the left-hand fork, and Valder realized that that must be the road to both Anaran's territory and the northern lands. Since the left fork headed due west and the right due north, he would have assumed otherwise, if not for the traffic, but among those coming down the west fork were men and women in clothes far warmer than the climate called for, some with mining tools on belts or backpacks.

Those who had stopped for the night were strewn haphazardly along the wayside with whatever supplies they had brought, which hardly seemed to indicate the presence of an inn anywhere on the road. Valder had brought nothing and still hoped to find shelter; he marched on past the fork and almost immediately felt a cool breeze that carried the scent of water—but not the salt tang of the ocean.

The fork had been on the side of a low rise, with the west fork following the contour of the land, while the north headed directly up over the crest. Valder pushed on over the ridgetop to where he could see what lay beyond, could see the broad river that lay at the bottom of the slope, the widest river he had ever seen just half a mile further down the road.

That meant fresh water, though perhaps not the best, unless the river was somehow too polluted to drink from. There might well be fish and edible plants of some sort, rather than the endless grasses that covered most of the countryside.

The road itself ran on across the river by means of a bridge—a bridge Valder judged to be a prodigious feat of engineering, one that quite possibly had required magic in its construction, since the river was very wide indeed. Men were standing on the bridge; perhaps, he thought, he had finally found some clever farm folk cashing in on the steady stream of traffic by selling their produce. Exhausted as he was, he stumbled down the slope toward the river.

CHAPTER 21

The men on the bridge were soldiers, in full uniform and heavily armed. They stood in front of a gate that blocked the south end of the bridge. Pitched nearby was an army-issue tent.

They did not appear to be there to sell vegetables. After a glance at them, Valder left the highway and made his way down the bank to the river. He drank his fill, wiped the sweat from his face and arms, splashed a little water on his tunic to cool himself down, then sat and rested for a few moments.

The last daylight was fading; on the bridge above him the soldiers were lighting torches. He glanced up at the hiss as the first one caught fire, and watched the procedure with interest.

This was obviously a toll bridge. He had heard of such things, though in wartime they had been illegal outside the borders of Old Ethshar—or rather, the Small Kingdoms, since Old Ethshar had apparently collapsed before Valder was born. Toll bridges might have interfered with the movement of troops or supplies, so they had not been permitted.

The war was over, however, and that law seemed to have been repealed—assuming this group was here legally. With four of them and Valder alone, he had no intention of questioning their rights.

He glanced at the river. Already the far side was invisible. He could not possibly swim so far, he knew, and he doubted that a river of such a size could be forded anywhere within twenty leagues. Certainly, no one would get any goods across without using either a bridge or a ferry. He saw no ferries. All trade, then, would use the bridge. The toll collection should prove profitable.

When he was feeling somewhat less exhausted, he got to his feet and climbed slowly back up the bank to the highway.

No traffic was moving. Three small parties, perhaps a dozen travelers in all, were camped along the roadside up toward the fork, with campfires burning. The only other people in sight were the soldiers on the bridge; in addition to their torches, they had a small cooking fire in front of their tent.

Valder was at a loss as to what he should do next. He was tired, hungry, and lonely, with no idea what would become of him; these common problems seemed more important at present than his unique one of being linked for life to a magic sword he did not trust. The sword was strictly a long-term problem, while the others were all immediate.

He could handle his weariness by trampling out a circle in the grass and going to sleep—in fact, he could probably find an abandoned campsite and save himself the trouble of trampling one out. Food, however, was becoming a very serious concern, and the sight of a soldier hanging a kettle over the cookfire decided him. He trudged up onto the bridge.

The soldiers saw him coming, despite the gathering gloom. Two had cocked crossbows in their hands, but did not bother to aim or release the safety catches, while a third dropped his hand to the hilt of his sword. Valder saw five in all; the fourth was the man tending the kettle, and the fifth was dozing nearby.

"Hello there!" Valder called.

"Hello," the swordsman replied.

"What are you doing here?" His assumption that they were toll collectors was, after all, only a guess.

"Guarding the bridge."

"Guarding it against what? The war is over!"

"Guarding against unauthorized crossing. It's one copper piece to cross for veterans or their families, and no one else is welcome."

"On whose orders?"

"Lord Azrad's."

That made sense. In fact, Valder respected Azrad for thinking of it. Not only would it add to the coffers, but it would keep the people of the Small Kingdoms—who would not be veterans, since the army had not been responsible for the homeland and had long ago moved all operations, including recruiting, elsewhere—from coming to Ethshar and further increasing the crowding in the cities. While the war had continued, none would have dared to venture into the war zones and military lands without a good reason, but now that peace had come and the war zones were transformed into the Hegemony of Ethshar, some might think there were opportunites to be exploited.

Valder had no intention of crossing the bridge until morning, when he could see the other bank and decide whether it was worth a copper piece, but he was very much interested in food and conversation before he slept. "What's cooking?" he asked, pointing to the kettle. "It smells good."

"Just stew; Zak caught a rabbit this afternooon."

"Might I join you? I haven't eaten in almost two days; I can't afford the prices in the city."

The swordsman glanced at his companions, and, although no objections were spoken aloud, Valder sensed reluctance all around.

"I'll pay a fair price, if you want; I've still got my back pay. I just wasn't willing to pay those robbers in the city what they wanted."

"I can agree with that," one of the crossbowmen

remarked. "If I had any doubts about staying in the army, those prices cured them. Silver bits for ale, they wanted!"

"Four the pint at the Overflowing Chalice, and worse in Westgate Market!" Valder agreed. "I can't pay that! Better to drink seawater!"

That broke the ice, as the soldiers all chimed in with complaints. A moment later the whole crew, Valder included, was clustered around the kettle, dishing out rabbit stew. No matter where or when, soldiers loved to complain, and Valder had given this group an opportunity for which they were properly grateful.

They even forgot to charge him for the stew.

The food did not stop the conversation. Between bites, Valder exchanged accounts of wartime action seen, commanders served under, and so forth. Coming as he did from the extreme west, Valder's tales seemed strange and exotic to the guardsmen, even though he avoided any mention of his work as an assassin. Their stories, in turn, seemed odd to him; they had lived and served without ever seeing northern troops. Their only action had been against magical assaults, either sorcerous or demonic, or against rebellion among the civilian population.

Valder had never lived in an area where there *were* civilians, other than camp followers and perhaps a few traveling merchants or coastal fishermen. He had never heard of civilian rebellions and could not really picture how or why they might occur.

His lone scouting patrols through empty forests were just as alien to the southerners, of whom four of the five had never seen a forest. Also, it seemed that Azrad's command structure was far tighter and more complex than Gor's. When Gor had needed something done, he had pointed to a person and told him to do it; when Azrad had needed something done, he had formed a committee to study the problem and set up the appropriate chain of command. Both systems had apparently worked. In fact, as the soldiers described it, once Azrad had all his systems established, they ran themselves, leaving him free to devote his time to his own amusement, where Gor had remained closely involved with day-to-day operations.

This was all new to Valder; it had never occurred to him that there could be such variation within Ethshar, either Hegemony or homeland. He found great delight in this new learning.

When war stories began to wear thin, around midnight, Valder asked, "Why are there so many people in the city? Why doesn't someone do something about it?"

"Where else can they go, and what can anyone do?" a soldier asked in reply. "Ethshar's the only real city there is, and only soldiers are fool enough to sleep in tents. All these veterans want roofs over their heads, and the only solid roofs in the Hegemony are in Azrad's Ethshar, so that's where they go. Sooner or later, they'll realize they can build their own, I suppose, but for now they go to the city."

"The supplies are running low there, I think."

"Of course they are! Even before the war ended, supplies were running low and, with all the eastern farmlands blasted to burning desert, supplies are going to run even lower until someone starts farming all this grassland we're sitting on. What food there is is probably sitting in warehouses, rotting because the distribution system has all come apart with the end of the war!"

Valder glanced around at the darkness beyond the torchlit bridge. "Who owns all this land, anyway? Is it really free for the taking?"

Manrin, the swordsman, shrugged. "Who knows? I guess it is. After all, it was wilderness before the war and it's been under military law ever since. The highway Azrad's keeping for himself, but the proclamation said the rest was available to anyone who would use it."

"Yes," Saldan, the cook, said. "But who knows how to use it? Everybody has grown up learning to be soldiers, not farmers."

A vague idea was stirring in the back of Valder's mind, but he was too tired to haul it forward and look it over. Instead, he tossed the last well-gnawed rabbit bone into the river and announced, "It's been a pleasure talking, and my thanks for the meal, but I need some sleep."

"It's time we all slept," Zak, one of the crossbowmen,

agreed. "Manrin's off until noon, but the rest of us are supposed to be up at dawn. Somebody kick Lorret awake; he's supposed to take the night watch."

Valder left the soldiers to their own business and walked off a few yards into the darkness. He found a spot where the grass seemed less scratchy than most, curled up in his blanket, and went to sleep.

He was awakened three hours later by fat raindrops on his face. He rolled his blanket out from under him, draped it over himself instead, and went back to sleep.

He awoke again just as the first light of dawn seeped through the clouds. The rain was still falling in a thin drizzle; his blanket was soaked through and stank of wet wool. He flung it aside and stood up, still tired, but unable to sleep any more without shelter.

"Somebody," he muttered to himself as he staggered toward the bridge, "ought to build an inn here."

He stopped, frozen in mid-step.

"Somebody ought to build an inn here," he repeated.

That was the idea that had been lurking in the back of his mind during the night's conversation. Somebody really should build an inn here, convenient to the river, the toll bridge, and the fork in the highway. All the land traffic in and out of Azrad's Ethshar and the southern peninsula had to pass by this spot. All the traffic crossing the lower reaches of the Great River would use this bridge. All boats coming down the Great River to the sea—and Valder was sure there would be plenty in time—would come past. It was almost exactly one day's walk from Westgate, just where northbound travelers would be ready to stop for the night.

Could there possibly be a better site for an inn in all the World? Valder doubted it. Only the war had prevented one from being built here long ago, he was sure. The land had belonged to the military, and the military was not interested in inns.

Somebody should build an inn here, and Valder was somebody. He had his accumulated assassin's pay for capital. He had wanted a quiet postwar job other than farming, and innkeeping seemed ideal. He could undoubtedly recruit all the labor he needed in the Hundred-Foot Field.

He could scarcely believe his good fortune. Could he really have been the first to think of it?

He imagined what it would be like—a comfortable little place, built of stone since no forests were nearby, with large windows and thick cool walls in the summer, a wide hearth and blazing fire in winter. Wirikidor could hang above the mantel; surely that would be close enough to him that the sword would not object, particularly if he placed his own chamber directly above, and no one would think it at all odd or inappropriate for a veteran to keep his old sword on display, even in peacetime.

He peered through the gloom and rain and tried to decide exactly where to put such an inn. The best spot, he decided, would be right at the fork, between the west and north roads. He could claim a strip of land along the roadside from there to the river and build a landing for river traffic.

Or perhaps the inn should be right on the river? There might be some difficulty in claiming half a mile of road-side.

No, he decided, the river traffic would not be as important as the west road, since boatmen could sleep in their boats. If he could not have his landing, he was sure he would still get by with the land traffic.

How, he wondered, did one go about claiming a piece of land? Perhaps the soldiers would know, he thought. He headed eagerly for the bridge.

Not surprisingly, most of them were still asleep, but Lorret, the night man, was bored and tired and glad to talk. He knew nothing of any official methods, but made suggestions and provided a few materials.

By the time the rain stopped at mid-morning Valder had marked off his claim with wooden stakes and bundled grass, all marked with strips of green cloth, his name written on each stake and each cloth with char from the night's cookfire. He had paced off room enough for a large inn and a good-sized stable, a decent kitchen garden, and a yard and then arbitrarily doubled each dimension—after all, if the land was free, why stint? He had indeed claimed his landing site near the bridge, but had decided against taking the entire half mile of roadside. He did not really need it, after all, and there was no need to be greedy. His customers could come up the hill on the public highway readily enough.

That done, and with assurances from the soldiers that they would enforce his rights for him until his return, he set out for Azrad's Ethshar to hire a construction crew.

PART THREE

Valder the Innkeeper

CHAPTER 22

*V*alder *gazed at the room with calm satisfaction. It* was almost exactly as he had pictured it four months earlier, when he had first staked his claim to the land at the fork. The windows were shuttered, since he had not yet been able to buy glass for them, and the furniture was mostly mismatched and jury-rigged, the tables built of scrap and the chairs upholstered in war surplus tent canvas, but the wide stone hearth, the stone chimney, oaken mantel, and the white plastered walls were all just as he had wanted them. A fire blazed on the hearth, keeping out the autumn chill, and a dozen lamps lighted the room.

In the rest of the inn, every room, upstairs or down, was taken for the night, and no one had complained of the accommodations or the fare at supper—even though the only wine he had been able to get was truly horrible, and as yet he had no ale at all. The most popular beverage was river-water filtered through five layers of canvas, surely an unheard of situation in any roadside inn!

He wondered whether he should sink a well. The river water seemed safe enough so far and did not taste bad at all, either before or after filtering, but he did not entirely trust it. There were just too many people upstream who might be pouring garbage, sewage, or poisons into it.

Geting ale and decent wine was more important, of course. He had appointed half a dozen of his erstwhile construction crew as agents and sent them out looking, in various directions, for suppliers. One was permanently posted in Azrad's Ethshar at no pay, but with a promise of three pieces of gold if he found a reliable supplier—a sizable sum now that prices had come back down to more reasonable levels, though they were still higher than in wartime. The other five had been given expense money and scattered across the Hegemony of the Three Ethshars, as the name now seemed to be, and the Small Kingdoms.

Valder's original supply of money had given out long ago, since he had paid generously at first in the interest of speed; but even before his inn had a roof, customers had been at his door, eager to pay for a night's shelter. He foresaw no difficulty in earning a living and paying for any improvements he might care to make.

Of course, the original flood of traffic had not lasted. Within a month of the war's end, the southbound flow into Azrad's Ethshar had thinned to a trickle. By then, however, the northbound exodus was in full flood, as the new arrivals finally convinced themselves that the city was not the golden land of limitless opportunity.

That, too, had passed, and Valder had had a bad six-night or two when business slowed drastically. He had used it as an excuse to cut his bloated, overpaid crew in half, and then in half again. Initially, he had wanted as many men as he could find work for, since speed in construction was more important than economy, and hauling stone from the riverbed took plenty of manpower. Once the walls and roof were in place, however, speed was no longer essential, as most customers asked no more than to get in out of the rain and the cool night air. His sixty-man crew, lured by the prospect of a copper piece a day, free water, and whatever food he could find for them, was an unwanted expense.

He had been glad to be rid of most of them. A man did not require much in the way of character or intelligence to drag rocks from the riverbed to the building site and drop them in place, so he had just taken anyone who volunteered when he shouted out his offer. The interior work, furniture, and finishing, however, called for more skill, skill that most of the men did not have and could not learn quickly.

He had kept a crew of fifteen, even when that meant paying out more than he took in—he had refused to give in to temptation and had set his charges to his customers roughly at wartime levels, rather than the absurd rates that had been asked in Azrad's Ethshar during the great confusion. He had been convinced that traffic would increase again and that the completion of the inn would prove worthwhile. He had been right. Refugees and wandering veterans were no longer arriving in any significant numbers, though a few still drifted in every so often, but merchants and tradesmen had begun to appear, bringing supplies into the city or skills and goods out. He had bought the foul stuff that passed for wine from one such commercial traveler, and the surplus canvas had come from an enterprising young ex-sergeant who had bought up hundreds of old tents cheap when the border camps were disbanded.

After the merchants had come the farmers bound for market and the would-be farmers searching for land. As yet, the farmers were few and their produce unimpressive, and the would-be farmers were invariably poverty-stricken, but Valder was sure that within a year that would change dramatically. The war had not ended until well after planting season, after all, so that crops had not been planted on schedule.

Now his income once again exceeded his expenses, though not by as much as he might have liked. He had cut his payroll once again by dispatching his six agents. Of the nine men who remained, seven were making other plans. One had taken a fancy to the river and was waiting for a berth on a barge. Another was saving his pay and working odd jobs for guests with plans to become a brewer, which pleased Valder quite well, as that might assure him of a supplier. The other five were still vague, but three had been foresighted enough to stake out claims on land in the vicinity while the opportunities were still there, and all were among the cleverer and more skilled of his original group; Valder had no doubt they would find suitable work when the inn was finished.

One of the two men planning to remain was Tandellin. Valder had been utterly astonished to find his old friend among the mob in the Hundred-Foot Field, and delighted as well, and had wasted no time in signing him on with the other volunteers. Sarai had been with him, and, although she was too small to be of any real help in hauling stone, she had helped out considerably on lighter jobs. She had been the only woman on the site, and some of the other men had grumbled mildly about her presence and exclusive attachment to Tandellin, but there had been no serious problems involved.

Only after three days of work had the couple been willing to admit that they had followed Valder, taking the next ship after his, rather than turning up in Azrad's Ethshar by sheer coincidence. Tandellin would give no reason, but Sarai explained, "You always seemed to know what you were doing, and nobody else did. The moment you had your pay, you were gone, as if you actually knew where you were going to go and what you were going to do. We had been sitting around for three days arguing, without coming up with a single idea we could agree on, until you left—then we agreed to come see what you were doing, and here we are." She shivered. "Things looked pretty bad there in the city, when we lost track of you."

It came as a surprise to Valder that he had seemed to know what he was doing, as he certainly had not thought he did, but when he said as much, Sarai simply pointed out that everything had worked out well enough.

Valder had to agree with that.

Tandellin and Sarai were not the only ones to follow Valder's lead. His inn acted as a spark or a seed; once he had claimed his piece of land, others took to the idea, and farmhouses were abuilding all along the highway between the bridge and the city. Customers told him that other inns were springing up, as well, further up the road.

He was pleased by that, particularly by the proliferation of farmers determined to plow under the grassland. He had gotten by at first by hunting small game and fishing, or by buying what others caught, but his supplies were always low. Some food came down the highway or the river, mostly fruit from the orchards around Sardiron of the Waters, in what had been the southwestern part of the Northern Empire, and Valder bought what he could afford of that to augment his catches. He suspected that people were starving in Azrad's Ethshar, though he knew supplies were reaching the city by ship. If farms were in production all along the highway and throughout the countryside, that would change.

For the present, he was getting by, and the future looked bright, with the inn built and paying customers in every chamber. He was well pleased as he looked about the dining room. Wirikidor hung above the fireplace on pegs driven into the stone; he smiled at it. He had no intention of ever drawing it again, and looking at it now only reminded him of the unpleasantness he had left behind and how lucky he was to be free of it and doing well. He had never thought he would be fortunate enough to outlive the war, but here he was, alive and thriving, and the Northern Empire was no more than a memory. The sword's enchantment might complicate his life eventually, with its supposed grant of immortality but not freedom from harm, but that was far from urgent. He enjoyed being an innkeeper, able to hear the news of the World from his guests without leaving home.

A knock sounded, though everyone else in the inn had retired. Valder turned and hurried to the door, hoping that, late as the hour was, the new arrival would be someone selling something he could use. He would settle for a customer willing to sleep on the dining room floor, though.

Two men stood on the threshold, wearing the tattered remnants of Ethsharitic uniforms, huddled together against the cold wind. As yet, no snow had fallen this year, and the locals assured him that often years would pass without a single flake in this region, but winter was assuredly coming and the winds were cold, even this far south.

"Come in!" Valder said, trying to conceal his disappointment. Ragged as they were, these two were not likely to be selling anything, nor to have enough money to be worthwhile as customers. Still, an innkeeper had obligations; everyone must be made welcome.

The two entered. One made directly for the fire on the hearth, but the other hesitated, staring at his host.

Disconcerted, Valder stared back. Something was very familiar about the man. Undoubtedly they had met somewhere before, but Valder could not place where.

"I know you," the man said.

"Valder the Innkeeper, at your service," Valder replied. "Welcome to the Inn at the Bridge." He saw no reason to deny his identity if the man did know him; but on the other hand, he was not in the mood for reminiscing about good old days that had, for him at any rate, been relatively miserable. Calling himself an innkeeper made clear that he lived in the present, not a nostalgic, glorious past such as many veterans seemed to prefer.

Of course, peace appeared to have treated this pair far worse than the war had; they were thin and hungry, and their clothes had obviously been lived in for months, probably months without shelter.

"Valder?" The man stared at him. "You mean Valder of Kardoret?"

"That was I," Valder admitted.

"The man who killed a *shatra* in single combat?"

Startled, Valder asked, "How do you know about that?"

"I was with the party that found you standing over the corpse. Gods, that was a weird thing! That body had all this strange black stuff in it—I'll never forget it. When we burned it, it stank like nothing I have ever smelled. And it was *you*! It was! You look different now, without the uniform, and you've put on a little weight, I think, but it's you."

"Yes, it is," Valder agreed.

"And you're an innkeeper now? Valder of the Magic Sword, an innkeeper?"

"Better than starving, isn't it? The war is over—not much call for magic swords anymore." He smiled.

The other grimaced. "Anything is better than starving, I'd say. I've had a little more experience of it than I like. Still, a man like you—you weren't any common soldier, you could have made your way in the World."

"I *am* making my way in the World. I own this inn and the landing on the river, don't I?"

"Oh, but you could have been *rich*! A man who could kill a demon, you could have done almost anything!"

"It was the magic sword that killed the *shatra*, not me; I'm happy here."

The man shrugged. "If you say so," he said.

"I say so. Now, what can I get you? Supper was over hours ago, and there isn't any ale, but I can find some cold food, if you like, and we have wine and good clean water."

The man looked embarrassed. He called out to his companion, "Hey, Tesra! Have you got any money?"

Valder sighed inwardly. These two were obviously not going to make him rich.

Tesra produced five copper bits, and after a little dickering Valder conceded that that was a fair price for staying the night on the floor by the hearth with a meal of scraps and water. When that was settled and the two tattered veterans were gnawing on pigeon bones—rabbits had become quite scarce, due to extensive hunting, but pigeons made a decent pie—Valder asked, "Where are you headed? You must have been on the road quite some time."

Tesra looked up at him. "We thought we'd try our luck in Azrad's Ethshar; it's been no good anywhere else. We've been on the road since the war ended, been up to Sardiron of the Waters and on through the Passes, and then came down the Great River from there."

Valder felt a twinge of guilt. "Was that five bits your last money? Ethshar's expensive these days, and, from what I hear, there isn't much work."

"Oh, we'll get by," said Selmer, the man who had recognized Valder. "We're not picky."

Valder shrugged. He had made his gesture, given his

warning; if the two of them chose not to heed it, that was not his problem. Rather than continuing with the subject, he asked about Sardiron. He had heard of the town, captured almost intact from the Northern Empire when it fell, but he knew little about it.

He talked with the pair until almost dawn. Tesra fell asleep, utterly exhausted, while the conversation continued, but Selmer lasted several hours before his eyelids, too, drooped. Finally Valder rose and left the two of them asleep on the floor. He left a brief note for Parl, the man who was to handle morning business, saying the two had paid in advance for the night but not for breakfast, and then retired.

When he awoke, the sun was high in the eastern sky, and the two veterans were gone. Parl reported that they had left an hour or so earlier, hoping to reach the city by nightfall.

Valder knew they would not manage it; one had to leave the inn within an hour after dawn to reach Ethshar before dark, traveling on foot. He wished them well and forgot about them.

At least, he forgot about them for a sixnight or so.

Supper was being dished out, a thick chowder and stale bread being all that Valder had on hand, when a late arrival knocked. Valder happened to be free, so he answered the door himself, admitting a party of four. First in the door was a young woman in flamboyant red velvet trimmed with white fur; behind her came two huge men wearing what looked like military uniforms, but in a pattern and color Valder had never seen before. Last came another woman, this one short and plump and wearing blue satin.

"Welcome, all!" Valder said. "Supper is just being served, if you would care to join us. The meal is a copper each with water, or a silver bit with wine. I'm afraid we have no ale or strong spirits."

"We did not come here to eat," the woman in red announced.

"A room, then? We have a few still available, two coppers the night."

"We are looking for someone."

Valder noticed that the woman spoke with a peculiar accent. He had taken it to be nervousness at first, but now thought she might be from somewhere where the language was spoken differently. He had noticed a slight difference between the people of Azrad's south and Gor's northwest previously, but this was far more marked. It made judging her tone difficult. Valder guessed she was from some obscure corner of the Small Kingdoms.

"This is my inn," he said. "And I want no trouble. You will have to tell me whom you're looking for and why."

"We seek Valder of the Magic Sword."

The woman insisted on speaking quite loudly, and the entire population of the room—three of Valder's employees and fourteen guests—were now listening closely, the chowder forgotten for the moment.

"I'm Valder, now the Innkeeper," he said. "Come inside and close the door." He had no idea why anybody might be looking for him and was not at all sure he wanted to find out. This group hardly looked like anything Gor might send after him. He remembered Tesra and Selmer, who had insisted on calling him Valder of the Magic Sword, and wondered if they had anything to do with it.

He was about to suggest a more private conference when the thought struck him that Gor of the Rocks might not care to send anyone obvious on a mission to deal with his former assassin. Gor was tricky enough to have contrived a group like this. Valder decided abruptly that privacy was not called for. When the woman in blue had closed the door, he led the way to an unoccupied table and gestured for the newcomers to sit.

The woman in red hesitated, and the others were all obviously following her lead. "Is there no place more private?" she asked.

That convinced Valder that he did not want to be alone with his group. "No," he said. "We speak here if you wish to speak with me at all."

Reluctantly, the woman in red nodded and took a seat; her companions followed, and Valder, too, sat down.

"I am Sadra of Pethmor, Pethmor being the rightful capital of all Ethshar. We have come seeking your help."

Valder interpreted this to mean that Pethmor was indeed one of the Small Kingdoms. Most of them claimed to be the ancient capital. "What sort of help?" he asked.

"We came to Azrad's city to find someone who might be able to help us, and two men there told us where you might be found. They said that you were the greatest fighter that had ever lived, that you had slain a northern demon in single combat. Is this true?"

"No." Valder was reluctant to elaborate.

"No?" Sadra was taken aback. "But you are Valder of the Magic Sword? They *swore*..."

"They swore? What did they swear?"

"One of them swore that you had slain a demon..."

"Oh. Well, yes, I did kill a *shatra*, which is half demon, but I'm hardly a great fighter. I had a magic sword." It seemed unwise to mention that he still had the sword and that it was in fact hanging in plain sight not ten yards away.

"Ah. The sword is gone, then?"

Valder shrugged.

"Of course it is, or you would not be an innkeeper— but perhaps you could get it back? Or perhaps you might help anyway?"

"You still haven't said what sort of help you want."

"Oh, it is quite simple. There is a dragon, a rather large one, that has been scorching the fields..." Again, as seemed to be a habit with her, she let the sentence trail off.

"You want me to kill a dragon for you?"

"Yes, exactly."

Valder put his palms on the table as if to rise. "I'm sorry, Sadra, but I can't help you. I wouldn't stand a chance; the only time I ever fought a dragon single-handed, I wound up running for my life."

"Then you have fought dragons before?"

"Just a little one and, I told you, it almost killed me. I will not fight your dragon for you. Talk it out of burning your fields, or hire a dragon-tamer from the city, if no one will fight it. Now, will you have supper here, or a room for the night, or will you be going?"

The party from Pethmor stayed for supper and for the

night, and for breakfast as well. Sadra made several more attempts to enlist Valder as a dragon slayer, but without success.

In the morning, as she was about to depart, Sadra stopped and turned back. "Selmer told me you were a hero," she said. "That you would be glad of an excuse to give up this dreary inn. I think he misjudged you badly."

Valder nodded agreement. "I think you're right. I like it here."

Sadra nodded in turn, plainly disgusted, and left.

Valder thought that was the end of the matter—until the next party turned up, trying to recruit him. This group was not after a dragon, but intended to loot the ruined cities of the north and wanted to hire Valder as a guard. A few surviving *shatra* were said to linger still amid the ruins, and what better protector could they have than the only man who had ever slain one in fair fight?

Valder got rid of them politely and marveled at how nobody acknowledged the part the sword's magic had played. They all credited him with far more prowess than he actually possessed. They wanted to believe in heroes, not ordinary, everyday magic.

Valder was no adventurer, no great warrior; he was just an innkeeper and glad to be one. He said as much to anyone who asked. Yes, he had a magic sword once, and yes, he had killed a *shatra* with it, and yes, he even admitted to having served as an assassin when that story finally surfaced—but all he was now was an innkeeper.

That was what he told the doddering wizard who wanted to hire him to fetch the ingredients for a certain unspecified spell and what he told the self-proclaimed mercenary captain who was trying to raise a company of war heroes to fight in the continuing border squabbles in the Small Kingdoms. From what Valder had heard from his guests, these little conflicts were too small to be considered real wars. The "captain," who had never risen above sergeant in the Great War, believed a small group of experienced men could make a big difference. Valder suspected he was quite correct in that, but was not interested in being one of those men and said as much.

He liked being an innkeeper. He enjoyed hearing his guests talk of their travels, their hopes, their goals. He enjoyed seeing the weary to bed, feeding the hungry, and serving drink to the thirsty, and watching their faces relax as their problems faded. As an innkeeper, he took no great risks. True, he made no great gains, but that did not bother him. He had not killed anyone since the end of the war, nor had anyone seriously attempted to kill him—he discounted a few drunken threats from men who could barely stand, let alone fight. The worst problem he ever confronted as an innkeeper, once he had found reliable suppliers of food and drink, was an occasional boisterous drunk, and the one advantage he saw in his growing fame as Valder of the Magic Sword was that troublemakers who had heard of his reputation avoided him. As the inn's proprietor, he was his own man; admittedly, he took orders from his customers, but only when he chose to. It was nothing like the military.

Yes, he liked being an innkeeper. It was infinitely more enjoyable than being an assassin or an adventurer. He preferred Wirikidor over the mantel, not on his belt.

He had to repeat this often. The talkative Selmer and the various guests who had overheard his conversation with Sadra or with others who had tried to coax him away spread his fame far and wide. In general, Valder did not mind; he rather enjoyed being famous and suspected that his reputation drew business that might otherwise have passed up the Inn at the Bridge in favor of other, newer inns that had sprung up along the highways.

He turned down offers that ranged from dull and dangerous to downright bizarre, requests for aid from silk-robed aristocrats and starving children—the latter leaving disappointed, but always well fed. He refused to rescue princesses, slay dragons, depose tyrants, locate lost siblings, kill pirates, loot tombs, battle wizards, terrorize witches, dispose of demons, settle boundary disputes, and search for everything from ancient magical treasures to a missing cat. Whenever possible, he tried to suggest someone who might serve in his stead. He was dismayed that, even safely sheathed, Wirikidor was still affecting his life.

He suspected that nobody ever believed him when he said that he enjoyed innkeeping, that many thought him a coward or a fraud. When a messenger from Gor of the Rocks came to ask if he had reconsidered his retirement, Valder turned him down politely, as he had all the rest, and was relieved when the man departed peacefully, apparently convinced that Valder was a harmless coward.

Nobody, not even Tandellin, believed that all he wanted was to be an innkeeper, but it was the entire truth.

CHAPTER 23

The Inn at the Bridge flourished. Valder flourished with it, and in fact all the World seemed to be doing well once the initial confusion had passed.

In 5000 the three overlords of the Hegemony of the Three Ethshars announced that the last northern stragglers had been eliminated and the last vestiges of the Empire destroyed. In celebration, the annual Festival that began 5001 ran for seven days instead of the traditional five. A few realists pointed out that this corrected astrological errors resulting from wartime neglect of the calendar, but they were generally ignored in the widespread merry-making.

That was the year that Valder finally got glass panes in all his windows.

In 5002 the northern territories surrounding Sardiron of the Waters refused to acknowledge the rule of the Hegemony when tax collectors came around. Instead they set themselves up as an array of baronies under the erstwhile officers of the occupying armies, with a high council meeting at Sardiron itself. The triumvirate, well aware that the people of the Hegemony wanted no more war, did nothing about it. The rumor circulated that Azrad and Gor had decided to wait, outvoting Anaran, in hopes that the baronies would tear themselves apart in petty rivalries as the Small Kingdoms had done, allowing the Hegemony to move in and pick up the pieces. If the rumor was true, this appeared to be a miscalculation; no reports came of internecine strife in the north. Instead, caravans came down the highways and barges down the Great River, filling Valder's guest rooms and his purse.

Valder heard all the news and all the rumors from his guests, but paid little attention. That was the year he finally considered his cellar to be adequate, with thirty wines, a dozen ales and beers, and both brandy and *oushka* in stock. One of his former workmen now ran a brewery and provided much of his supply. His staff was down to just himself, Sarai, Tandellin, and Parl.

By 5005 virtually all the veterans were settled, and the offer of free land was discontinued. Almost all the old battlefields were now farms, and the vast grasslands that had stretched from the Great River to the western ocean had been plowed under and sown with corn and wheat and barley. Ethshar of the Rocks and Ethshar of the Sands were real cities now, rivals—but never quite equals—of Azrad's Ethshar, now called Ethshar of the Spices in recognition of its most profitable trade. The Small Kingdoms were still splintering and fighting amongst themselves, and most of the people of the Hegemony had come to think of them as barbaric. It was hard to remember that they had once been the heart of civilization, Old Ethshar. But then, nobody mentioned Old Ethshar any more. The past was forgotten, and the Hegemony and its three capitals were the only Ethshar.

That was the year that Valder tried unsuccessfully to start a ferry service in competition with Azrad's toll bridge. A torch "accidentally" dropped from the bridge onto the ferry one night and burned it down to the waterline, putting an end to that enterprise. Valder decided against rebuilding; the next stray torch might have hit his inn. The walls were stone, but the roof was thatch.

In 5009 the northern coast followed Sardiron's lead and declared itself the independent Kingdom of Tintallion, with joint capitals on the mainland and on the island from which it took its name. Valder calculated, after much discussion with travelers who had been there, that the mainland capital was just about on the site of the camp where he had served prior to the desperate enemy drive to the sea that had left him stranded alone in the woods.

That was the year an incompletely tamed dragon accidentally burned down Valder's stable. Terrified by the results of its actions, the dragon had smashed its way out through the wall and vanished, never to be seen again. Fortunately, the dragon's owner did not get away in time to avoid a generous cash settlement for the damages, and the only injuries were to two boys knocked down and bruised when they attempted to catch the other animals fleeing through the hole left by the dragon's departure.

In 5011 Anaran of the Sands died at the age of sixty-three, and, after a month or so of widespread concern, Azrad and Gor declared Anaran's ten-year-old son Edaran of Ethshar to be the new overlord of Ethshar of the Sands. Since would-be commanders could no longer prove themselves in battle, the surviving overlords had decided to make their positions hereditary. Nobody seemed to object, Valder noted, and it did ensure peaceful transitions. Azrad and Gor both had sons to succeed them, and no one seemed very concerned about having a mere child as coruler of the Hegemony.

That was the year that someone tried to rob the Inn at the Bridge.

It was a slow night in deep winter, the fourth day of the month of Icebound. Enough snow was falling to discourage the neighbors from dropping in for a meal or a drink, and no trade came down the highway from the north at this time of year. The river never froze this far south, but, as it happened, no boats had stopped that day, and no travelers from the Small Kingdoms to the east or the Hegemony's other cities to the west had happened by. Tandellin and Sarai had gone home to the house they had built for themselves on the other side of the highway, and Parl had gone off, as he often did, with a young woman. He might not be back for days, but in winter he was rarely needed. Valder sat alone in the dining hall, keeping the fire alive and contemplating the coals, not thinking about anything in particular.

A knock sounded; startled, Valder looked up. He did not particularly want to leave the hearth and get a faceful of cold air, so he bellowed, "It isn't locked! Come in!"

For a moment he thought that the latch must have frozen or the new arrivals had not heard him, but then the door swung open.

He did not much like the look of the two men who came in. The first one was short, with dark hair that looked curiously lopsided; it took Valder a moment to figure out that the man had been wounded on the scalp and that no hair grew from the resulting scar tissue, leaving him partially bald on one side and not the other.

The second man was huge, perhaps six and a half feet tall and disproportionately broad. Both wore battered breastplates—not standard army-issue—and carried old swords on their belts, unusual in these peaceful times. The larger man had one of the strange, black, Northern helmets jammed onto his head, the first such helmet Valder had seen in years. Both had the look of men who were perpetually broke and always blaming others for it, though what money they acquired would invariably go for *oushka* or inept gambling. Valder had seen enough of the sort and did not like them. Such men usually felt that because they had served a few years in the army the World owed them a living.

Valder judged this pair to be his own age or a year or two younger—mid-thirties, certainly. That would mean they had only served a few years each, probably not a decade between them. No one owed them anything.

Still, he was an innkeeper. "Welcome!" he said. "Come in and get warm! What can I get you?"

The two looked around for a moment. The big man remembered belatedly to close the door.

"Cold out there," the small man remarked. "Have you got something that will warm a man's gut?"

"Brandy or *oushka*," Valder answered. "Two coppers, or a silver piece for a bottle."

"*Oushka*," the little man replied, as Valder had expected. These two did not look like brandy drinkers.

He nodded and headed for the kitchen. He had not expected any customers tonight and had stored the keg away earlier than usual. "Make yourselves comfortable," he called back over his shoulder. He decided silently to be as quick as he could, so that he would be back before this pair could cause any trouble. There was little to steal in the big room, but they might decide it would be fun to smash a few tables.

"Hey, innkeeper," the big man called after him before he had reached the door. "Is your name Valder?"

Valder stopped and turned. "What if it is?"

The big man shrugged. "Nothing; we just heard that this place belonged to someone named Valder of the Magic Sword, supposed to be a war hero."

Valder sighed inwardly. These two were obviously not just going to express polite interest in his wartime experiences. They undoubtedly wanted something from him, probably aid in some unsavory scheme, and might get ugly about it.

Well, he could take care of himself. "I'm Valder," he admitted. "I was in the war; I fought and I killed a few northerners, but I don't know that I was a hero."

"What was this magic sword, then?"

"I had a magic sword; got it from a crazy hermit out on the west coast."

The big man waggled a shoulder in the direction of the hearth. "Is that the sword, up there?"

Valder did not like the sound of that. "What if it is?"

"Hey, just asking. I never saw a magic sword up close before."

"Well, that's it. Take a look, if you want, but I wouldn't try touching it." He hoped the vague threat would discourage the pair. He was not particularly worried. Unless he had been sleepwalking and killing people without knowing it, nobody else would be able to draw Wirikidor, and no other weapon could kill him.

"What about that *oushka*?" the smaller man demanded.

"I'll get it," Valder answered. He marched out through the door to the kitchen, leaving it open so that he could hear anything that happened.

He heard nothing but low voices and quiet little bumps that could be chairs being moved about. That was fine, then, if the two were settling down at a table. He filled two crystal tankards with *oushka*. Most inns avoided using glass due to its high cost and breakable nature, but Valder was convinced that strong spirits did not taste right in anything else and had gone to considerable expense to have a wizard shatterproof his glassware. He had thought the expense was worthwhile, as his customers appreciated such nice little touches. Some of them did, anyway.

He arranged the tankards on a tray and headed back into the main room, where he found the big man standing on a chair on the hearth, tugging at Wirikidor.

Since Valder had had no intention of ever taking the sword down, he had wired it securely to pegs set into the stonework. He suspected that, if he had not, the two would already have gotten it down and vanished into the snow.

"Oh, demons drag you to Hell!" he said. He did not want to deal with this sort of unpleasantness. He put the tray down on the nearest table and demanded, "Leave that sword alone! You can't use it anyway."

At the sound of his voice the small man whirled, drawing his sword. The big man heaved at Wirikidor's scabbard, and with a twang of snapping wire ripped it from its place.

"Oh, we can't?" the small man said.

"No, you can't," Valder replied. "Ever hear of the Spell of True Ownership?"

"No," the little thief said. "And I wouldn't believe it if I did. If that sword's magic, I can use it."

"Go ahead and try," Valder replied. "Try and draw it." He suppressed a sudden flash of terror at the possibility that Darrend and his compatriots had somehow miscalculated the duration of the sword's attachment to him.

The smaller man did not move. He remained facing

Valder, his sword at ready, as he said, "Draw it, Hanner."

Hanner was trying to draw it, without success. "I can't," he said. "I think he's glued it into the scabbard."

"No glue," Valder said. "Magic. It's part of the enchantment on it."

"I think we'll take it anyway," the small thief said.

"It will come back to me; that's part of the spell."

"Oh, is it? How nice for you. What if you're dead, though? We didn't come here just for the sword, innkeeper. You must have a tidy little heap of money tucked away somewhere. I don't think you'll be geting much business tonight; if we kill you now, we'll have until dawn to find where you hide it. And even if we don't find it, we'll still have the sword and we can sell that for a few bits of gold, whether we can draw it or not. If you help us out, make the sword work for us and tell us where your money is, we might let you live."

"You can't kill me," Valder replied.

"No? What's going to stop us? There are two of us, with swords that aren't enchanted but they've got good edges nonetheless. You're all alone and unarmed, unless you've slipped a kitchen knife under your tunic. We've been watching this place. You haven't got a single customer, and your helpers left hours ago."

Valder felt a twinge of uneasiness. His situation *did* look bad. The only thing in his favor was the magic of a sword that had not been drawn in more than a dozen years—and an untested aspect of the enchantment, at that. The army wizards had said that he could not be killed, but he had naturally never put it to the test. He stood for a moment, trying to think of something to say. Nothing came.

"Hanner," the small thief said, "I think it's time we convinced Valder of the Magic Sword to help us out, don't you?"

Hanner grinned. "I think you're right," he said. He took Wirikidor in his left hand and drew his own sword with his right. Side by side, the two thieves advanced slowly across the room, winding between the tables without ever taking their eyes from Valder's face.

Valder watched them come, tried to decide whether there was any point in retreating into the kitchen, tried to think of something he might use as a weapon, and watched Wirikidor, clutched in the big man's hand. The thief, Valder thought, was making a mistake; the smart thing to do would have been to leave Wirikidor behind somewhere, well out of reach. He remembered the odd compulsion that had made people bring him the sword whenever it left his possession back in General Karannin's camp and wondered if Hanner was aware that he was holding the scabbard.

Idiotically, he also found himself wondering what the smaller thief's name was.

As the two drew near, Valder moved as quickly as he could, snatching up the tray of *oushka* and flinging it at the pair. Two swords flashed, and tray and tankards were knocked harmlessly aside, spraying good liquor across the floor. The crystal vessels bounced in a truly alarming manner, but the thieves were not distracted by this unnatural behavior. Either they had seen enchanted glassware before, or they were so intent on their victim that they had not even noticed anything unusual.

All Valder's effort had done was prove that both men knew how to use swords and that the wizard who had charmed the tankards had not cheated him. He stepped back, not toward the kitchen, but toward the wall.

The two advanced another few steps, then stopped. Hanner's sword inched up to hover near Valder's throat, while the other's blade was pointed at his belly.

"Now, innkeeper," the small man said, "tell us about that sword and, while you're talking, tell us where you keep your money."

Valder watched from the corner of his eye as Hanner's left hand moved forward, apparently without its owner's knowledge; his own right hand was open and ready. "The sword's name is Wirikidor, which means 'slayer of warriors.' Nobody knows exactly what the spells on it are, because the wizard who made them vanished, but they're all linked to a Spell of True Ownership, so that nobody can use it except me, until I die." He was talking primarily to keep the two thieves occupied; Wirikidor's hilt was less than a foot from his hand.

Suddenly he lunged for it, calling out, "Wirikidor!"

Hanner tried to snatch it away as he realized what was occurring. Valder was never sure exactly how it happened, whether the sword had really leaped from its sheath under its own power or whether he had made a lucky grab, but the sword was in his hand, sliding smoothly out of the scabbard.

Hanner reacted with incredible speed, chopping at Valder's wrist with his own blade. Wirikidor twisted about in a horribly unnatural fashion, so that Valder felt as if his wrist were breaking, but it successfully parried the thief's blow.

The smaller thief was not wasting any time; his sword plunged toward Valder's belly. Valder dodged sideways, but not quite fast enough; the blade ripped through his tunic and drew a long, deep cut in his side. Blood spilled out, and pain tore through Valder's body. He hardly saw what happened next.

Wirikidor, now that it was free again, seemed to be enjoying itself. It flashed brilliantly in the lamplight as it swept back and forth, parrying attacks from both thieves. Valder made no attempt to direct it; his hand went where the sword chose to go.

The character of the fight quickly altered; rather than two swordsmen bearing down on a mere innkeeper, it became two swordsmen fighting for their lives against a supernatural fury.

Hanner's guard slipped for an instant; Wirikidor cut his throat open. A return slice removed his head entirely, spraying blood in all directions.

With that, Wirikidor lost all interest, and Valder found himself in a duel to the death with a swordsman smaller than himself but far more skilled and obviously much more practiced, not to mention partly armored. Realization of his peril helped him to ignore the intense pain in his side as he concentrated on parrying a new attack.

The small thief, noticing a change, grinned. "You're

getting tired, innkeeper—or has the sword's magic been used up?"

Valder tried a bluff. "Nothing's used up, thief," he said. "I just thought you might prefer to live. Go now, and I won't kill you. Your partner's dead; isn't that enough?"

"Hanner's dead?" In the intensity of his concentration on the fight the thief had failed to comprehend that. He glanced at his comrade's headless corpse and was obviously shaken by what he saw.

Valder seized the opportunity and swept Wirikidor in under the other man's guard, aiming just below the breast-plate.

What should have been a killing stroke was easily deflected as the man recovered himself and made a swift downward parry. Still, the attack disconcerted him, and he stepped back.

Valder pressed his advantage, but the thief met his onslaught easily. Even so, Valder noticed that the man was no longer taking the offensive, but only defending himself.

"I'm holding the sword back," Valder lied. "But the demon in the steel is getting stronger. I don't like feeding it more than one soul at a time; it might get *too* strong someday. Go now, while I can still control it." He was grateful for the popularity of legends about vampiric swords.

The thief glanced at Wirikidor, then at the body on the floor, and his nerve broke. "Keep it away from me!" he screamed as he turned and ran for the door.

Valder let him go, but quickly wiped Wirikidor's blade on Hanner's tunic, then picked the scabbard up off the floor and sheathed the weapon. If the thief returned, he wanted to be able to draw the sword again and use its magic.

The thief showed no sign of returning. The pain in his side was growing with every movement, but Valder made it across the room and slammed the door that the fleeing man had left standing open. He leaned against it, tempted just to slide down into oblivion on the floor, but he forced himself to pull off his tunic and wrap it around himself, forming a makeshift bandage over the wound. That done, he looked around the room, at the broken wires on the pegs above the mantel, at the severed head rolled into one corner, at the lifeless corpse by the kitchen door, and at the blood, Hanner's and his own, that was spattered everywhere. He looked down at the sheathed sword he held.

"Damn that hermit," he said.

Then he fainted.

CHAPTER 24

The door hit him in the side and he awoke in agony.
He rolled over, groaning, away from the door and whatever was pushing in against it.

Tandellin slipped through the opening and looked down to see what was blocking him.

"Gods!" he said. "What happened?" He bent down to try and help.

Valder looked up at him and feebly waved him away. "I'll be all right, I think," he said. "I need something to drink."

"Right," Tandellin said, "I'll get you some ale." He looked up to see where the nearest keg might be, and for the first time noticed the rest of the room.

"Gods!" he said again and then decided that that wasn't strong enough. "By all the gods in the sky, sea, and earth, Valder, what happened here?"

"Ale," Valder said. He did not feel up to explaining yet.

"Oh, yes," Tandellin agreed. He stood and headed for the kitchen, making a careful detour around Hanner's corpse and the surrounding pool of blood. Valder sank back and closed his eyes until he heard footsteps returning.

He opened his eyes and tried to sit up, with his back to the wall. After a brief struggle, he managed it and accepted the mug Tandellin offered.

The ale helped. After he drank it, his throat no longer seemed to be stuffed with felt and his breath was no longer actively painful, if he kept it shallow. His side was still roaring with pain, and his head throbbed, but he felt better.

"More," he said, holding out the mug.

Tandellin fetched more.

After that, Valder felt almost human again. He arranged himself more comfortably against the wall. "Know any healing spells?" he asked.

Tandellin shook his head.

"Know any good wizards who might? Or witches, or theurgists?"

"I can find someone—but healing spells are expensive."

"I have money," Valder said. "That's not a problem."

"You weren't robbed? There was just the one man?"

"There were two, but the other one ran. I don't think he took anything, unless he sneaked in the back way while I was unconscious, and I doubt that he did that, because, in that case, he would have tried to finish me off."

"Oh. Well, you certainly took care of that one; his head's clean off. Was he the one who wounded you?"

"I know his head is off, Tan; I'm the one who took it off, remember? And it was the other one who cut me; they both attacked at once."

"Oh," Tandellin said again. "How sporting. What should we do with this one? We can't just leave him there."

"Of course not. Look, get me another mug of ale and see if there's something I can eat cold, and then you can start cleaning up. I think we can bury him out back; I don't want to take the trouble and the wood to build a proper pyre. I'm not very concerned about seeing that his soul is freed to the gods, if you see what I mean." He glanced down at Wirikidor, lying innocuously at his side, and a thought struck him.

"Leave the head, though. I think we'll put that on a pike out front, to discourage any other thieves who get ideas about this place." He had not seen a head on a pike in years, not since he was a boy, but he thought it would make for a fine warning.

"We'll probably have to sand down that floor to get the bloodstains off," Tandellin remarked.

"Might be easier just to replace the boards, or paint over them," Valder suggested.

The door behind him opened again, admitting Sarai. As was her custom, she had arrived later than Tandellin because she took charge of feeding their daughter, Sarai the Younger, before leaving home.

She looked down at Valder, sitting on the floor bare-chested with the bloodstained remnants of his tunic wrapped about his middle, then looked around the room, taking in the headless corpse, the spattered blood, and the general mess.

"I take it you had a rough night," she said.

Valder stared up at her for a moment, then burst out laughing. The laughter was cut short by renewed pain in his side, but he smiled up at her and said, "You could say that, yes."

After that, his problems somehow seemed less serious. He pulled himself up into a chair and supervised the cleaning up, the disposal of Hanner's body, and the disposition of the head. No pikes could be found anywhere in the inn, but Tandellin improvised one from a boathook from the landing and set it up outside, near enough that its connection with the inn would be apparent, but far enough away that odor would not be a problem. Below the head he tacked up a sign that read, "THIEF," in large black runes, in case anyone might miss the point.

When the inn was again fit for customers, Tandellin set out to find a wizard who could heal Valder's wound, leaving Sarai to attend to the handful of travelers who drifted in, despite the cold and slush. Valder himself did not feel up to moving about much. Instead, he sat back and watched and thought.

He had not expected anyone to try to steal Wirikidor, or for that matter to try robbing him at all, though he did keep a goodly supply of coin securely hidden in his own bedchamber. The possibility had simply never occurred to him.

That, he realized, had been foolish.

The thief's head would probably serve to discourage further attempts for a time, but it would also remind people that there might be something worth stealing. Something would have to be done about that.

He had heard that there were people in Ethshar of the Spices who would guard one's money, for a small fee; they called themselves bankers. That suddenly seemed like a good idea. He had enough gold and silver tucked away to tempt an entire horde of thieves, he realized. He had nothing in particular that he wanted to spend money on, now that the inn was properly finished and supplied, so it just accumulated. He would do something about that.

The only other theftworthy item, really, was Wirikidor. It was far too late to quash the stories of his magic sword, and he would never convince anyone it was gone while a sword still hung over the mantel. That meant he would have to dispose of it somehow, if he didn't want some young idiot to cut his throat while he slept in order to steal the fabled Valder's weapon. He would not die of a cut throat, if Wirikidor's enchantment held true, but he doubted he would enjoy the experience.

That was rather a shame; he had liked having it on display above the hearth.

The next question was what to do with the sword. Its magic was still strong and still as quirky and inconvenient as ever. He had not died, as the spell had promised he would not, despite losing an incredible amount of blood—but he had been seriously wounded. The sword would still fight for him, but only against men and only until he had killed one. The ownership spell still linked it to him;

he was not sure whether it had actually jumped into his hand, but Hanner had been unable to draw it, and he could not imagine any reason the thief would have been stupid enough to bring Wirikidor within reach had the spell not been working.

He shifted in his chair, and his side twinged. That reminded him of his wound all over again. What good was a magical spell that guaranteed his life, if he could still be cut to pieces? That might be worse than death. That infernal old hermit had promised the sword would protect him, but he thought he might well have been better off without any such protection as this. He smiled bitterly.

He should, he thought, have been able to avoid the blow. The little thief was a good swordsman, true, but Valder had once been at least competent, and he had possessed size, strength, and reach in his favor. He sighed. He was getting older and out of shape. He had not drawn a sword in more than a decade; no wonder he was out of practice! His reflexes had slowed, as well; he was thirty-seven, no longer a young man.

Not that the thief had been much younger, but even a few years could make a difference. Besides, the thief had obviously kept in practice.

Thirty-seven—he had not thought about his age much, but he was undeniably growing older. What did that mean as far as Wirikidor was concerned? Obviously the sword would not prevent him from aging, any more than it had saved him from being slashed. What would happen when old age came? Would he just deteriorate indefinitely, unable to die, growing weaker and weaker, losing sight and hearing, until he was little more than a vegetable? He had heard tales of men and women still hale and hearty past a hundred years of age—probably exaggerated—but, as he understood Wirikidor's enchantment, the spell had no time limit on it at all. He might live not just one century, but two or three or a dozen, if he never again drew the sword. No, not *might* live that long, but *would*. He could theoretically live forever—but would he want to, if he kept aging?

That was an unpleasant line of thought, one that did not bear further exploration just at present. He was only thirty-seven; he had decades yet before the question became really important.

He would, however, want to be very, very careful to avoid maiming or blinding or any other sort of permanent injury. He had once asked himself what sort of a life one should lead when one could live forever; he answered himself, "A cautious one."

For now, he intended to put Wirikidor somewhere out of sight, where it would tempt no one. He might bury it, or throw it in the river; he knew that the Spell of True Ownership would prevent it from being carried downstream away from him. He was sure that he would be able to recover it should he ever want to.

Perhaps, he thought, I should hire a wizard to break the spell and live out my life normally. The war is long over; why do I need a magic sword?

He remembered then that Darrend had thought the spell was unbreakable. Well, Darrend could have been wrong. It would undoubtedly take a very powerful wizard to break the spell, of course, and wizardry was expensive—not just because of the greed of its practitioners, but because so many of the ingredients needed for charms were so difficult to obtain. He recalled when a call had gone out, years earlier, for the hair of an unborn child, needed for some special spell Azrad had wanted performed; he wondered if any had ever been found. Other ingredients were said to be even more difficult to acquire. By ordinary standards he was well off, as the inn was successful, but, if he tried hiring high-order wizardry, his savings could easily vanish overnight.

He resolved to ask whatever wizard Tandellin might bring back about the possibilities of hiring powerful countercharms, but for the present he had no intention of actually having the spell broken. Wirikidor could be useful. Dangerous, but useful. He could safely draw it at least fifteen more times, perhaps as many as twenty-three, by his best count. That was still a safe margin.

When it dropped to single digits he might reconsider—or when his health started to go.

He would mention it to the wizard—assuming Tandellin did not bring a witch or theurgist instead—but for now he would simply bury the sword out back.

Two days later, his wounds magically healed, he did just that, working alone late at night by the light of a lantern, using a patch of ground that he had thawed with a bonfire that day.

The earthquake that followed a sixnight later was small and localized. It broke a few windows, emptied a shelf or two, sent a wine barrel rolling across the cellar floor, and, of course, split open the ground and flung Wirikidor up, to lie against the inn's kitchen door.

Valder considered throwing it in the river only until he had estimated how much damage would be caused by a flood big enough to carry the sword half a mile up the slope to the inn. The flood might not come, but he was not willing to risk it.

He wondered idly what a concealment spell would cost, but finally just tossed the sword under his bed and forgot about it.

CHAPTER 25

The news of the death of Gor of the Rocks in 5034 sent Valder into a brief depression. He had admired Gor once, but that admiration had largely worn away, starting with the overlord's request that Valder serve as his personal assassin in peacetime. The loss of the territory where Valder had served, when it became the Kingdom of Tintallion, had been another blow. The Hegemony of the Three Ethshars, which had once seemed so pure and all-embracing, had been corrupted and whittled down.

Gor's part in putting Edaran of Ethshar on his father's throne had not raised Valder's opinion any; it had left the entire central region that Anaran had once controlled at the mercy of Gor and Azrad, who had taxed it heavily. Gor had gotten an edge over Azrad by marrying off his son and heir, Goran of the Rocks, to Edaran's sister Ishta of the Sands in 5029, despite Ishta being eleven years older than the boy.

Over the years Gor had gone from being virtually an object of worship in Valder's eyes to just another conniving tyrant, but still, his death was not welcome news.

It removed any possibility of further difficulty over Valder's long-ago refusal to serve as an assassin, but it also removed the last vestige of his boyhood hero.

Gor had been only a dozen years older than Valder, at that, and yet he was dead of old age. Valder still felt strong and healthy, but Gor's death was another reminder that he, too, was growing old and that Wirikidor was doing nothing to prevent it.

Goran was now overlord of Ethshar of the Rocks, a young man in the prime of life—and he had not even been born until thirteen years after Valder built his inn. The thought of that oppressed him as he sat in a corner staring at the half-dozen patrons in the dining room, every one of them too young to remember the Great War.

Perhaps, Valder mused, part of the depression was because he had never taken a wife and, to the best of his knowledge, had sired no children. He had had women, certainly, but none had stayed. When he had been a soldier, none of his pairings had been expected to last by either party, because most did not in a soldier's life, and since becoming an innkeeper the only women he saw were those with the urge to travel. Some had stayed for a time, but all had eventually tired of the calm routine of the inn and had moved on.

It seemed a bit odd that Tandellin, who had always seemed rowdy and irrepressible as a youth, had been happily married for thirty-seven years, while Valder, who had always thought of himself as dull, ordinary, and predictable, had never married at all. It went against the traditional stereotypes.

He knew that he could have found a wife in Ethshar of the Spices, had he ever wanted to; but since the completion of the inn, he had never once returned to the city. He disliked the crowds and dust and knew that swords were no longer worn openly there, save by guardsmen and troublemakers, so that the necessity of carrying Wirikidor would mark him as a stranger.

He had always done well enough for himself without visiting the city. His lack of a family had never really bothered him; Tandellin and Sarai and their children had been his family in many ways.

He mulled all this over, sitting in the main room with a mug of ale that Sarai the Younger kept filled for him. As he glanced up to signal her for another pint, his eye fell on Wirikidor, hanging over the hearth.

The sword had lain neglected beneath his bed for scarcely a month before he restored it to its place. He had gotten tired of questions about its absence from familiar customers; too many had gone away convinced that the thieves had indeed gotten away with it, even if they had lost one of their number in doing so. Although that might have deterred thieves on the grounds that there was nothing left worth taking, it grated on Valder's pride. Besides, Valder had gotten tired of seeing the empty pegs and could not think of any way to remove them short of sawing them off as close to the stone as possible.

So he had returned Wirikidor to its place of honor, but devised another approach to the problem of removing temptation. He held contests whenever the inn was crowded, offering ten gold pieces to any man or woman who could draw the blade. This served as good entertainment on many a night and demonstrated to all present just how useless the sword was to anybody else. Rather than suppressing details of the sword's enchantment, as he had before, Valder made a point of explaining that it was permanently linked to him and that every time he drew it a man died.

That had discouraged any further attempts at theft. After all, who cares to risk one's life for a sword that nobody can use, knowing that, if it *does* leave its scabbard, someone will die—and that that someone will not be the sword's owner?

He had not mentioned that the spell was limited to another score or so of uses, however, nor that it would then turn on him. He did not mention his theoretical immortality, lest someone be tempted to test it.

He stared up at the dull gray of the scabbard and the tarnished black hilt. Wirikidor was such a very ordinary-looking sword; how could it have such power over him?

That is, if in fact it actually did. At times Valder was uncertain whether he should so trustingly accept the assessment made so long ago by General Karannin's magicians. Karannin was long dead; Valder had heard that he had been knifed ignominiously in a brawl in 4999 or 5000. He had no idea what had become of the wizards. Sometimes it seemed as if most of the World's wizards had vanished after the war; once the army's control was gone, the Wizards' Guild's compulsion for secrecy, which had done so much to restrict wizardry's effectiveness in the war, had taken over unrestrained. Now even simple spells could be difficult to obtain or prohibitively expensive. Certainly there were still wizards around, but most seemed to be severely limited in what they would undertake.

That virtually eliminated the possibility of having Wirikidor's enchantment removed, even if he decided he so wanted. When last he had sent an enquiry to the city, he had been told that no wizard in Ethshar would attempt to remove an eighth-order spell for less than a thousand pieces of gold. Valder was not sure whether Wirikidor's enchantment was in fact eighth-order, but he remembered a mention of that number. A thousand pieces of gold was considerably more money than he had ever had in his life and far more than he had at present, as business had trailed off slightly. Furthermore, as he grew older, he turned more and more of the work over to his helpers, which meant he needed more helpers—all three of Tandellin and Sarai's children now worked for him—and that meant more money. He had more than enough to live comfortably on, but he was not rich.

Karannin was dead. Gor was dead. Anaran was dead. Terrek was dead. It seemed as if all the men who had fought the war were dead or dying. Valder had not seen a man in a wartime uniform in decades; the soldiers of the Hegemony, such as were posted in the guardhouse at the bridge, had long ago switched to a new one, with a yellow tunic and a red kilt replacing the old familiar brown and green and with no breastplate at all.

Azrad was still alive, of course, and still ruled over the seas and the southwestern portion of the Hegemony, from the Small Kingdoms halfway to Sardiron—but he was a doddering old man now, three-quarters of a century old and showing it. He had not aged well.

And Valder of Kardoret still lived, no longer the young scout, or the desperate assassin, but the aging proprietor of the Thief's Skull Inn—the skull had fallen and been buried years ago, but the name still lingered. Valder wondered if his younger customers even knew the name's origin; he rather expected that the name would soon change again, perhaps back to the Inn at the Bridge.

He finished his ale and put down the mug, signaling that this time young Sarai was not to refill it. A pleasant young woman, that, more like her father than the mother she was named for.

Life was still good, Valder told himself, and as long as it remained so, he need do nothing about Wirikidor. Gor's death did not change anything.

Still, he could feel himself growing older. He knew that he would have little chance in a fair fight, either with swords or unarmed, against almost anyone. He would not stay healthy forever.

When the time came that his health was irretrievably going, he promised himself, he would take decisive action to free himself from Wirikidor's curse. There was always a way out; he had only to find it.

He reminded himself of that resolve periodically from then on and even wrote it down, lest he forget. When the time came, six years later, that he could no longer deny that he was losing his sight, he made his decision.

He could put it off no longer. His vision was slowly deteriorating, and he was certain that in a year or two he would be blind. The thought of spending an eternity helpless in the dark was more than he could take, particularly when he realized that he would become a perpetual invalid, with no prospect of dying, and that Tandellin and his family would be forced to care for him indefinitely. He had heard—his hearing was still good—his patrons speak with scorn of old Azrad, who still clung to his life and his throne despite his eighty years of age and poor health. He did not care to engender similar scorn. Azrad could abdicate, if he so desired, and be taken care of in luxury for as long as he lived; Valder did not have that option. Tandellin and Sarai were not his family and had no obligation to stay on if he fell ill, but he was sure, nonetheless, that they would. They were far from young themselves, as evidenced by the recent birth of their second grandchild; where else would they go? They had lived their lives as his helpers at the inn; it was all they knew. If he became an invalid, they would have little choice but to tend him for as long as they could. He would not saddle them with a blind old fool who would live forever; that would be unforgivably unfair.

And if he were to reach a point where death became preferable to living on, how could he die, if he had grown too old and feeble to draw Wirikidor?

He saw only one course of action. He would take Wirikidor and go to the city. He would seek out a wizard there, or several wizards, and learn whether Wirikidor's enchantment could be removed, allowing him to live out a normal life. Once that was done, finances permitting, he would also have his fading eyesight restored, so that he might live out his remaining years more pleasantly. He was ready and willing to pledge everything he owned toward the cost of such spells.

If the enchantment could not be broken, then he saw no option but suicide. He refused to live out all eternity as a blind, senile cripple. Blindness alone he might learn to live with, were he still young and healthy, but in time he knew his other faculties would go. He would have to kill himself with Wirikidor while he still had the strength to do so.

If Wirikidor would not kill him immediately, he knew he might have to kill however many other men it would take to use up the spell. That might be difficult, but he was sure he could manage it somehow.

With that firmly resolved, he made his plans and preparations. On the third day of the month of Greengrowth, in the year 5041, he set out for Ethshar of the Spices, riding as a paying passenger on an ox-drawn farm wagon, with Wirikidor on his hip.

CHAPTER 26

The wagon's owner knew nothing about magicians of any sort and, in fact, expressed doubts as to the authenticity of most spells, so Valder thanked him politely and disembarked as soon as they reached Westgate Market. The guards at the gate were more helpful, but the directions they gave him to reach the Wizards' Quarter were not as detailed as he had hoped. He was to follow High Street for half a league or so—he had forgotten the city was that big—and then turn right onto a diagonal cross-street, a big one called Arena Street, and follow it past the Arena itself and on into the Wizards' Quarter, down toward Southgate. That sounded simple enough, but there were so very many cross-streets that he was not at all sure he would know the right one when he found it.

The guards had also strongly advised him against carrying his sword openly on his belt. The overlord did not approve of such martial displays, and some people took it upon themselves to enforce the old man's whims, even though at the moment there was no valid decree in effect on the matter. Valder thanked them, but left Wirikidor where it was. He thought that the sword might discourage thieves who would otherwise be tempted to attack an old man with a fat purse. He had brought all his accumulated funds from forty-odd years as an innkeeper; magic, he knew, did not come cheap.

The crowds and dirt and noise were overwhelming at first, particularly as he was already weary from his long ride. Oxen were slow-moving beasts, and the farmer had been in no great hurry, so the trip had taken a day and a half. He had arrived at mid-afternoon of the second day, the fourth of Greengrowth, his back aching from toes to shoulders. He had not realized, sitting around the inn, just how much age had affected him.

Objectively, he knew at a glance that the crowds were nothing compared to the mobs that had overwhelmed the city when first he saw it, but he still found them daunting as he made his way along High Street, watching for the diagonal cross-street the guards had described.

He passed inns and taverns clustered around the gate-side market and assorted disreputable lodgings. He passed block after block of varied shops, built of stone and wood and brick, selling everything imaginable, from fishhooks to farm wagons and diamonds to dried dung—but very little magic, and none of the signboards boasted of wizardry or witchcraft. A passing stranger, when asked, told him that these shops made up the Old Merchants' Quarter; there was also a New Merchants' Quarter to the south. The Wizards' Quarter was much further on.

He came to a broad diagonal avenue that he took at first for Arena Street, but it was angled in the opposite direction from what the guard had led him to expect, so once again he asked, this time inquiring of a shopkeeper dealing in fine fabrics. The shopkeeper explained that this avenue was Merchant Street and that Arena Street was further on, past the New City district.

Valder trudged on along High Street and found himself passing mansions. Some faced upon the street, their rich carvings and gleaming windows plain to be seen, while others were set back and hidden behind walls or fences. A few stood surrounded by gardens, and one boasted an elaborate aviary. The streets in this area were not crowded at all, and most of the people he did see were tradesmen; only rarely did he spot someone whose finery was in accord with the opulence of the buildings.

The fine houses stopped abruptly, replaced by a row of shops facing onto a diagonal avenue, and Valder knew he had found Arena Street. He paused in the intersection to look around.

Far off to his left, at the end of the surprisingly straight avenue, he could see the overlord's palace. He had caught quick glimpses of it once or twice before on Merchant Street and again on one of the streets in the New City, but had not stopped to look at it.

That was where Azrad the Great lived, now more than eighty years old but still holding on to his absolute power as overlord of the city and triumvir of the Hegemony. He was said to suffer from bouts of idiocy, to have lost his teeth, and to drool like a baby in consequence. Valder shuddered at the thought. It was not that Azrad's current condition was so very unpleasant, but that it had come upon him in a mere eighty years or so, while Wirikidor could perhaps keep Valder alive for eighty centuries.

And for that matter, how pleasant could Azrad's life actually be? His elder son Azrad had died as a youth, in the waning days of the Great War. His wife was long dead. His surviving son, Kelder, was middle-aged and said to be a dreary sort. One grandson had died at the age of fourteen of some unidentified disease, and another was just coming of age. There were three granddaughters as well.

How happy a family could it be? Did any of those still living really care much for the old man? Kelder was surely waiting to inherit the throne, and the others had known Azrad only as a sick old man, never as the brilliant leader he had once been.

Still, he had a family. Valder had only employees.

He hunched his shoulders and turned onto Arena Street. The guards had not said how far it was to the Wizards' Quarter; he hoped it was not far. The sun was already low in the west.

The Arena itself, a large and impressive structure, was roughly a mile from High Street, Valder discovered. A block beyond it, he saw the first sign advertising a witch's shop. A witch, of course, would be able to do nothing against a sword enchanted by a wizard, but it provided encouragement.

In the next block was a theurgist's shop, and Valder was tempted. The gods, after all, could do anything—if they could be convinced to pay attention at all, and if you contacted the right god. He was unsure just how effective theurgy actually was since the gods had gone into their self-imposed exile, however, and he preferred to stick to the more straightforward approach.

The next two blocks were full of gaming houses, but, beyond that, Valder's search was abruptly rewarded with greater riches than he had anticipated. The street was suddenly lined with magic shops of every description, advertising all manner of wizardry, witchcraft, theurgy, even demonology and sorcery, as well as arcane arts Valder could not identify, on a profusion of boastful signboards. "Abdaran of Skaia," one read, "Miracles of Every Description." "Intirin the White," the next read, "Your Prayers Answered or Your Money Back." One bore no boasts but simply a black outline of a hand superimposed on a red eye and the name Dakkar—Valder thought that was rather ominous and probably represented a demonologist.

He walked on, following what seemed to be the thickest grouping around a corner to the right, and finally spotted, "Tagger, Tagger, and Varrin, Counterspells and Cures for Every Purpose." That sounded like exactly what he was after.

The iron-studded door was closed, the windows draped with heavy dark velvet; he hesitated, but then knocked loudly.

He waited for what seemed a reasonably long time and was about to knock again when the door swung open and he found himself facing a small, black-haired man in a red robe and hat.

"Hello," Valder said, "I need to have a spell removed."

"Oh," the red-clad man said. "Come in, then. I'm afraid the others are both out just now, but I'll see what I can do. I'm Tagger the Younger."

"Valder the Innkeeper," Valder replied, nodding politely.

"The one with the magic sword?" Tagger asked.

Startled, Valder nodded.

"Ah! Come in, come in! What can I do for you?" He swung wide the door and escorted Valder inside, leading him to a comfortable, velvet-upholstered chair. He then sat down in a similar chair on the opposite side of a small table.

It took Valder a few seconds to gather his wits sufficiently to reply. He looked around the shop, which was furnished much like a small parlor, with many dark woods and rich fabrics, predominantly red. "Since you already know about the sword," he said when he had composed himself, "I don't suppose I need to explain everything after all. I want the spell removed from the sword."

It was Tagger's turn to be disconcerted. "Why?" he asked. "I thought the sword protected you and made you a formidable warrior!"

"It does to some extent, but what does an innkeeper need with that? It also happens to include a sort of curse that I'd like to be rid of."

"Ah, I see! What sort of a curse? Do you know?"

"Do you really need to know?"

"It would probably help considerably."

Valder paused. "Could we leave that for later?"

"I suppose. In that case, what can you tell me about the sword? Do you know who enchanted it or what spells were used?"

"The spells were put on it by a hermit in the coastal marshes north of what is now Tintallion..." Valder began.

"After it was forged?" Tagger interrupted.

"Oh, yes, of course; it was just a standard-issue sword for at least three years."

"Ah. Good, then we shouldn't have to destroy it. Go on. Did you know this hermit's name?"

"No; he never told me. I don't believe I told him mine, either, for that matter."

"And what was your name at the time? Surely you weren't an innkeeper then."

"No, I was Valder of Kardoret, Scout First Class."

"Go on." Tagger shifted in his chair.

"I saw part of his work when he was enchanting the sword, but I didn't pay close attention, and he never explained any of it to me or told me anything about it. Even if he had, it's been more than forty years now, and I wouldn't remember much. When I got back to Ethshar, the army wizards tried to analyze it and they said that it included the Spell of True Ownership and some sort of animation; that's all I remember. Oh, yes, I think they said it was eighth-order magic."

Tagger started. "Eighth-order?"

"Yes."

"Oh, dear."

Valder did not like the sound of that. He waited for the wizard to continue.

"I can't do anything for you, I'm afraid. My father might be willing to try, though, if you can pay enough; he'd stand a good chance of succeeding, I think, and would almost certainly survive the attempt, but I'll admit frankly that you might not."

"Why?"

"Because your life-force is linked to the sword by the Spell of True Ownership; tied to it, as it were, by an invisible knot. The wizard who made the connection in the first place, or any really extremely powerful and skilled wizard, might be able to untie that knot—but you don't know who the original wizard was, and *I* don't know of any wizards skilled enough to handle an eighth-order linkage properly, which is what it would be if the True Ownership were applied as part of the eighth-order spell rather than as a separate enchantment. If my father were to make the attempt, he wouldn't be untying so much as cutting the knot, and that would mean possibly cutting away part of your life. To carry the analogy a step further, the severed ends are likely to lash about, and one might strike him and harm or kill him. Naturally, that means a high price is called for."

Valder was already pretty certain that he did not want to pursue this route, but asked, "How high?"

"I can't speak for him, really; at least ten pounds of gold, though, I'm sure."

That settled the matter, since Valder did not have that much.

"Would you by chance know of anyone who might attempt it for less?"

Tagger shook his head. "No, I'm sorry, but I really don't. High-level magic is expensive. Besides, you know, the really powerful wizards don't need to make money by selling their talents; they provide for themselves by other means. I don't suppose I should admit it, since it's hardly good business, but since I've already told you we probably can't help you, I might as well go on and tell you that we're all second-raters here, all of us shop-keepers in the Wizards' Quarter. If I could untangle an eighth-order spell, I could probably conjure up a castle in the air and live in luxury for the rest of my life, instead of spending my days removing impotence curses or curing baldness and scrofula and so forth."

That made a great deal of sense, but also presented another possibility. "But such powerful wizards do exist?"

"Oh, yes, there's no doubt about that; the ones who can still be bothered with mundane affairs run the Wizards' Guild, so I've met a few—but never by their true names, and probably not even wearing their true faces."

"Where could I find such a wizard?"

Tagger shrugged eloquently. "I haven't any idea at all. Certainly not running a shop in Ethshar of the Spices, unless you find one visiting to remind himself what he need no longer tolerate. And before you get any high hopes built up, let me remind you that a truly great wizard would have no particular reason to help you by removing the enchantment from your sword."

"He'd have no particular reason *not* to help me, though."

"Laziness comes to mind—and even for a really powerful wizard, undoing an eighth-order spell is likely to involve considerable difficulty and even some risk."

"I see," Valder said. He started to rise.

"Before you go," Tagger said, "would you mind explaining to me just what this curse is you're so eager to avoid? Perhaps we can find a way around it."

Valder settled back again. "What do you mean?"

"Well, for example, we had a client once who had been cursed with what seemed like a simple enough spell; he had been given a really unpleasant odor, so that nobody could stand to go near him for very long. It's a standard little curse, useful for revenge or blackmail—but in this case, the wizard had been feeling particularly vengeful, and had booby-trapped the spell, linking it to some very complicated wizardry we couldn't be bothered untangling for any price the victim could pay, so that we couldn't use the usual countercharm. Instead, we put *another* curse on the poor fellow, one that stopped up the sense of smell of anyone near him—and just to be sure, we gave his wife a love potion strong enough that she wouldn't mind the stink, even if it reached her. There are still some effects—for example, dogs and other animals can't go anywhere within a hundred feet of him, so he has to travel entirely on foot—but at least he's not totally isolated."

Valder considered, looking at the little wizard's face; the man seemed quite sincere, and there was always some way out, if only it could be found.

"All right," he said. "The curse is that I can only die when slain by the sword, Wirikidor; nothing else, not even old age, is supposed to be able to kill me. That's what Darrend of Calimor and the rest of General Karannin's wizards said, at any rate. However, I still age, can still be wounded, and I'm still going blind."

"We can cure the blindness, I think," Tagger said.

"That's not the real point, though. I'm still going to age; I'm going to get older and older, weaker and weaker, and I won't die. Ever. I don't think I can face that."

"You can kill yourself with the sword, though."

"Not if I get too weak to lift it."

Tagger looked thoughtful. "That's a good point. I'm not sure how that would work, not knowing the exact spell."

"I'm not sure either—and it's my *life* that's in question here."

"Have you tested your supposed immortality?"

"No; how can I test it? I can still be harmed, after all."

"You might take poison and see what it does."

"And perhaps spend the rest of my days with my belly burnt away? That's just the sort of thing I want to avoid."

"Oh, come now, there are plenty of deadly poisons with no long-term side effects. Still, I see your point. You haven't tested it, in short."

"No."

"And you want some way out of your current situation, where you believe you will age normally, but never die of it."

"Exactly."

"You would consider suicide acceptable?"

"I am not enthusiastic about it, but it seems preferable to the alternative."

Tagger stared at him thoughtfully. "Could you really find it in yourself to do it? Killing oneself with a sword is not easy."

Valder shifted uncomfortably. "I'm not sure," he admitted.

"You could hire someone to kill you, I suppose."

"No, not really; nobody else can use the sword while the spell holds, and the spell still has several deaths to go."

"Several deaths? How do you mean that?"

"Oh, I didn't explain the whole enchantment; it's complicated. Between my acquisition of the sword in its enchanted form and my death, every time I draw it, it must kill a man, up to about a hundred times, and then it will turn on me and kill me. I had figured that I could live forever by simply not drawing it any more—but now I think that looks worse than death, as I've told you."

"If I understand you, I feel obliged to warn you that I don't think you will be able to kill yourself with the sword. I'm familiar with spells of that type, though not quite that form; they were discovered right about the time the Great

War ended. The sword is semianimate, with a will of its own, is it not?"

"Yes."

"Then it will not permit you to kill yourself until it has served out its full quota of deaths in your hands; your own determination aside, it's physically impossible for you to commit suicide with that sword; I'm sure of it. You will have to kill however many men remain to the predetermined allotment, and then the sword will claim a new owner, who will kill you; no other outcome is possible while the sword and spell exist."

Valder mulled that over; somehow, he was not surprised. He thought that he might have suspected it to be true all along, on some unconscious level, or perhaps had once heard it explained, long ago, by a wizard studying the sword.

At last he rose, saying politely, "Thank you for your help; I have one more favor to ask. Could you direct me to a good diviner or seer?"

Tagger, too, arose. "Certainly; I would recommend either Sella the Witch, across the street and down two blocks to the east, or Lurenna of Tantashar, four blocks west."

"Lurenna is a wizard, or another witch?"

"A wizard. There are also a few theurgists who deal in prophecy and divination..."

"No, a wizard is fine." Valder bowed and departed.

He paused for a moment at the door, noticing for the first time that full night had arrived while he spoke with the red-clad wizard; he was footsore and weary, feeling his age, and he considered for a moment simply finding a place to sleep and continuing in the morning.

The streets, however, were torchlit and inviting, the shop-windows mostly aglow, and he decided he would pursue matters now, having delayed so long already. He would find Lurenna of Tantashar, not in hopes that she might remove the sword's enchantment, but rather that she might be able to locate for him a more powerful wizard who could. Tagger had said that such wizards existed.

True, he had little to offer in compensation—but he would deal with that problem when he had to. He would find a way.

Tagger watched the old man with the sword march away, then returned to the shop parlor to find that Varrin had slipped in the back way, unnoticed.

"Who was that?" the older man asked.

"Oh, an old veteran with a magic sword with a curse on it—nothing I wanted to deal with, though. Eighth-order, he said."

Varrin shook his head. "Those idiots during the war didn't know what they were doing, throwing around spells like that; it's amazing we survived, let alone won."

Tagger, who had not yet been born when the war ended, shrugged. "I wouldn't know," he said, reaching for the candy jar.

CHAPTER 27

Valder found Lurenna's shop only with difficulty; reading signs by the flaring, uneven torchlight was more than his weak eyes could handle readily, and hers was small and discreet, a simple panel reading, "Lurenna of Tantashar: Your Questions Answered."

Fortunately, the window was still lighted, behind heavy wine-red draperies. The blue-painted door, however, was securely locked; he knocked loudly.

It was a long moment before the latch slid back and the door swung in. A thin woman in a lavender gown— a color Valder had never before seen used for an entire garment—peered out at him.

"I have closed for the night," she said.

"My apologies for disturbing you, then, but I have come a dozen leagues today to find answers to my questions."

"Then you must be Valder the Innkeeper, here to ask about Wirikidor." She seemed to hesitate for a moment, then said, "Come in—but I warn you, I can't help you."

"I have not yet said what I want."

"I know—but I know that whatever it might be, although I will answer your questions, the answers will not be the ones you seek."

"How can you know that?" Valder said before he could stop himself; no wizard, he still knew exactly what her reply would be.

"It's my business to know things; why else would you come to me? I can answer my own questions as well as anyone else's and I like to know who my customers will be and whether I will please them—though I had neglected to ask when you would come and had not expected you until morning. Now, come in and be seated."

Valder followed her into a small room hung with wine velvet and sat down in a velvet chair by a small table. Lurenna seated herself opposite him and reached for a small velvet pouch.

"My price is fixed; I will answer three questions for a gold piece and guarantee the answers to be correct and complete. For a silver piece I can answer one question with no guarantees save that what I then tell you will be the truth."

Valder hesitated; that was more than he had expected to pay. Still, he needed answers. He fished out one of his carefully hoarded gold pieces and tossed it on the table.

"Good; now, what are your questions?"

"Are there any limitations? Must answers be yes or no?"

"No, of course not—I would not dare charge gold for that! However, be careful just what you do or don't ask; I will probably answer only what you say, not what you intended to say."

That seemed fair enough. He thought for a long moment, composing his question.

"Who," he said at last, "of all those alive today, is capable of removing the enchantment from the sword Wirikidor, which I carry?"

"And your second question?"

"Will depend upon the answer to my first."

The wizard looked displeased. "That makes it more difficult for me, but I'll get your answer. Wait here." She rose and vanished behind one of the velvet draperies.

Valder waited, growing ever more bored and ever more aware of the pain in his overworked feet and his general weariness; finally, after what seemed like days, Lurenna emerged.

"I have a list of some eighty or ninety names here," she announced. "Do you want them all?"

"I might," Valder said, pleased.

"Have you decided upon your second question?" Lurenna asked.

"No; I hadn't expected so long a list."

"If I might make a suggestion, what would be the consequences of removing the enchantment?"

"I had been thinking rather of where I might find the one of those ninety wizards most willing to perform the removal, but I have two questions left; very well then, what would be the consequences?"

"I have already asked that, in anticipation and to satisfy my own curiosity; you would die, and, of the wizards listed, only one, a hermit living on the Plains of Ice beyond the old Northern Empire, stands any chance of survival. The number of innocents in the area who would also die could reach as high as thirty-three."

Valder sat, stunned.

"I told you that you would not be pleased by my answers; when the first seemed so promising I could not resist asking my own questions." The wizard seemed almost to be gloating.

"This hermit in the far north—what of him?"

"Is that your third question?"

"No! No, it isn't. Wait a moment."

"The hermit knows you of old, apparently, and would probably refuse to aid you in anything whatsoever. Furthermore, because his surprisingly powerful magical aura interfered with my spells, I could not determine the extent of harm that might be done to you or to him if he were to try to remove the sword's spells. I give you this answer free of charge, and you have one question left."

Valder sat for a moment, then finally asked what he realized should have been his first question. He had more gold, if necessary, and could ask further questions.

"My question is this: What are all the possible ways in which I might be freed of the enchantment linking me to the sword Wirikidor?"

Lurenna smiled. "That's a much better question; it may take some time, however. Would you prefer to return tomorrow?"

"I'll wait," Valder replied.

"As you wish," she said as she rose and again vanished behind the drapery.

The wait this time seemed even longer than before—and in truth, it *was* longer than before. Unable to sit still, Valder at last rose and went to the door, only to discover that outside the street was dark and empty, the torches doused or burned out, the shops shuttered tightly, their lamps extinguished, and the people gone to their homes. The sky was clouded with the city's smoke, so that he could not judge the hour from the stars, but Valder guessed it to be midnight or later. He had, he remembered, arrived at this shop shortly after full dark; whatever spells Lurenna might be working, they obviously took time.

There was nothing to see on the deserted street; he returned to his chair and waited.

He had dozed off before Lurenna returned; he awoke with a start to find her staring at him, a sheet of parchment in her hand.

He stared back for a moment, then said, "Well?"

"No, I'm afraid it is not well at all." She held up the parchment. "I had to ask a second question, for which I will not charge you. The answer to your original question was very brief, very simple; you may only be free of Wirikidor with your death. No other possibility exists anywhere that wizardry holds sway—and wizardry, of course, holds everywhere. My second question, then, was by what means might you die—I promised you a complete answer, after all, and you paid me on that basis. There are only two ways in which you can die; I was surprised, I will admit, to find that out, since most men may die in any number of ways. You, however, may be slain only by another's hand drawing and wielding Wirikidor, or by a magical spell powerful enough to break the enchantment, thereby killing you, destroying the sword, and slaying the spell's wielder in an explosive release of the arcane forces pent in the sword. The wizard who cast the original spell, whether intentionally or not, booby-trapped it quite effectively."

Valder continued to stare at the wizard for a long moment. "You're certain?"

"Absolutely. I'll swear it by any terms you might choose."

"You said that I might be slain only any *another's* hand; can I not kill myself?"

"No; the sword must be drawn and wielded by another—and a man, at that."

"But no one else can draw the sword!"

"Not until you have slain another nineteen men."

"Nineteen? Exactly?"

"Could be eighteen, could be twenty, but it's probably nineteen."

"Darrend wasn't that exact."

"Darrend analyzed the sword a long time ago, without the spells I know, and when the spell was fresher and more chaotic."

"I'm sixty-six years old; how am I going to kill nineteen men?"

"One at a time," Lurenna replied with a shrug.

"There is no other way out?"

"None known to wizardry."

"Damn wizardry!" Valder said as he turned and headed for the door.

He had forgotten, in his anger, how late it was; he looked at the empty streets in annoyance, then headed back toward Westgate, looking for an inn. He knew that he might be closer to inns near the city's other gates, but preferred not to wander randomly in search of them.

As he walked, his anger cooled; and as his anger cooled, he thought over possible courses of action.

He could, of course, let things remain as they were

and sink gradually into senility and decay that would last for as long as wizardry remained effective—forever, in short.

Or he could find one of the eighty or ninety high-level wizards capable of undoing the spell and perhaps convince him to make the attempt, thereby condemning himself, the innocent wizard, and probably others to a messy death. That assumed, of course, that one of those eighty or ninety wizards would be foolish enough to make the attempt, which seemed unlikely; surely they would be able to do their own divinations and would see the danger. The possibility that one of that group might be suicidal was too slim to bother pursuing.

That left dying on Wirikidor's blade as the only way out, unappealing as it was; and, according to the wizards, he could not kill himself, but must use up his ownership of the weapon and then wait to be murdered. He resolved to test that theory—but not immediately. He did not feel quite ready to die yet. Besides, if he drew the sword and the wizards were right, someone else would have to die, and he had no good candidates.

If the wizards were right—and he believed that they were—he would have to kill nineteen more men, give or take a few. In peacetime that was not going to be easy.

He could, of course, do what he had been asked to do so often and go join one of the warring armies in the Small Kingdoms—but wars could cripple and maim as well as kill. Besides, old as he was and with poor eyesight, what army would want him, magic sword or not? And he did not care to kill people just because they were fighting a war; he would want to be on the side that deserved his help and he had no idea how to go about choosing the morally superior side in a petty border war where the truth about the causes of the conflict would be almost impossible to get at.

There must, he told himself, be some way of finding people who deserved to die and killing them.

That was an executioner's job, of course, killing convicted criminals. Once before, he had slain a prisoner with

Wirikidor and, although he had found it repulsive, he could think of nothing better. He resolved that, come morning, he would go to the Palace and apply for a job as an executioner.

He reached this decision somewhere in the Old Merchants' Quarter but was distracted temporarily by the necessity of finding an inn still open for business at this late hour. By the time he found a rather dirty and unappealing one a few blocks from Westgate, its sign weathered blank but shaped in a rough approximation of a gull, he had so thoroughly accepted the idea of becoming a headsman that he was wondering about such trivia as how much the job paid and what the perquisites accompanying the post might be.

CHAPTER 28

*H*e awoke late the next morning with innumerable itches and the unclean feeling that comes from sleeping in a bed already inhabited by a great many assorted vermin; as he alternately scratched and pulled on his clothes, he thought over the events of the night before.

He had been exhausted, he realized—perhaps so much so that he had been too tired to realize just how tired he was. Still, in reviewing what he had said and done, he could find nothing he would have done very differently, had he been more alert. His questions to Lurenna might perhaps have been better used, and he wondered whether he might have talked down the price, but what had been done was done, and he had the answers he needed. Although his outlook on the world was somewhat different, now that he had slept and been eaten by bedbugs, and would presumably change somewhat more when he had himself eaten, he had no doubt of the wizard's veracity. She had been recommended by Tagger, after all, whom Valder had trusted because he had not claimed to be able to do more than he could. For that matter, were Lurenna less than she claimed, she would most likely have given him more encouraging answers and would not have stretched his three questions to the five she had actually answered.

That meant that there was no easy way out of his situation; he would have to kill nineteen men before he himself could be murdered, and the only way he could see to do that without the slaughtering of innocents or undue hardship for himself was to become an executioner.

In the cold light of morning, however, as he struggled to pull his boots onto swollen feet, becoming an executioner did not seem quite so simple. Just how did one become an executioner? To whom did he apply? Could he just walk up to the Palace and ask? Or was that a military job, in which case he should ask at the gatehouse?

The gatehouse was certainly closer than the Palace; once he was dressed and had gathered his belongings, he headed downstairs with every intention of proceeding directly to the gate—until the smell of cooking bacon reached him and reminded him that he had not eaten, save for some stale bread and cheese at bedtime, since reaching the city. He had doubts about any food that this inn might provide, but decided to take the risk.

In the actual event, the food was not bad at all, and the few patrons of the Gull who were awake and present were pleasant enough. The ambitious had risen early and were already gone, while the unsavory still slept. Valder considered asking one of his more talkative tablemates about the city's executioners, but never found an opportunity in the conversation; beheading criminals was not a subject that sprang readily to mind in cheerful breakfast chatter. Before he had managed to bring up the topic, the sitting was over and the guests departing on their various errands, making way for the remaining late risers. He found the innkeeper, a huge, surly fellow, standing over him, a cleaver in one fist, and took this as a hint that his seat, too, was wanted—though he hadn't realized the inn held that many people that it would be needed.

The innkeeper, however, seemed as likely an informant

as any, and the cleaver brought the subject up as nothing else had.

"No need to use that thing, I'll be going," Valder said, trying to sound lightly amusing. "You've no call to chop off my head."

The innkeeper stood and glared silently; Valder stood.

"Ah . . . speaking of chopping off heads, I'm looking for work as a headsman—I've been trained in the art. Whom would I speak to about such employment?"

His only training had been the standard army training in combat and his rushed indoctrination as a scout, but he saw no need to limit himself to the absolute truth.

The innnkeeper's glare turned from simple resentment to puzzlement and wariness. "A headsman?" he said, uncomprehendingly.

"An executioner, then."

For a long moment the Gull's master stared in open disbelief at the master of the Thief's Skull. "An executioner?"

"Yes; whom must I talk to?"

"The Lord Executioner, I guess," the innkeeper said, still baffled.

"Where do I find him?"

The city-dweller shrugged. "Don't know; the Palace, I guess." He turned away, losing interest.

Valder watched him go, wondering how the man had ever become an innkeeper when nature had plainly intended him to be a thug of some sort, then shrugged and departed. He glanced in the direction of the gate wistfully as his boots struck the packed dirt of the street, but headed for the Palace.

Half an hour later he stood in the Palace Market, on the only stone pavement he had yet encountered in Ethshar of the Spices, staring at the home of Azrad the Great.

The Palace was immense; Valder could not see all of its facade from where he stood, but it was several hundred feet long and three stories high for its full length. It was gleaming white and appeared to be marble, ornamented with pink-and-gray carved stone. It stood on the far side of a small canal from the marketplace, connected by a broad, level bridge; at each end of the bridge stood huge ironwork gates, and at each gate stood a dozen guards.

The gates were closed.

That puzzled Valder; surely, he thought, there must be some way for people to get in and out in the ordinary course of day-to-day business, without having to open the immense portals. He could see none, however; the canal turned corners at either end of the Palace grounds, wrapping itself all the way around. The bridge was the only visible entrance.

With a mental shrug, he decided that the direct, honest approach was likely to be the most effective. He walked up to the gates and waited for the guards to notice him.

When they gave no acknowledgment of his existence before he came within arm's reach of the iron bars, he revised his plan and cleared his throat.

"Hello there," he said. "I have business with the Lord Executioner."

The nearest guard condescended to look at him. "Business of what nature?"

Valder knew better than admit the truth. "Personal, I'm afraid—family matters, to be discussed only with him."

The guard looked annoyed. "Thurin," he called to one of his comrades, "have we got anyone on the list for the Executioner?"

The man he addressed as Thurin, standing in front of one of the great stone pillars that supported the gates, answered, "I don't remember any; I'll check." He turned and lifted a tablet from a hook on the pillar. After a moment's perusal, he said, "No one here that I can see."

Before anyone could shoo him away, Valder said, "He must not have known I was coming; Sarai sent a message, but it may not have reached him in time. Really, it's important that I see him."

The guard he had first spoken to sighed. "Friend," he said, "I don't know whether you're telling the truth or not, and it's not my place to guess. We'll let you in—but I warn you, entering the Palace under false pretenses has been declared a crime, the punishment to be decided jointly by all those you meet inside, with flogging or death the most common. If you meet no one, it's assumed you're a thief, and the penalty for robbing the overlord is death by slow torture. And that sword isn't going to make a good impression; we can keep it here for you, if you like. Now, do you still want to get in to see the Lord Executioner?"

With only an instant's hesitation, Valder nodded. "I'll risk it; I really do have to see him. And I'll keep my sword."

"It's your life, friend; Thurin, let this fellow in, would you?"

Thurin waved for Valder to approach; as the innkeeper obeyed, the guard knelt and pulled at a ring set in the stone pillar.

With a dull grinding noise, one of the paving stones slid aside, revealing a stairway leading down under the great stone gatepost; trying to conceal his astonishment, Valder descended the steps and found himself in a passage that obviously led, not *over* the bridge, but through it. He had never encountered anything like this before; in fact, he would not have guessed the bridge to be thick enough to have held a passageway and he wondered if magic were involved.

The pavement door closed behind him, and he realized that light was coming from somewhere ahead; he walked on and discovered that in fact the bridge was *not* thick enough to conceal the corridor, but that the corridor ran below, rather than through, the center of the bridge; this central section of the passageway consisted of an iron floor suspended from iron bars. It seemed rather precarious but gave a pleasant view of the canal beneath.

At the far side of the bridge, another set of stairs brought him up beside another stone gatepost, facing another guard.

"Destination?" the soldier demanded.

"I'm here to see the Lord Executioner."

"You know the way?"

"No."

"In the left-hand door, up one flight, turn left, four doors down on the right. Got that?"

"I think so."

"Go on, then." The guard waved him on, and Valder marched on across the forecourt.

Three large doors adorned the central portion of the Palace facade; Valder followed the guard's directions, through the left-hand door, where he found himself in a broad marble corridor, facing ornate stone stairs. He could see no one, but heard distant hurried footsteps. As instructed, he went up a flight, turned left at the first possible opportunity into another corridor—not quite so wide or elegant as the first, but lined with doors spaced well apart, with figures visible in the distance. He found the fourth door on the right and knocked.

For a long moment nothing happened, save that the people at the far end of the corridor disappeared. He knocked again.

The door opened, and an unhealthy young man peered out at him.

"Hello," Valder said, "I'm here to apply for a job as an executioner."

The young man's expression changed from polite puzzlement to annoyance. "What?"

"I'm an experienced headsman; I'm looking for work."

"Wait a minute." He ducked back inside, closing the door but not latching it; a moment later he reappeared, something clutched concealed in one fist. "Now, are you serious?"

"Yes, quite serious," Valder answered.

"A headsman, you said?"

"Yes."

"From out of town, obviously."

"Yes."

"Headsman, let me explain a few things to you that you don't seem to know, though any twelve-year-old child in the streets could tell you. First off, the Lord Executioner is the only official executioner in the city and has no interest in hiring others; if he did, he'd hire his friends and family first, not strangers who wander in. Understand?"

"But..."

"But what?"

"This is the largest city in the world; how can there be just one executioner?"

"That brings us to my second point. The post of Lord Executioner is not a very demanding one; after all, no nobleman likes to work. It's true that the Lord Executioner *could* hire assistants, as his father did before him, but there's no call for them, because hardly anybody manages to require an official execution. Generally, captured thieves and murderers are disposed of quite efficiently by the neighborhood vigilance committees; they don't come to us. All we get are the traitors and troublemakers who have contrived to offend the overlord himself, and the occasional soldier guilty of something so heinous that his comrades aren't willing to take his punishment into their own hands and that can't just be dealt with by throwing him out of the guard and out of the city. This comes to maybe one execution every two or three sixnights, and it will be a long time before the current Lord Executioner is too feeble to deal with that himself. Which brings me to my third point—you don't look like much of an executioner in any case. You must be sixty, aren't you?"

"Sixty-six."

"Did your former employers retire you, perhaps? Well, in any case, the Palace is not a village shrine for old men to gather at."

"I didn't think it was, but I can guarantee that I would have no difficulty in carrying out the job."

"Ah, but there remains my fourth and final point, which is that we have no use for a headsman in any case. Were the Lord Executioner too old or feeble or ill or lazy to do his own work, or were there a hundred convicts a day to be disposed of, and were you forty years younger, we would still have no use for a headsman; the last beheading in this city was more than thirty years ago, when the first Lord Executioner was still in office and his son too young for breeches. Lord Azrad long ago decided that beheadings were too messy and too reminiscent of the Great War; we hang our criminals here. I had thought that custom had become the fashion almost everywhere by now.

Our own headsman's axe has hung undisturbed on the wall behind me for as long as I can recall. Now, are you satisfied that there's no place for you here? Leave immediately and I won't have you arrested."

Dismayed, Valder stepped back. "A question, though, sir—or two, if I might."

"What are they?"

"Who are you, and what have you got in your hand? How am I to know that what you say is true? I confess I don't really doubt it, but I am curious."

"I am Adagan the Younger, secretary to the Lord Executioner, and incidentally his first cousin. I hold a protective charm—you might have been a madman, after all, and you're obviously armed. As for how you know what I say to be true, ask anyone; it's common knowledge, all of it."

"And you wouldn't know of any place that does need a headsman? This sword I carry is cursed, you see; I can only remove the curse by killing nineteen men with it."

"Perhaps you're a madman after all . . ."

"No, truly, it's cursed—it happened during the war."

"Well, maybe it did; many strange things happened during the war, I understand. At any rate, I can't help you; I know of no place that still beheads its condemned, let alone with a sword rather than an axe."

Reluctantly, Valder admitted himself defeated. "Thank you, then, sir, for your kindness." He bowed slightly and turned to go.

"Wait, old man; you'll need a safe conduct past the guards on the bridge. Take this." He held out a small red-and-gold disk. Valder accepted it, noting wryly that the man's other hand still held the protective charm.

"Thank you again." He bowed and marched off down the hallway. He heard the clunk of the door closing behind him, but did not look back.

The guard at the inner gate demanded the little enameled disk before allowing him into the tunnel under the bridge and gave him a slip of paper in its place, which was in turn collected by the guard at the outer gate when Valder knocked on the paving and was released into the marketplace once again. It struck him as odd that it was more difficult to get out of the Palace than in, though he could see the logic to the system; after all, someone with legitimate business might be unable to obtain a pass to enter, but anyone who departed without some sign of having had such business could be safely assumed to be a fraud or worse. It still seemed odd, though.

He managed to distract himself with such trivia for the entire trip out of the Palace and across the market square; it was only when seated in a quiet tavern and sipping cold ale that he allowed his thoughts to return to his problem.

One reasonably positive aspect of his situation had occurred to him rather belatedly. If he could not kill himself, but must wait to be murdered, then he might live for a good long time after he had killed all his nineteen victims; he had no intention of being a willing victim, and that meant that his killer might not be able to get at him until he had sunk irretrievably into senility, or blindness, or some other incapacity, by which time he thought he would prefer to die in any case. He would, he thought, be a rich enough victim to attract a cutthroat fairly quickly, once he was known to be helpless, so that he probably would not be left to linger unreasonably long. He might even leave instructions with Tandellin that he was to be killed when he had sunk far enough, without hope of recovery, to make his life miserable.

That was an interesting idea, actually; he rather liked that. The idea of suicide was one that had never really appealed to him, nor had he cared for the idea of allowing some scoundrel to do him in and take possession of Wirikidor. Allowing Tandellin or some other worthy fellow to put him out of his misery, however, was not so bad.

That still left him with the necessity of killing nineteen men. He might yet find a job as a headsman, he supposed, but it would mean travel, extensive travel, to find such a post. He was not at all sure he felt up to any such travel; he felt his age, though perhaps not as much as most men of his years. It would be far more pleasant to find his victims here in Ethshar.

A thought struck him. He was not able legally to dispatch condemned criminals, but if what Adagan had told him was correct, there were neighborhood vigilance committees that didn't always bother with legalities. He might join such a group, perhaps—or perhaps he could simply track down criminals on his own and let their removal be credited to the vigilantes. That was an idea with great promise.

When the taverner came by with a refill, he asked, "What do they do with thieves around here, anyway? One almost got my purse this morning."

"Depends who catches them," replied the taverner, a heavy man of medium height, bristling black beard, and gleaming bald pate. "If it's the city guard, by some miracle, they are hanged—assuming they can't bribe their way out of it. Usually, though, it's just the neighbors, and they'll beat a little honesty into them, even if it means a few broken bones—or broken heads."

"The neighbors, you say?"

"That's right; the landowners have the right to defend their property, old Azrad says."

"Landowners only, huh?"

"Yes, landowners; can't have just anyone enforcing the law, or you'll have riots every time there's a disagreement."

"So if I were robbed here—I can see you run an honest place, but just suppose some poor desperate fool wandered in off the street and snatched my purse—what should I do? Call you?"

"That's right; we'd teach him a lesson, depending on what he'd stolen, and from whom, and whether we'd ever caught him before; if he lived through it, that would be the end of it—assuming he gave back your money, of course."

"What if I caught him myself?"

"Well, that's your affair, isn't it? Just so you didn't do it in here."

Valder nodded. "Good enough."

It was, indeed, good enough. If he could contrive to be robbed or attacked, then he would have every right to defend himself. He was an old man, with a fat purse—

or fat enough, at any rate. If he were to wear his purse openly, instead of beneath his kilt, and were somehow to make Wirikidor less obvious while still ready at hand, he would be very tempting bait. It would be unpleasant, and he might receive a few injuries, but it seemed the quickest and best solution to his problems.

He thanked the taverner, finished his ale in a gulp, paid his bill, and left. He turned his steps back toward Westgate; he was heading for Wall Street.

CHAPTER 29

Wall Street had changed in detail since Valder had spent a night there forty years earlier, but not in the essentials. The law still required that no permanent structures be erected between Wall Street and the city wall itself, and that meant that the Hundred-Foot Field was still there and still the last resort for the homeless. Those had been confused veterans when Valder had first seen it, men suddenly displaced from the only life they had known since childhood, but the majority had still been honest men who simply had not yet found their places. Now, however, all such had long since departed, either finding themselves better homes or dying, leaving behind the human detritus of the city and the Hegemony, the beggars, cripples, outcasts, and simpletons. The tents and blankets of the veterans had given way to shacks and lean-tos; where the soldiers had been almost exclusively young men, the current population came in both sexes and all sizes, shapes, and ages.

And among these derelicts, Valder had heard, hid the worst of the city's criminals. The guard did not willingly come into the Hundred-Foot Field, and there were no land-owning vigilantes, since it was entirely public land, so that it served as a final refuge for scoundrels and black-guards who had been driven from all the more comfortable places.

With that in mind, it was Valder's intention to stroll the length of Wall Street with his purse plain on his belt and Wirikidor serving as a cane. That, he was sure, would attract thieves, and any such lurking along Wall Street might reasonably be assumed to be no great loss to any-one, should he kill them in self-defense. Whether he would be able to lure nineteen of them to their deaths he did not care to guess, but he did expect to make a good start.

He walked south from Westgate Market an hour or so after the sun passed its zenith, a good meal in his belly and feeling reasonably rested. The day was warm but not hot, and a strong wind blew from the east, tugging at his clothes and keeping him cool. He expected the first attack within an hour.

It did not materialize; rather than being attracted by the harmless old man, the people who noticed him at all stared and actively avoided him.

Perhaps, he thought, he was being too obvious about it. Thieves would suspect a trap of some sort. He tucked the purse into a fold of his kilt, as if he were unsuccessfully attempting to hide it, and trudged onward.

Another few minutes brought him to Newgate Market in the city's southwestern corner; although far smaller and less active than Westgate Market, the square was lined with inns and taverns, and he stopped into one for a drink and a rest. He intentionally chose the one that looked worst, in hopes that a drunken brawl might start and provide an opportunity for swordplay. He promised himself he would not be the first to draw a weapon in such a situation and that he would not actively provoke a fight—but should one begin, he was ready and eager to join in, sixty-six or not.

No fight began, and after an hour or two he moved on, heading from Newgate into Southwark. This gave every appearance of being a quiet and respectable residential

area, despite its proximity to Wall Street and the Hundred-
Foot Field, where Westgate, Westwark, Crookwall, and
Newgate had all been more colorful. The population of
the Field seemed thinner here, and the shacks and huts
fewer and more substantial.

Another hour found him still plodding along unmo-
lested, well on his way to Southgate and inwardly fuming.
He had decided that Wirikidor was too obviously a sword,
rather than a cane. From what little he knew of the city's
geography, he judged himself to be nearing the southern
end of the Wizards' Quarter—assuming that district
reached the southern wall, which he doubted. He began
mulling over the possibility of purchasing a concealment
spell or an illusion to hide Wirikidor or make it appear
something other than itself.

Although the idea had a certain appeal, he marched
onward down Wall Street rather than turning aside; he
had no desire to become lost in the city's tangled streets.

It also occurred to him that perhaps he overestimated
the boldness of the city's thieves in expecting an attack
by daylight; he resolved that the next time he came to a
tavern or inn he would settle in, eat an early dinner, and
wait until dark.

The next inn, however, did not turn up until almost
half an hour later, in Southgate, as he drew near Southgate
Market. There he paused, glanced at the sun sinking behind
him, down nearly to the rooftops; with a shrug, he stepped
inside.

It was indeed well after dark when he stepped out
again, and he was slightly the worse for drink, but his
belly was full and his feet did not hurt quite so badly as
before, whether from the rest or from the liquor he was
not sure.

With fresh resolve, he strode onward toward Southgate
Market, past innumerable cookfires scattered among the
ramshackle shelters in the Field, and beneath the torches
that lighted Wall Street.

He had gone perhaps two blocks when a thought suddenly struck him; would a thief approach him on Wall
Street itself, where there were torches and campfires

lighting the way and any number of possible witnesses in the Hundred-Foot Field who might be bribed into identifying an attacker?

Far more likely, he decided, they would look for their prey in alleys and byways that were uninhabited and not as well lighted. With that in mind, he turned left at the next opportunity, into a narrow unlighted street.

He wanted to remain in the vicinity of Wall Street, however, so he doubled back at the next intersection.

For the next hour or so, he wandered the back streets of Southgate; several times he sensed that he was being watched, though no one was in sight, and once he thought he heard stealthy footsteps, but no one accosted him. Still, he was encouraged.

He was also tired; he sat down on the stoop of a darkened shop and caught his breath.

He reviewed his actions of the day and evening and decided that he had done the right thing so far—save that it had taken him far too long to realize that dark alleys were better places to find cutpurses than Wall Street, even if Wall Street might be their home. He wished he had thought of it sooner, if only for the sake of his poor abused feet and tired legs. He stretched them out, feeling the muscles twinge as he did so, and rubbed his calves.

If he were to be attacked, he thought, he wasn't certain he would be able to draw Wirikidor fast enough to prevent injury to himself when he was this tired.

It was with that in his mind that he heard a scream, suddenly cut off, and thrashing sounds from around the corner nearest him.

He leaped to his feet with the trained response of a man who had spent much of his life breaking up drunken brawls before they could damage the furnishings; without consciously intending it, he found himself rounding the corner into the alley whence the sounds came.

A smile twitched across his face as he saw what was happening; here he had been roaming the city looking for a robbery, and one had come to him while he rested. The light was poor, coming primarily from torches in a neighboring avenue, and his eyesight was not what it once was, but he could still plainly see that two men were attacking a woman. One held her from behind, one hand holding a knife to her throat and the other clamped over her mouth, while the other man was pawing at her skirt, searching for her purse or other valuables.

Valder had found himself a target and without luring anyone to himself. He drew Wirikidor, dropping the scabbard to the road and hoping that the second man would flee, rather than fight.

Hearing his approach, the man who had been kneeling at the woman's skirt whirled and lost his balance, tumbling awkwardly to the street. The other released the woman, flinging her aside and whipping a sword from its sheath.

He had time to get a good look at Valder in the flickering torchlight before the two swords met with a clash of steel. "Ho, old man," he said, starting a jibe of some sort; Valder never heard the rest of it, as Wirikidor whirled back to the side and slid under the thief's guard so fast that he probably never even saw it coming and certainly had no time to parry. The blade, sharper than any razor, sliced through leather tunic, flesh, and bone with ease, spraying blood in an arc across the entire width of the alley.

Valder could not see the thief's face; the light was behind him. All he saw was a black outline that slowly crumpled to the ground, the sword still clutched in the dead fingers. He brought Wirikidor up into guard position and looked for the woman's other assailant.

That man had scrambled to his feet even as his comrade fell and had out his own sword now. Valder watched him warily.

The thief looked down at his dead companion, then back at Valder. "I don't know how you did that, old man," he said. "I guess you surprised him. I'm ready for you, though; you won't take me by surprise. Maybe you're better than you look, but you're still old and weak and slow."

Valder forced a grin. "I've killed fourscore better men than you, fool; run while you can."

"So you can hit me from behind, perhaps? No, I've a

friend's death to avenge and avenge it I will!" With that, he lunged forward, sword extended.

Valder stepped back, suddenly realizing just how much trouble he was in as the other's blade slid past his neck; he *was* old and slow, just as the man had said, and yes, without Wirikidor's aid, he was almost defenseless. The sword sagged in his grip as he flailed helplessly, trying to fend off the next attack. He wouldn't die—the curse assured that—but it looked to him very much as if he were about to be badly cut up, with eighteen men yet to kill. He saw the blade approaching and knew that his parry would not stop it before it drew blood and weakened him further; he tried to duck and felt himself losing his balance.

Then everything vanished in a sudden violent blaze of intense golden light; he staggered and fell, dazed, to the street.

He lay there for a long moment on his back, staring up at the polychrome aftereffects of the flash, streaks and stars of every color superimposed on the smoke-stained night sky of the city; then a shadow slid over him.

"Are you all right?" a woman's voice asked.

"I'm not sure," he managed to reply.

"Can you move?"

Valder tried and discovered he could; he forced himself up on his elbows. "I think so. What happened to the man I was fighting?"

The woman gestured. "I took care of him."

Valder sat up and looked where she indicated, but could distinguish nothing but a vague black shape. "I don't understand," he said.

"Here, let me give you some more light." She gestured again, this time not pointing at anything, but making a curious pass in mid-air with her hand. A white glow appeared in her palm, lighting the whole alleyway.

"You're a wizard?" Valder said.

He could see her face now in the light that came from her hand; it was a young, attractive face. She smiled. "Yes, I'm a wizard."

He looked again where she had indicated and saw that

the black shape was exactly that, a charred black lump roughly the length of a man, with protruding fragments that resembled arms, legs, and a head. Valder gagged as he saw the distinctive shape of a human skull beneath a coating of ash and realized that this was all that remained of his foe.

"Not very pleasant, is it?" she remarked. "But then, they weren't very pleasant people; I suppose they were going to rape me and kill me, if I resisted."

"Did they know you were a wizard?"

"No, of course not; I don't walk the streets wearing a sign proclaiming my profession, after all."

"Why didn't you fry them both right away?"

"They caught me by surprise; I couldn't reach any of my magics, or move my hands to gesture, once they grabbed my knife and held it at my throat." She held up the dagger that Valder's first opponent had used, and he noticed for the first time that it had the white gleam of silver rather than the gray of steel and that the hilt was carved of bone.

"What were you doing in this alley in the first place, and without any protective spells?"

"Well, if you must know, I took a wrong turn; I'm lost. I had hoped this alley was a shortcut. I was sightseeing, you might say, reacquainting myself with the city; it's been quite some time since I last visited Ethshar of the Spices. As for protective spells, I had forgotten that I might need them. Foolish of me, I know—but I never claim to be free of human foolishness." She sheathed the dagger on her belt, then asked, "For that matter, what were *you* doing here?"

That reminded Valder of his own situation; he looked about, spotted Wirikidor's scabbard, and got to his feet to retrieve it. The sword itself, under the influence of the Spell of True Ownership, had never left his hand. When he had the sheath, he turned back and answered, "I was looking for thieves and murderers."

"It would seem you found them," she replied with a smile. "You'll have to tell me all about it—but not here. Do you have any idea where we are?"

"Roughly; Wall Street lies three blocks that way, if I'm not mistaken, and we're not very far from Southgate Market."

"Ah! Lead on, then."

"You haven't any magic to find your way?"

"Not with me; I didn't expect to need it. I grew up in this city, back when it was called New Ethshar; I hadn't realized how much it had grown and changed."

Valder looked at her curiously at that; he had judged her to be in her early twenties, from what he had seen of her, and, though he knew well enough that the city had changed greatly in his own lifetime, he had not thought that any great part of the change had been in the past two decades. Furthermore, he had never heard it called New Ethshar.

That was none of his concern, though. He buckled the scabbard to his belt, sheathed the sword, and then led the way to Southgate Market. They arrived there without further incident, and the wizard then took the lead, in her turn. Valder followed without protest, but did ask, "Where are we going? From what you've said, you don't live in the city."

"No, but one of my former apprentices does."

Once again, Valder found himself puzzled; how could so young a wizard have a former apprentice? She seemed scarcely older than an apprentice herself. Still, he walked on in amiable silence, his feet aching with every step, discovering bruises from his fall that had not been immediately apparent.

He had lost track of time, but it was obviously quite late, once they were two blocks from the market, the streets were deserted, and the torches were burning low, some already out. He felt rather burned out himself; it had been a very long and trying day. For a moment, he wondered why he was following the wizard, but that passed; after all, she owed him a favor for his help and might at least save him the price of a night's lodging.

They arrived, finally, at the door of a small shop in the Wizards' Quarter, whose sign read "Agravan of the Golden Eye, Wizard Extraordinary." A light still burned in the window. Valder's guide knocked twice, and a moment later they were admitted to a young man who did, indeed, have one golden eye, the other being a watery blue.

"Mistress!" he exclaimed. "What kept you? And who is this?"

"I will tell you all about it, Agravan, but first, something to drink, and I think a soft bed would not be amiss— would it, friend? Your questions can wait until morning."

Valder, who was only semiconscious by this point, managed to nod agreement; he made it up a flight of stairs, then collapsed upon the offered cot and was instantly asleep.

CHAPTER 30

Valder awoke, uncertain of where he was. The night's events returned gradually, and a glance around reminded him that he was in the loft room of a wizard's shop. The room was cluttered with books and arcane paraphernalia, jammed on shelves and overflowing from tables; his cot was squeezed into one corner. An unreasonable surge of hope welled up briefly; here he had found himself with a wizard in his debt. Perhaps something could be done about Wirikidor!

That hope faded quickly, however, as he recalled Lurenna's words. There was nothing that could be done about the sword.

He might, however, have his eyesight restored, if the wizard he had rescued were really grateful. That would be a relief and might stave off the day when death would be preferable to an enforced life.

He got to his feet and wished he hadn't; he had done far too much walking in the past few days and had slept with his boots on. His legs and feet were aching, itchy, and swimming in sweat. He found a filled pitcher his host had thoughtfully provided and pulled off his boots to swab his feet.

He was involved in this inelegant task when Agravan appeared on the stairs.

"Good morning, sir," the young wizard called.

"Hello," Valder replied. "And my thanks for your hospitality."

"Oh, it's nothing; I owe Iridith more than I can ever repay, and you've put her in your debt, it seems."

"It's kind of her to say so."

"Would you care for breakfast? Iridith is awake, and I'm sure we all have much to tell one another."

"I would be delighted," Valder replied, though he was unsure just what he would have to say that would interest the wizards. He pulled his boots back on and followed his host downstairs.

The breakfast was good, but Valder found himself carrying the conversation, explaining in detail Wirikidor's nature and how he had come to have his sword enchanted in the first place and his attempts to remedy his situation.

When he had finished, Iridith asked, "Do you really want to die?"

"No," Valder admitted. "But it does seem preferable to the alternative."

"Is there only one alternative, though?"

"I told you that I consulted wizards on the matter and was told that the spell can't be broken without killing me."

"That's probably true; certainly I wouldn't know how to go about it," Iridith said, spreading butter on a biscuit. "However, as Tagger the Younger told you, there must be a way around it. I've never met the lad, but he sounds like a sensible person."

"How can there be a way around it? I'll live as long as I own the sword and I'll own the sword for as long as I live; there isn't any way out of that. I'll just grow older and older forever unless I kill another eighteen men and allow myself to be murdered. I don't mind the idea of living forever, but not if I continue to age."

"Ah, but then why should you continue to age?"

Valder wondered if the woman was being intentionally dense. "I don't have a great deal of choice in the matter," he retorted.

"That's where you're wrong, though. You *do* have a choice. Others might not, but you do; you just don't know it."

Valder was not sure if the wizard was speaking in riddles or just babbling outright nonsense. "What are you talking about?" he asked politely. He was tempted to be harsher, but the wizard had saved him from injury the night before, as much as he had saved her, and besides, offending wizards was never a good idea.

"How old do you think I am?" she asked.

Playing along with the apparent nonsequitur, Valder answered, "Oh, twenty-one or so." An honest reply would have been twenty-five.

She smiled, and Valder, who had not really had a chance to see her clearly the night before, was startled by how beautiful her face became when she smiled. "I'm two hundred and eighty-eight."

Valder could think of nothing to say in reply to such an outrageous claim. He had heard tales of immortal wizards, of course—everybody had—but he had never paid much attention to them. He had seen wizards die and knew them for mere mortal humans; two of his childhood friends had taken up careers in magic, one as a theurgist and one as a wizard, yet both had remained ordinary people outside of their magical abilities.

"I don't think you believe me," Iridith said, reading his face. "But it's true. I served as a combat wizard for a century under Admiral Sidor and Admiral Dathet; I was retired long before Azrad came to power, and before you were born. I grew up here before the city wall was built, before the Palace was built, before the New Canal was dug. There are spells to restore or preserve youth indefinitely."

"Why haven't I ever heard of them, then?" Valder asked skeptically.

"You've never heard of wizards centuries old?"

"Certainly I have, but just rumors—and most of those wizards were supposed to look old, not young and beautiful."

She smiled again. "My thanks for the compliment; my face is my own, only my age is of thaumaturgical origin. Not all wizards who can restore youth choose to do so; many prefer to stay the outward age at which they learned the spells that prevent aging. Since that's usually not until one is sixty or seventy years old, many of the ancients like myself still look old. I was vain enough—and weary enough of eating with false teeth—that I chose otherwise. I was . . . let me see . . . seventy-four when I learned the secrets."

"That doesn't explain why I never heard more about these spells, though."

"They were secret, of course—the Wizards' Guild saw to that. Even during the war, when we let the army know so many secrets, we kept that one for ourselves."

"But why?"

"Isn't it obvious?"

"Not to me."

"The spells are very difficult, the ingredients very expensive, and they consume an inordinate amount of magical energy. If everyone knew that such spells existed, everyone would want them; who wouldn't want to be young forever? However, that's not practical. First off, if no one were to die of old age, the world would become very crowded very quickly. And besides, we simply *couldn't* enchant everyone; there isn't enough to go around of some of the ingredients, and the spells would use up so much magical energy that it might affect the whole balance of reality. But do you think most people would believe that? Most people distrust wizards enough as it is. In the face of something like eternal youth being denied them, they'd surely accuse us of keeping it for ourselves out of evil motives." She paused, then added, "Besides, there are plenty of people around I'd just as soon not see still alive a century hence."

Valder had to agree with that sentiment, but asked, "What about some of the really important people, though?

Why haven't you restored Azrad's youth, if it's possible? He's a great man and, as overlord of the world's richest city, he could certainly afford to pay for the ingredients, however rare they are."

"Oh, certainly, we could restore his youth, and he could afford to pay for it—but we don't want to. He's been a good enough overlord, and a good admiral before that, but, if he were to live forever, he might not stay one. What sympathy would he have for ordinary people once he, himself, were free of the fear of death? Besides, he would then have an unfair advantage in his competition with his fellow triumvirs, don't you think? He would have all eternity to plot and plan and carry out his schemes; what mortal ruler could compete? In a century or two, he'd rule all the world—including the wizards, perhaps, and we don't want that. Nor do we care to treat all rulers equally with our youth spells; we'd be preserving the bad along with the good and isolating them from their people. This is without even mentioning that we could scarcely keep the spells secret if we used them on Azrad or any other public figure. If old Azrad were to appear in the next parade looking like a man of thirty again, that would make it rather obvious that youth spells exist, wouldn't it? Assuming, that is, that everyone actually believed him to be Azrad and not a brash young imposter."

Valder had to admit the truth of these arguments.

"Well, then, you see that there is a way around your curse; all you need is a perpetual youth spell."

"And just how am I to get one? Why would these immortal wizards you speak of allow *me*, a mere innkeeper, what they would not permit Azrad? And just who are these people, anyway? Plenty of wizards grow old and die; I've seen it happen. Who decides who will be made young?"

"Oh, that's simple enough; anyone who can handle the spells is permitted to use them. After all, how could we stop them? The difficulty is that the spells involved are all of a very high order; the one that I used was an eleventh-order spell. From what you've said of your difficulties with Wirikidor, I'm sure you know that very few wizards ever become capable of handling such spells in the course of a normal lifetime. Among those who do, the spells are not secret; in fact, any member of the Wizards' Guild who asks is given whichever recipe he might choose. In most cases, since failure usually results in a messy death, wizards wait until they are either capable of handling the magic involved or are old enough to be desperate."

"You mean all the wizards know about these youth spells?"

"Most of them, anyway."

"How can you keep secret what so many know?"

"Oh, well, that's an advantage of being wizards; the Guild has ways of keeping secrets that don't bear explaining."

"Why don't the wizards object to not being given immortality, then?"

"But they all have the opportunity to earn it, you see, if they're good enough at their craft. Most aren't—but that possibility is always there. If we were to cast the spell on every poor fool who manages to survive an apprenticeship, the world would fill up with wizards until there was no room for anyone else."

"And how am I to earn it? Are you suggesting I become a wizards' apprentice at the age of sixty-six and hope that by some miracle I live long enough to learn an eleventh-order spell?"

"It would hardly take a miracle, with Wirikidor involved; but no, that's not at all what I propose. I intend to enchant you myself."

"But you just finished explaining why the spell wasn't given out!"

"It's not given out to just anyone, Valder, but you're a special case. You saved my life last night, and, after two hundred and eighty-eight years, I consider my life rather precious. Besides, for forty years you've lived quietly, despite owning a sword that could have put you on a throne in the Small Kingdoms or otherwise cut a swathe in the world's affairs; I don't think the Guild need worry too much that you'll upset anything or take unfair advantage of extended youth. In fact, you already have immortality, and that's the hard part; all I'll be doing is restoring your youth, not extending your lifespan. I'll be saving eighteen other lives, as well; you'll have no need to draw Wirikidor again, no reason to want to be murdered. More than eighteen, since after your death the sword would take a new owner, who would have to kill his own quota before he could die. That's a very nasty sword you have there, and I'm sure that taking it out of circulation indefinitely is a good enough reason to grant you your youth. I'm certain my Guild colleagues will agree."

"Just because I haven't done anything stupid? A life is a life, that's all, and I never saw any reason to treat mine differently because of Wirikidor."

"Ah, but that's what makes you special! *Most* people would have shaped their lives around the sword."

"You can't just remove the spell somehow?" Valder was not sure whether he wanted to be young again; the idea was strange, unfamiliar, and he needed time before he could accept it fully.

"I could, actually, but we would both die as a result, and I am not in the least interested in dying."

Valder was not interested in dying, either. Here, finally, was his way out, if he could only accept it. He would be young again—he would live forever, if he chose. He could not help but think that there was some trick to it, some hidden catch; it had been wizardry that had complicated his situation in the first place, when the hermit had wanted to get rid of him. Now another wizard was volunteering to interfere with his life, and he was sure there would be drawbacks—but he could not think of any. After several minutes of thought, he reached a decision. He would not be deterred by his previous experience. He would accept this incredible gift being offered him. Perhaps with new youth, his eyesight would return to what it had once been; he would like that.

"All right," he said, pushing his chair back from the breakfast table. "What do we do now?"

Iridith smiled. "Come with me."

CHAPTER 31

The house by the seaside was pleasant enough, with its covered porches and wooden walkways down to the beach, but it was not at all what Valder had expected of a centuries-old wizard capable of eleventh-order magic. He had been expecting a glittering palace, not a ramshackle old house with walls of rough wood and fieldstone and a roof of thatch.

He mentioned this to Iridith, who replied, "I had a palace once; it seemed the thing to do at the time. This is more comfortable."

Valder found that hard to believe at first, looking over the cobwebbed furnishings and feeling the cool, damp sea breeze blowing through the chinks, but he had to admit that, after Iridith had cast a restorative spell or two and conjured up a blazing fire, the house was quite cozy.

The main structure, not counting the sprawling verandas and terraces, contained just four rooms—an immense workshop filled with the arcana of the wizardly trade occupied the entire western end, a fair-sized bedroom the southeast corner, a small kitchen the northeast, and a small parlor faced south toward the sea at the center. Each room was equipped with a vast stone hearth and cavernous fireplace; when all four were lighted, the moist chill that had bothered Valder vanished in a matter of moments.

They had arrived shortly before midday; the flight from Ethshar of the Spices had been quite brief, just across the peninsula to the southern shore. It had been Valder's first flight in more than forty years and quite a refreshing experience; he had forgotten how exciting it was to soar above the landscape and remembered wryly how he had taken it for granted during his time as an assassin.

"You'll sleep in the parlor," Iridith told him, "if you have no objection."

"I'm scarcely in a position to object," he replied. "But how long do you expect me to be staying here?"

"I can't really say; until I've gotten the approval of the elders of the Guild and gathered the ingredients I need for Enral's Eternal Youth Spell."

"Oh? What are the ingredients?"

"I don't remember them all; I'll need to look it up. I do know that I'll want powdered spider, blue silk, cold iron, dried seaweed, candles colored with virgin's blood, and the tears of a female dragon; I don't recall the others offhand."

"Virgin's blood and dragon's tears?"

"I think you'll be staying for a while; those are the easy ones."

"Oh." He looked around. "The parlor should do just fine."

He had been at the wizard's house for five days, days spent strolling along the beach enjoying the fine spring weather or reading the many strange books that she loaned him from her workshop—in addition to assorted grimoires and magical texts, she had a wide variety of histories and books of philosophy. She, in turn, spent her time in the workroom, consulting with other wizards by various magical methods and trying to locate the needed ingredients for the spell. In addition to those she had remembered, she needed the ichor of a white cricket, the heart of an unborn male child, and the hand of a murdered woman.

"It could be worse," she had told him at dinner that first night, a dinner she had prepared herself by perfectly natural methods and which they ate in the kitchen. "Any woman killed by another person will do, I think. She needn't have been a virgin, or a mother, or whatever. I should be able to find one eventually. And an aborted or miscarried child should work."

He had agreed without comment.

"Don't worry," she said, sensing unease. "I'm not going to kill someone myself just to help you. I'm not that sort of wizard."

That had relieved him somewhat; the remainder of the meal had passed in amiable silence for the most part.

Since then he had seen only brief glimpses of her, other than at meals. At breakfast she would usually be planning the day's investigations, and by supper she would be too tired to talk much, but at luncheon she chatted freely, exchanging reminiscences of the war and the changes that they had both seen in their lifetimes. She reacted to his admission that he had been an assassin with a sort of horrified fascination, even while admitting that it was certainly no more morally repugnant, logically, than her own wartime work of more straightforward wizardly slaughter. After that first dinner, his own longstanding habits prevailed, and he played host, preparing and serving the meals.

Between meals she was always in her workshop, using various divinations to try and locate what she needed. Powdered spider, cold iron, and candles colored with virgin's blood she had on hand; she explained that all three were useful in many spells. The iron was meteoric in origin, but, she assured him, that could only add to its efficacy. Blue silk was easily acquired in a short jaunt back to the city. The seaweed Valder provided himself after a walk on the beach, bringing back a mass of dripping weed to hang over the workshop hearth and dry.

That left the dragon's tears, cricket's ichor, baby's heart, and severed hand. Iridith was cheerfully optimistic about all of them. "I found them once," she said repeatedly.

That was how things stood on the fifth day, when she emerged unexpectedly from the workshop in the middle of the evening, holding a small pouch.

"What's that?" Valder asked, looking up from a book that purported to describe the now-dead religion of the ruling class of the Northern Empire. "Find something?"

"No," she answered. "But I now have explicit consent from enough of the Guild elders to go ahead with the spell, and besides, I thought I needed a break, so I made this as a sort of celebration and a token of my esteem."

"What is it?"

"It's a bottomless bag, made with Hallin's Spell."

"What's a bottomless bag?"

"Well, I'll show you. I noticed that that sword seems to get in your way sometimes, but that you don't like to leave it lying around—and as you probably noticed back in Ethshar, it's not the fashion these days to wear a sword, in any case. So you can put it in this." She held up the tiny pouch, smaller than the purse he wore when traveling.

"Oh, one of those!" he said, remembering. He had seen bottomless bags in use during the war, though he had never known what they were called; an entire army's supply train could somehow be stuffed into one and then pulled out again as needed. It made transport over rough country much easier. The major drawback was that the only item one could retrieve was the one most recently put in, so that, if a great many items were stuffed into it, getting out the first one could take quite awhile. Careful planning was needed to use such a bag efficiently.

He accepted the bag and managed to slip it onto the end of Wirikidor's sheath. He watched with amused wonder as the full length of the sword slid smoothly into the little pouch, vanishing as it went. When it had entirely disappeared, leaving only a small bulge, he tied the pouch to his belt.

"Much more convenient," he said. "Thank you."

"You're quite welcome," Iridith answered.

He looked up at her; she was smiling warmly.

"I don't really understand why you're being so generous with me," he said. "You're doing far more than you need to."

"Oh, I know," she said. "But I like to be generous. I have everything I could ever want, you know; why shouldn't I share it? I've spent too much time alone; wizards have a tendency to do that. So many spells require isolation or such strict concentration that one dares not allow anyone else near! And it's so depressing to be around other wizards, who all distrust one another and want only to learn new spells without revealing any of their own little secrets, or around ordinary people, who are frightened half to death of me, and who I know will grow old and die in just a few years."

"I'm an ordinary person," Valder said.

"No, you aren't! You aren't going to die, are you? That sword won't let you. And you aren't afraid of me."

"Why should I be afraid of you?"

"That's just it, you shouldn't! I could roast you in an instant with a fireball, just as I did that thief, but I'm not going to, any more than you would turn that unbeatable sword on a friend—but so many people don't understand that. They only see my power; they don't see that I'm still a person. The power isn't important; you'd be just as dead stabbed with an ordinary pocketknife as with a wizard's dagger, or killed in a brawl instead of mangled by some high-order spell. Anyone is dangerous—so why should people be scared of wizards more than of each other?"

"I don't know," Valder said, thoughtfully. "I suppose it's just that it's unfamiliar power, unfamiliar danger. Everyone understands a sword cut, but most people have no idea how wizardry works. *I* don't have any idea how wizardry works."

Iridith grinned. "Do you want to know one of the great secrets of the Wizards' Guild? Most of us don't, either."

Valder grinned back.

CHAPTER 32

Iridith located the dragon's tears the day after giving Valder the bottomless bag; a wizard in Sardiron had a bottleful and was willing to trade. The same wizard was able to direct her to a cave where white crickets could be found and had a friend with a bottled fetus on hand, taken from a woman dead of a fever.

That left only the hand of a murdered woman.

The two celebrated the evening of this discovery by drinking a bottle apiece of an ancient golden wine Iridith had stored away a century or so earlier. The stuff was past its prime, but still potable, and the wizard got quite tipsy, giggling like a young girl at Valder's every word. Valder himself had long ago developed one of the necessities of the innkeeper's trade, the ability to consume vast quantities of alcohol without suffering noticeably from its effects, and watched with great amusement as the usually calm and mature magician deteriorated into kittenish silliness. Around midnight she dozed off; Valder warily picked her up and carried her to her bed, his aged muscles straining. He had half feared that some protective charm would strike him for daring to touch her, but nothing of the kind happened.

He stared down at her, marveling that this handsome, fresh woman could be more than four times his own age, then turned and found his way to the divan where he slept.

The next morning Iridith was far less pleasant; her curative spells prevented an actual hangover, but she obviously regretted her juvenile behavior. "We haven't got them yet," she pointed out over breakfast. "I still have to go to Sardiron and fetch them. Something could go wrong."

Valder shrugged. "Certainly it might," he agreed.

She looked at him rather sourly, as if annoyed that he was agreeing so calmly, then realized how absurd that was and broke into a crooked grin.

"You know, Valder the Innkeeper, I like you; you don't let things upset you."

He shrugged again. "I learned long ago to accept things the way they are; usually, they're pretty good. I've had a good life, overall, better than I expected—I never thought I'd live to see the end of the Great War, and here it's been over for two-thirds of my life. If things go wrong now, I still don't have any cause for complaint."

"A healthy attitude—and a very, very unusual one." She pushed her chair back. "I had best be going."

The journey to Sardiron took three days in all, even flying; Valder found himself wandering aimlessly about the house on the shore, unable to interest himself in reading anything, while Iridith was gone. Meals seemed particularly lonesome.

He tried to tell himself that he was simply homesick and wanted to return to the Thief's Skull, but he didn't entirely believe it.

On the third day, Iridith returned safely, with the heart in a sealed jar, a flask of tears—Valder was surprised to see they were a faint yellowish green, rather than clear as he had always supposed tears to be, regardless of their origin—and a large, loudly chirping box of crickets. "I'm not sure how much ichor I need," she explained.

With all but one of the ingredients, the two of them settled down to wait for an opportunity to arise to obtain the hand of a murdered woman. "People are killed in Ethshar every day," Iridith said. "Sooner or later, I'll find one that will do. I don't know why I haven't already."

"I don't either," Valder replied. "Surely, a woman's been murdered somewhere in the World in the past few days!"

"Oh, certainly," Iridith answered. "But I need one whose family is willing to sell her hand; I mustn't steal it. That sort of thing gives wizardry a bad name. The Guild wouldn't like it. That baby's heart was sold by the woman's husband—I suppose he was the child's father."

"Oh," Valder said, startled; he had not realized she was being so scrupulous.

For the next several days, she spent each morning in her workshop, checking her divinations, and then spent the afternoon with Valder, sitting about the house and talking, or walking on the beach, or levitating to an altitude of a hundred feet or so and drifting with the wind. On one particularly warm day, as they were strolling along the shore, Iridith suddenly stopped and announced, "I'm going swimming."

"Go ahead," Valder said. "I never learned how, really, and I'm too old to learn now."

Iridith smiled as she pulled her tunic up; her face vanished behind the cloth as she tugged the garment up over her head, but her muffled voice was still audible. "You won't always be," she said.

"Then maybe I'll learn, someday."

"You'll have plenty of time, Valder, I promise you that." She had her tunic off and reached down to remove her skirt.

Valder watched admiringly. "Lovely," he said. "If I were twenty years younger I'd do something about it."

"Don't worry," she said. "You will be—but whether I let you do anything about it is another matter entirely." With that, she tossed him her clothing and ran splashing into the surf.

On an evening a few days later, as they were walking up to the house with feet wet from splashing in the tidal pools, Iridith asked, "What are you planning to do when I've completed the spell?"

"I'll go home, of course," Valder replied.

"To Kardoret?"

Startled, he almost shouted, "No!" Calming, he added, "I'm not even sure it's still there; it wasn't much of a place to begin with. No, I meant my inn, the Thief's Skull—or the Inn at the Bridge, as it was originally called."

"Sounds dull."

"Oh, no! It isn't, really. We get travelers from all over, from Sardiron and the Small Kingdoms and all of the Hegemony, and hear their stories. Every sort of person imaginable stops at an inn sooner or later, and after a day on the road most are eager to talk, so it's never dull. I hear news that never reaches the city and get many of the great adventures described firsthand. It's a fine life. This house you have here, it's a splendid house, but it's rather lonely, isn't it? Your nearest neighbors are fishermen a league down the coast in either direction, or farmers half a league inland."

"I got tired of people decades ago," she answered. "After the war, I didn't think I ever wanted to see ordinary people again. I've taken on apprentices, of course; I wasn't really lonely here."

"I see," Valder said as they reached the steps to the veranda.

They crossed the plank flooring of the porch in silence, but, as Valder opened the door to the parlor, Iridith said, "You know, nobody will recognize you when you go back. They know you as an old man, not a young one."

"I hadn't thought of that," Valder admitted.

"You had best claim to be a relative of some sort— you'll have a strong family resemblance, after all."

"Will anyone believe that?"

"Certainly! Why shouldn't they?"

"Oh, I don't know. Of course, I don't think I really have any relatives still alive; I haven't heard from any in thirty or forty years and I've told people that."

"All the better; none will turn up to dispute your story. Surely you could be an illegitimate son, or long-lost nephew, or something!"

"I suppose I could; I'll want to warn Tandellin, though. He had probably thought that he would inherit the place; he may not be overjoyed to have a new heir turn up."

"He'll have to live with it. Nothing's perfect; giving you eternal youth can't solve *all* your problems for you."

Valder smiled. "It's a good start, though."

CHAPTER 33

The eighth day of the month of Longdays, a sixnight after Valder made a visit to the inn to reassure his friends that all was well, was rainy and gray, but the wizard and innkeeper paid no attention to such trivia; Agravan had sent a message that he had at last acquired the final ingredient. A young streetwalker had run afoul of a gang of drunken soldiers and died in consequence; her body had been sufficiently abused that her brother saw no reason to object to further mutilation, if the price was right. The circumstances were depressingly sordid, but the precious hand was finally in their possession.

Valder was pleased to hear that the soldiers responsible were to be hanged; the Lord Executioner would have a busy day, for once.

The hand was safely delivered that evening, and Iridith then locked herself in her workshop, telling Valder to eat well and rest; the spell would require twenty-four hours without food or sleep and would make great demands upon both mind and body.

At midday on the ninth, while rain splashed from the

eaves, Iridith called for Valder to join her in the workshop, and the spell began.

Most of it was meaningless to him; following the wizard's directions he sat, stood, knelt, swallowed things, handled things, closed his eyes, opened his eyes, spoke meaningless phrases, and in general performed ritual after ritual without any idea of the underlying pattern. Around sunset he began to feel strange, and the remainder of the enchantment passed in a dreamlike, unreal state, so that he could never recall much about it afterward. All he knew, from about midnight on, was that he was growing ever more tired.

When he came to himself again, he was lying on his couch, feeling utterly exhausted. He looked out the nearest window and saw only gray skies that told him nothing save that it was day, not night—yet something seemed wrong. His vision seemed unnaturally clear.

He got to his feet, slowly, feeling very odd indeed. His every muscle was weak with fatigue, yet he felt none of his familiar aches and twinges; it was as if he had become another person entirely.

That thought struck him with considerable force; if he were another person, then was he still Wirikidor's owner? He reached for his belt and found no sword. He looked down.

His hands were young and strong, fully fleshed, no longer the bony hands of an old man, and he seemed to see every detail with impossible clarity—yet the hands seemed completely familiar, and he found the little pouch at his belt that, he now remembered, magically contained Wirikidor despite its size. He opened the drawstring, reached in, and felt the familiar hilt.

He was obviously still Valder—but he was also obviously a young man. The spell had worked.

He found a mirror and spent several long, incredulous minutes admiring himself and being pleased, not just by what he saw but by how well he saw it. He appeared twenty-five or so—scarcely older than when Wirikidor was first enchanted.

Tandellin would never have recognized him; he congratulated himself on having taken Iridith's advice and informed his employees on his recent visit that he was retiring and leaving the business to his nephew, Valder the Younger. Tandellin had not been happy about it and had in fact demanded to know why he had never heard of this nephew before, but he had conceded Valder's right to do as he pleased with his property.

At last he managed to tear himself away from the mirror. He was, he realized, ravenously hungry—which was scarcely surprising, now that he had a young man's appetite and had not eaten in at least a day. He strode into the kitchen, reveling in his firm, effortless stride.

Iridith was sitting at the table, devouring a loaf of bread and a thick slab of cheese.

"Catching up?" he asked, aware that she, too, had been unable to eat during the spell.

"Oh, I already did that, really; this is just breakfast."

"Is it morning?" Valder was surprised; he knew the spell had been complete around midday on the tenth and had assumed that it was still that same afternoon, not the morning of the eleventh.

"Yes, it's morning—and of the sixteenth of Longdays. Eat; you must need it." She shoved the bread and cheese across the table toward him.

He accepted them and quickly began wolfing them down, while the wizard watched in amusement.

When he had taken the edge off his appetite, he slowed down in his eating and looked at his hostess. She looked back, then rose and crossed to the cupboard to fetch further provender.

He watched the movement of her body, remembering all the conversations he had had with her over the past month and more.

She returned with another loaf, a pitcher of beer, and assorted other items, remarking, "That spell does take quite a bit out of one, but it's worth it, wouldn't you say?"

Valder nodded, looking at her.

"Yes," he agreed, "I would definitely say so."

They both ate in silence after that; when they had eaten their fill, Iridith led the way out to the porch, where they could watch the morning sun struggle to force an opening in the clouds.

"My debt is paid," Iridith said. "And your problems with the sword are solved."

Valder nodded agreement. "So they are," he said. He watched a beam of sunlight stab through to the foam at the water's edge, then added, "I have another problem, though—one that I never solved. I never found myself a wife, and now I'm young enough again to want one—but what kind of a life would it be, having a wife who would grow old and die while I stayed young?"

"It's not pleasant," the wizard agreed.

"If I could find a wife who wouldn't grow old, of course, that would be ideal."

"Of course," she said. "Strictly for practical reasons."

"Naturally, I would let her lead her own life if she chose; I've never believed in the theory that a wife should be a chattel. A companion, though, a comrade through the years, would be welcome."

"I'm sure."

He was silent for a moment.

"Do you think you might want to be an innkeeper's wife?" he asked at last.

She smiled. "Oh," she said lightly, "I think I could stand it for a century or two."

EPILOGUE

Valder stared at the white-haired little man as he came through the door of the inn. "I know him," he muttered to himself. "I'm sure I do." He watched as the old man found his way to a table and carefully seated himself.

Young Thetta headed toward the new arrival, but Valder waved her off; something about this person fascinated him. He crossed the room slowly to give himself time to remember and, by the time he reached the table, he thought he knew who the man was.

It was very hard to believe, though, after so long.

"Hello," he said, "I'm Valder; I own this inn. What can I do for you?"

The old man looked up at him, and Valder thought he saw a flicker of recognition in the ancient eyes. Then the old man looked away again and shook his head, as if telling himself he was imagining things. "Wine," he said. "White wine."

Valder fetched him wine and, after placing the cup before the old man, he sat down across the table from him. "Pardon me, but I believe we've met before, a long time ago."

The old man peered at him. "That soldier? In the marsh?"

Valder grinned. "It *is* you!"

"I'll be damned," the old man said. "So you made it after all!"

"I never expected to see *you* again!"

"Didn't expect to see you, either—especially not after two hundred years." The wizard gulped his wine.

"Two hundred and twenty-one, to be exact."

"You keep count?"

"Well, it was a pretty important event in my life, getting my sword enchanted that way."

"Suppose it was." He gulped more wine. "Suppose I should apologize about that."

"Apologize about what?"

"About getting the spell wrong. Not really my fault, though; the sun was down when I got to that part, and everything was all sooty."

"Got to what part?"

"The Spell of True Ownership. I did it wrong. Conditions like that, who can tell a gold ring from a brass one?"

Valder stared for a long, long moment before he started to laugh.

ABOUT THE AUTHOR

Lawrence Watt-Evans was born and raised in eastern Massachusetts, the fourth of six children. Both parents were longtime science fiction readers, so from an early age he read and enjoyed a variety of speculative fiction. He also tried writing it, starting at age seven, but with little immediate success.

After getting through twelve years of public schooling in Bedford, Massachusetts, he tried to keep up family tradition by attending Princeton University, as had his father and grandfather. He was less successful than his ancestors and, after two attempts, left college without a degree.

In between the two portions of his academic career, he lived in Pittsburgh, a city he considers one of the most underrated in the country. It was at this time that he began seriously trying to write for money, as it seemed easier than finding a real job (he had previously worked in a ladder factory, as a feature writer for a small-town newspaper, as a sandwich salesman on campus, in a supermarket, and at other trivial tasks). He sold one page of fiction in a year and a half.

In 1977, after leaving Princeton for the second and final time, he married his longtime girlfriend and settled in Kentucky, where his wife had a job that would support them both while he again tried to write. He was more successful this time, producing a fantasy novel that sold readily, beginning his full-time career as a writer.